SCORELESS nights

KATIE RAE

Scoreless nights

Our parents wanted us to spend quality time together, but I'm not sure this is what they meant....

Cruz

As the goalie of Miami Inferno FC, it was my job to keep everyone scoreless.

So how did I end up being the one that couldn't score?

The answer: Lily Harris. My step sister, and apparently my new roommate. My dad thought I could keep an eye on her and protect her while she was in Miami.

But Lily and I weren't exactly one big happy family.

There was a reason I had barely spoken to her since the day our parents got married—a secret I would never tell.

Admittedly, having her there wasn't so bad, though.

Not once we worked out a few issues.

She even agreed to help me out and be my fake date to a dinner.

But that night changed everything.

My scoreless nights were over.

I just had to hope our parents didn't find out.

Because I would definitely be grounded for life if they knew the things I was teaching my innocent and overprotected little step sister.

A mis lectores. Espero esto les mantenga caliente durante sus noches solitarias.

For my readers. May this keep you hot on your scoreless nights.

Prologue

Lily

"I now pronounce you, man and wife. You may kiss the bride."

Looking across the altar, I saw the scowl on Cruz's face, the same one he always had when he looked at me. Ever since I met him, it was clear he didn't like me, but I thought he would at least be nice, especially during the wedding.

It was a big day, one I had been waiting for since the proposal almost a year ago. Sure, we were completely different people, but I honestly expected to see Cruz smile when the preacher said the magic words.

His eyes locked onto mine and they softened for a second before hardening again. Then he glanced away and I turned as well, not wanting to be embarrassed by his obvious disgust. He would be gone after the weekend, and I could deal with him until then.

The music started and we walked toward one another, then Cruz put his arm out like he was told to do. I hooped my hand through his arm for him to guide me down the aisle and we began to walk.

"This sucks," he groaned quietly through his fake smile.

"Shut up," I hissed. "Don't mess this up."

"It's already messed up."

I tried to dig my nails into him to shut him up, but his suit jacket was too thick. Instead, he thought I was holding onto him too tight and he looked down at me asking, *"What the hell?"*

We made our way to the end of the aisle and out the double doors, then Cruz dropped my arm and jumped into the limo that was parked along the curb. He didn't bother waiting for me, he just slammed the door in my face, and made me squeal when I thought my fingers were going to get caught in the crossfire.

"Lillian!" I heard my Aunt Frannie coming up behind me. Putting a smile on my face, I turned to greet her.

"Hi Aunt Frannie! I'm so glad you could make it."

"I wouldn't have missed this for anything. You looked so beautiful up there."

"Thank you," I blushed. Even from my aunt, hearing any sort of compliment felt good. I was at that age where words counted. She made me quickly forget about being annoyed at Cruz.

"How does it feel having a big brother?"

And just like that, I remembered Cruz, my so-called brother, sitting in the limo alone and probably hoping I tripped and fell flat on my face.

"He isn't my brother," I explained. "Cruz is just Ivan's son. He doesn't even live here."

"Well your parents are married now, Lillian. He'll be around more than you think and it'll be nice having a big brother."

I gave her a straight smile and decided to let her have her dream. She lived in New York anyway, and we wouldn't see her again until the next major event.

"Lillian," my mom called with her new husband close behind her. "Where's Cruz?"

I pointed to the car and rolled my eyes, making sure *she* knew how much he annoyed me. Mom gave me a knowing wink and then opened the car door. "Cruz, can you come with me? I want to introduce you to someone."

He reluctantly got out of the limo and slid his phone into his pocket. I followed them because I didn't know what else to do, but I instantly regretted it when my mom started praising Cruz for being the star soccer player at his school in Miami. So what if he could kick around a ball, big deal. I'd seen the same kind of thing at the circus being performed by animals.

When Mom was finally done gushing on Cruz, we followed our parents back to the limo and slid into the seat facing them. My mom had never looked so happy, and Ivan was a really good man.

It had just been us after my dad died when I was three. I barely remembered him, but Mom mourned him almost every day until she met Ivan. She also resented him, and many times her grief was laced with anger. My dad's absence affected every aspect of my life and I hoped that since she met Ivan, my life would become a tad easier.

"Cruz," Ivan spoke, getting his teenage son's attention away from his phone again. "When we get to the reception, you keep Lillian close. You two are sharing a dance."

His sigh of contempt was embarrassing, but I wasn't going to let his mood ruin my mom's day. My entire life had been spent placating my mom, so I was well practiced, and smiled, accepting whatever I had to do.

"Isn't it creepy to dance with your *sister*? Especially when she's only twelve?" Cruz fought against his assignment, and I secretly hoped he won because I didn't want to dance with him either.

"Lillian is only two years younger than you," Ivan admonished. "Stop acting like you're too good to help us celebrate today."

Cruz sighed again and mumbled, "*Fiiiine*," before putting his head back into his phone. Ivan and Mom smiled at me from across the limo, and I felt proud that even though I wasn't a soccer star, I was still the good child.

Once we were at the reception, we didn't have to wait long to get our part over with. We were quickly announced to everyone that was attending and then led to the dance floor with our parents next to us.

Dancing at our age consisted of swaying back and forth with our hands on each other's shoulders. We stood two feet apart and looked around the room—at anything but each other. But my young heart was beating fast, almost hurting inside my chest.

I didn't like Cruz because he didn't seem to like me. He was also my big brother now, though I would refuse to accept that for as long as I could. But it was also my first dance with a boy, and whether I wanted it to, or not, it made me feel heady and exhilarated.

Then the song ended and we went our separate ways, quietly agreeing to never speak again. Our parents were married, our duties were over, and he was headed back to Miami where he lived with his mom.

It would all be okay.

Chapter One

Lily

This was not okay.

Pacing the floor of my parents' house, I listened as Ivan called Cruz and asked him if I could stay at his place while I interviewed for jobs. What part of, *"I can get a hotel"* did he not understand? I had some money saved up and would be fine.

Meanwhile, my mother was hovering over Ivan, listening to whatever Cruz was saying on the phone. I could tell it wasn't pure delight at the idea, and I didn't blame him. I didn't want to be there either, at least not at his house.

It had been six years since I last saw Cruz and that was only because Ivan insisted he come up to Brooksville, South Carolina for my high school graduation. Cruz had avoided our small town since he went to college, and since becoming a huge soccer star, he had somehow still managed to keep his distance.

Mom expected me to stay with him like we were one big happy family. Ironically, the only thing Cruz and I had in common was how much we denied being *"one big happy family."*

Ivan clapped his hands when he hung up the phone and smiled. "Cruz is expecting you next week."

"You've got to be kidding me," I groaned. "Ivan, Cruz and I barely know each other. It'll be like staying with a stranger."

"No, it'll be like staying with your big brother. Cruz can keep an eye on you, show you around, make you feel comfortable, and most important, keep you safe."

Why did Miami have to have the best opportunities for an art dealer? Why couldn't Cruz get traded to Seattle?

"Plus," my mom chimed in, interrupting my thoughts. "We will be worried sick about you. For me, please accept Cruz's invitation to stay."

"He didn't invite me, Mom. Ivan strong-armed him into agreeing. Did you forget I've been standing right here?" *They were lunatics.*

"Cruz isn't a kid anymore," Ivan continued. "He understands the importance of family. He'll be thrilled to have you close by for a while. Then, if…no, when you get one of those jobs you're applying for, we'll only have to make one trip to see both our kids."

Mom smiled, but I could tell she secretly hoped I didn't get any of the three jobs I had applied for. She would prefer I stayed right there in Brooksville, no matter how suffocating that town was for an artist.

"You both realize I'm twenty-four, right? I'm not a kid and can look after myself."

Ivan stood and shook his head, not understanding why I was fighting him so hard on the matter. He would never be able to see how insecure Cruz made me feel or how nervous I was to try fitting into a world I knew nothing about. My only life experience had been my six years in college as an art major in Wilmington, which was still laced with overprotective parents just two hours away.

Miami had a whole vibe, and I knew I was going to stick out. Add in a famous step-brother who made me feel inferior without even trying, and I wouldn't stand a chance. Couldn't my mom and Ivan let me struggle without the added kick of having Cruz there as a witness?

"Just do this for us," my mom sighed. "You're my only child and have been sheltered your entire life. I know you're an adult, Lillian, but I will never stop being your mother. Cruz is family, and I know you two barely know one another anymore, and you're thinking it will be awkward, but it won't be. I promise."

"Fine," I relented, throwing my hands up in surrender. Not only because I was tired of listening to her go on and on, but also because it had been ingrained in me never to give my mom a reason to worry. She had hovered over me since I was young, and I knew it was hard on her to see me wanting to move away. How bad could staying with Cruz really be, anyway? We weren't kids anymore, and I doubt he still rolled his eyes and scowled every time he looked my way.

"He travels for away games," Ivan reminded me, taking a little more anxiety off my chest with his very valid point. Cruz traveled a lot, and chances were low that he would be there every single day. "And I've been to his place when I went down for a game. Real nice, and a great view of the ocean."

"I'm sold," I sighed. "Remember?" They were going to keep talking until I left, and I had no more fight left in me, so I turned and headed up the stairs to my room.

It had been a few months since I came home from college, but my boxes and suitcases remained packed. For most of the summer, I had been working as an art teacher for summer school, and looking for job opportunities in small art districts. I stayed with mom and Ivan to save money, knowing I wouldn't be there long enough to get my own place anyway.

Being a broker wasn't my first choice, but it was hard to

make it as a sketch artist. When one of my old professors told me he had contacts in Miami, it didn't matter that Cruz was there, I jumped on the chance to interview at places as prestigious as ICA, GGA Gallery, and DCG.

As long as I had freedom, I would take whatever I could get.

Hey! What's your ETA?

Leaving next Friday!

So excited to finally meet you face to face. I cleared out some room for you in my closet while you're staying with us.

I cringed, forgetting that I had yet to come up with a lie to tell Angel. I hated lying to my friends, but it was either them, or my parents, and I was not the kind of girl that lied to her parents.

Oh shoot, I forgot to tell you. My parents got me an apartment to stay in for a few weeks. Airbnb.

What? Tell them to save their money, you can stay with us.

The problem was, my parents didn't realize I had friends in Miami, so I guess I *had* lied to them a little. Since my mom was a worry wart, I hated telling her I made friends on the internet, much less that I was going to stay with them. She would probably die of a heart attack.

> They already paid for it. It'll be okay, though.
> You two have to work most of the time anyway.

> Hey, party at your place, then!!!

> Ha, yeah.

Dammit. No.

That wasn't happening. Telling them I was staying with my brother wasn't happening either. That would open a whole can of worms since I had never even told them I had a brother, because I didn't. It was complicated, and the last thing I wanted was my first real friends ever finding out my stepbrother was Cruz Martín. Especially since they had already told me they were huge Inferno fans. What if they only liked me because of him?

> Call me when you leave. I'm off Friday and we
> can talk all day to make the drive bearable.

Angel and I met in an online class that she was taking through Wilmington State University. We got paired up for a project and spent hours on zoom calls trying to plan out our presentation.

Eventually, our conversations went from schoolwork, to books and music. Her roommate would add to the topics in the background, and we all three became friends. We had a lot in common and I considered Angel my best friend, but I never even considered telling her about Cruz because I didn't really know him anyway. The lie by omission seemed innocent.

But staying with him was forcing me to deepen that lie and I felt sick to my stomach. Still, I wasn't going to say anything.

Not yet, anyway.

Chapter Two

Cruz

"*Ay papi, qué bien se siente.*"

"*Te gusta mi bicho grande, verdad?*"

"*Quiero este bicho grande sólo para mi. Sólo mío, Cruz.*"

Yeah, that wasn't happening. I had just met her twenty minutes before I put my dick inside her. Fuck, I didn't even know her name. I'm sure she told me her name, but her pussy wasn't memorable enough for me to worry about. She was just there and willing when I needed it the most.

When we had gotten to the bathroom of the club we were in, I pushed her hands against the wall so I didn't have to look at her. I wasn't even sure I cared if she came, I was just pushing myself to the finish line as fast as possible.

My pants were barely down and my t-shirt was still on. She was fully clothed except for the panties I tore off and her skirt was lifted to her waist.

"*Tu amas mi chocho, verdad papi?*"

Oh for fuck's sake. "*Tú sabes que si.*"

The next time I went looking for a quick hook up, I needed to vet her a little more and make sure she was fucking quiet.

There was too much tension in my body to keep speaking to her like I cared. I knew I was bordering on the line of being a complete asshole, but my life was about to be turned upside down and I needed that quick fuck to settle down before I completely lost it.

Finally, her words turned into moans, and I was able to push myself closer to my climax. Closing my eyes and ramming my cock into her from behind, I enjoyed how she squeezed me as she got ready to come.

"Oh..."

"Shhhh," I put my hand over her mouth to shut her up. I was there, so fucking close, but if she told me she wanted my dick to be hers again, I would have to pull out and leave–unsatisfied and fucking agitated.

My hips started losing rhythm as I spilled cum into the condom that separated us. The head of my cock stroked her a few more times and she clenched, coming while I kept my hand over her mouth.

Then I pulled out and backed away, wasting no time getting the condom discarded and my pants back up. She was straightening her skirt and licking her lips, like she was waiting on me to kiss her. Or...

"I cannot believe I just fucked Cruz Martin," she purred, in what I was sure was a sexy tone if I cared to pay attention. Her words just confirmed what I thought, though. She was using me as much as I was using her. Fucking me would be a story she told her friends later, one they probably wouldn't even believe.

Then she would try to call the phone number I gave her to prove it. Some poor guy or girl would answer their phone and have to tell her she had the wrong number. Dammit, I was being an extra-large asshole with a side of jerk, but I couldn't help it.

Opening the door, I turned to the girl whose name I couldn't remember and told her to call me, not waiting for a response. The longer it took to leave, the more guilt would eat away at me.

What was wrong with me?

It was no secret that I loved fucking, but I had become rabid, hoping to score every night with someone new just so I could work the pressure out of my body. Practice and games weren't enough to subdue the anxiety that had been bubbling up.

Ever since Dad asked if Lillian could stay with me, I'd been irritated and grumpy. I lived alone, and I liked it that way. My apartment was my safe space, no one outside of my friends and family ever infiltrated my space. Of course, Dad said Lillian was family. It wasn't the same as having a stranger come stay, but he didn't understand that Lillian *was* a stranger–to me.

Other than that, I had no good reasons she couldn't stay. Dad powered through every attempt I made to change his mind, and it only took minutes for me to realize he would get his way. He and his wife, Gloria, worried way too much about Lillian. She was a goddamn adult, but they seemed to be up her ass all the fucking time.

By the time I got home, I fell backward onto my couch and pulled my wrist up to check the time. Lillian was supposed to be getting into Miami late, and I was supposed to be the welcoming big brother that stayed up and made sure she was settled and comfortable. As if on cue, my phone buzzed in my pocket and I reached for it, seeing my dad's name flashing across the top.

"Hello?" My dad spoke Spanish, but chose not to when Gloria or Lillian were around. He felt like it was rude of him to leave them out of conversations, even if he wasn't talking to them, or about them.

"Cruz, you home, son?" His English told me Gloria was there next to him, and as much as I gave my dad shit for sending Lillian my way, I respected Gloria enough not to let her hear how big of a jerk I was being about it.

"Yeah, Dad. Just here, waiting for Lillian."

"I called you earlier but it went directly to voicemail."

Hmmm, must have gotten shitty reception in that dank bathroom.

"Well, I'm here."

"It's been a while, hasn't it?" He laughed, like we didn't discuss that exact thing the week before.

"Six years. Hope she doesn't think of me as a stranger." My subtlety didn't hit the mark and Dad just laughed.

"No, no. Time doesn't change sibling connections."

My dad was one of the smartest men I ever knew. He had more than one college degree, and was a supervisor at his job. But he was borderline delusional. Lillian was not my sibling. We didn't even grow up together. Her mom married my dad, but I lived in Miami with my own mother. I visited Dad until I went to college and since then, he was the one that visited me so he could watch me play.

Bottomline, Lillian and I were not close. He knew that.

"She's nervous," I heard Gloria speak into the phone. "Take care of her, Cruz."

"Sure thing," I promised through gritted teeth and a small snarl she couldn't see.

"Oh, she's calling now. Hello?" Gloria answered her own phone. Dad stayed quiet and I listened to her speak to Lillian in the background. I considered hanging up and acting like I thought we were saying goodbye, but refrained.

"Oh she said she's in Miami. GPS says one more hour to your address," Gloria squealed to all of us before speaking to Lillian again. "We are talking to Cruz now. You have his number right? You should call him."

Gloria made agreeable noises as I assumed Lillian was doing the talking, which was when I decided I really did have to go.

"Dad, I have to do something..." I hung up, hoping he didn't call me back.

Apparently, Lillian was an hour away and just knowing how small the countdown was made me antsy again. I needed to run. My apartment was across the street from the beach, so I could run on the sidewalk that lined the ocean no matter how late it was.

Throwing on my workout gear, I grabbed my keys and left my phone. It would be easier to relax if I wasn't worried about it ringing with my dad on the other end.

When I got down to the parking garage, I started to veer off toward the pedestrian exit when a woman doing jumping jacks caught my eye. Her back was to me but she had on jeans, which was why she drew my attention. *Jeans? A workout?* A lot of people in Miami were very eclectic, but no one worked out in jeans. It was too hot for that shit.

Whatever.

When I started toward the door again, the woman let out a growl, loud and echoing off the walls of the garage. She began pacing, and talking to herself, but I wasn't quite close enough to hear what she was saying. Something about her wouldn't let me walk away, though. I had never noticed her before, and as late as it was, I started to get a little worried that she was lost, or maybe even on something.

"Excuse me?" I asked, walking closer. The good Samaritan in me was eager to help her, but she didn't seem to hear me or even notice me approaching.

"You're not crazy," I heard her say. "You can do this. You're not a kid. Just go up there."

"Excuse me," I said again, a little louder.

She turned and faced me, her eyes wide, and her chest heaving from what I assumed was from her random workout. Her blonde hair fell around her face, and the shirt she was wearing dipped down low enough that her cleavage was on display. I licked my lips involuntarily, thinking that if she wasn't so crazy, I would charm her until her panties were around her ankles.

Recognition flashed in her eyes and that immediately told me she knew who I was. Fucking her would be easy. Two in one night would be better than a run, and it seemed I had the time.

"Oh...um..."

Her cheeks flushed with a hint of embarrassment, and I smiled at her as I got close. *"¿Estás bien, belleza?"*

Her eyes got even wider before she turned away from me and started talking to herself again. After a few mumbled words, she stopped and faced me again, lifting her shoulders back and her chin up.

"Cruz Martin?" She walked closer with a formality I didn't understand, and stuck her hand out. "Lillian Harris, nice to meet you."

Chapter Three

Lily

If there was a worse way to see your famous step-brother who intimidated you, and probably hated you, that you hadn't seen in six years, then I would like to hear that story. Because at that moment, it felt like a heart attack would have been better than the humiliation I felt when I turned and saw Cruz watching me panic.

Mom was calling me nonstop on my drive so I called her back and told her I was an hour away, but that was a lie. Technically, I was already there. I just needed more time to prepare myself before going up to see Cruz. The drive took all day, and I had energy to burn, and worries to shake out. I needed that hour to myself, even if it was in a strange parking garage in South Beach.

Belleza.

I knew enough Spanish to know that he called me beautiful. That meant he had no idea who I was, because the Cruz Martin I once knew would never call me that. So I did what any two strangers should do, I introduced myself.

But the way his forehead creased, and his body tensed,

made me feel like that was the wrong thing to do. I pulled my hand back and hid it behind me, hoping he didn't even see it. I could almost feel myself turning green from the need to vomit all over the place.

"Uh," I backed up, deciding to head to Angel's house and letting my parents deal with it. From the look on Cruz's face, I would be safer with "strangers" anyway.

"Lily?" He finally asked, his voice hoarse.

"I have friends I can stay with," I explained. "You and I are..." I trailed off without finishing my thought, "and this is weird. I'll tell Mom and Ivan, don't worry. And thank you for the offer, I should just—"

"It's midnight."

"Yeah, so here's the thing. My mother doesn't realize I'm all grown up, but ta-da, I'm a full adult. So it may be midnight, but I need to go."

I turned to race toward the driver door of my car, but Cruz snapped out of his dumbfounded trance and reached out to shut it. "Come upstairs. I've been expecting you, so it would be kind of rude to bail on me now. You can leave tomorrow."

"You looked like you were heading somewhere," I motioned towards his keys and clothes.

"You told your mom you had another hour, I was just going to jog until you arrived."

Oh yeah, he was talking to Ivan when I called my mom. *Shoot.*

"Don't let me stop you," I laughed, although it was more awkward than funny. "I can just, um..." I looked around, like I had a lot to do but all that was there was my car. "I gotta go."

"Like I said," Cruz grabbed my keys from my hand and pushed the button on the trunk. He grabbed a few bags before finishing his thought. "You can leave tomorrow."

I nodded, and gave up. Our parents were expecting to see us together, so for one night, I would stay and let them have their way. Cruz didn't want any part of their craziness either, he never had, so one night was good for both of us.

Grabbing a few more bags from my car, I followed him to the elevator. He hit the number twelve once and we rode the lift up in an awkward silence. There were only two doors on the twelfth floor, and he took me to the one farthest away.

"No one lives there," he pointed to the first door. "But they have been showing it to possible buyers so you may hear them coming in and out a lot."

"I'll be gone in the morning," I reminded him.

Cruz just scoffed and shook his head as he unlocked the door. He carried my luggage across the big condo and down a short hall on the left side of the living area. "This is where you can stay. My room is across the living room, on the other side. There is no food here because I don't cook. I'm gonna get that run in. Tell Gloria you're fine so my dad doesn't threaten to come down here."

Then he was gone, back out the front door, leaving me to take stock of where I was. The room was amazing, even if there wasn't much besides a bed and a desk. But the space looked clean and Zen, with a window that faced the ocean. It would be perfect for one night, and with Cruz all the way across the apartment, I doubt I'd even see him before I left the next day.

I sent my mom a quick text letting her know I was here. She questioned my timeline, but I assured her I'd read the GPS wrong, and was safe at Cruz's. I also added that I was exhausted, and she spared me another phone call for the night.

Before Cruz got back, I wanted to be showered and in bed, so I rushed to get some things from my bag, and found the bathroom across from my room. For a second bathroom, the shower was amazing. Two shower heads, a massager, and a warmer that kept the room toasty until I could get dressed again.

I snuck back to my room afterward and peeled the covers back on the bed. The quilt was a sage green, with matching sheets, which I could tell were brand new. I tried to picture Cruz putting them on by himself and it made me glad I stayed at least one night so that effort didn't go to waste.

Just as I was starting to fall asleep, the door slammed and I could hear Cruz toss his keys onto the kitchen counter. His footsteps made their way across the tile and I heard his bedroom door close soon after. I let out a deep breath and relaxed back into my pillow.

Admittedly, as awkward as it was seeing Cruz again, I was thankful to be somewhere safe and comfortable for the night. In the morning, I would quietly sneak out and head to Angel's, who had reminded me during my whole drive that I was welcome to stay with her and Jackie. At least she seemed to genuinely want me around. Cruz had always been stand-offish with me, barely saying a few words.

Growing up, he only stayed with us a week at a time, and I usually ended up hiding in my room as much as I could. As I closed my eyes again, I thought back to when we were kids and he had come back to see his dad for the first time since our parents got married.

"Lillian," my mom yelled up the stairs. "Come down here and eat with us. We are having a family dinner."

I rolled my eyes to myself and set my drawing aside. I pulled on a hoodie to cover my body and hide my insecurities, then made my way down to the dining room.

Cruz was quietly sitting in the spot I usually sat in, and I snarled at him, letting him know that was my seat. He chose to shrug and smirk, but didn't move, and before I could open my mouth to tell him that he was in my spot, Ivan came in with bowls of my mom's leek and potato soup, with a huge smile on his face.

"I love having us all together. Lillian, maybe you can help me convince him to move up here full time."

I shook my head, but stayed quiet, as I took the seat I wanted Cruz to move to. He was eyeing me with humor in his eyes, feeling like he won since I chose to sit down. But really, I just hated being around him. He was a good looking boy who spoke two languages, and got praised for how well he did at soccer. I was an insecure, rat-looking girl with hardly any friends, and overprotective parents.

"Mamá me necesita, tú sabes," Cruz spoke to Ivan.

"English!" Ivan commanded, making Cruz roll his eyes. He didn't repeat himself, but I knew he said something about his mom.

Cruz's mom, Mariana, ran a Cuban restaurant in Miami that he helped with sometimes. Ivan thought highly of Mariana even though their marriage didn't work out, and often told us how much he loved Cruz getting experience by helping her at the restaurant. It was the main reason I knew Ivan would never really fight to have Cruz come live with us.

Ivan and Mom carried the dinner conversation on their own. Cruz ate the entire bowl of soup, and then had seconds, sitting quietly until he was excused. I could barely eat, but had to do the dishes before I was allowed to go back to my room.

When I did, Cruz was in his room on the phone. I could hear him speaking to someone he called Deon about how it was torture being around "Lily," which he called me instead of Lillian, to get under my skin. Tears formed in my eyes and I didn't stick around to hear anything else.

He stayed a whole week, and not once did he say a single word directly to me. It set the tone for all his trips, and even though I wasn't much better than he was, I blamed our dislike for one another on him.

Chapter Four

Cruz

Once I realized the crazy girl in the parking lot was Lillian, I moved on autopilot. She tried leaving, and I should have let her, but I knew there would be hell to pay if I did, so I just rushed her up to her room.

Then I ran for almost an hour, trying to get rid of the anxiety she gave me.

I knew as kids, I wasn't always fair to her. She didn't ask her mom and my dad to get married, and I didn't really resent her for their decisions. But Dad tried making us a big happy family, and that wasn't how my life really worked. I was an only child, whose dad took a job twelve hours away when he was ten, and shit was never the same.

As an adult, I knew my dad had done the right thing. He was able to provide for me more than he would have had he not taken that job and moved. But as a kid, I was resentful, and I hated that Lillian got to have my dad in her life while I only got to see him two times a year.

Somehow, as soon as my dad asked if she could stay with me, I got all those old feelings back. I was angry for no reason and had anxiety about how to speak to her without being an asshole. Having her in my space was going to be tiresome.

Especially after I accidently called her beautiful.

Because she was definitely fucking gorgeous.

Lillian always had a beauty to her that was hard to deny. She was blonde, with bright blue eyes, and almost everyone I met that knew her thought she was a miniature Barbie doll. Now that she was all grown up and filled out, she looked better than Barbie herself, yet had an innocence that came from having Gloria and Dad fuss over her every move.

Miami was going to eat her up and spit her out.

With an early practice the next day, I didn't think I would see her until I got home, but when I opened my bedroom door, she was fully dressed with her shoes in her hand, and her bags dragging behind her toward the door.

"You leaving?"

She jumped and turned around, like she had been caught stealing. "What are you doing up?"

"I have a job. What are you doing? It's Saturday."

"Well, I know how awkward it is having me here. I swear this wasn't my idea. And I told you I would leave."

"Do you have any idea how much shit our parents will give us if you go to a hotel?"

"I have friends," she stood up straighter. "They said I can stay with them."

"And Gloria?" I asked.

Before Lillian could answer, her phone started ringing and she gasped when she saw the caller ID. She dropped her shoes and bags, then ran toward me and pulled me down next to her on the couch.

"It's our parents on Facetime. Smile. Be happy."

"Hey Mom!" Lillian said when she answered. She held the

phone up on herself only until I could get my brain to function again. Then I heard Gloria asking where I was. "Right here!"

The camera moved to my face, and I smiled, trying to look happy like Lillian told me to do. "Hi!"

"Oh, seeing you two together again warms my heart."

"Uh, yeah, it's good having her here," I mumbled, not fooling anyone except Gloria, who always saw roses and glitter, even when it was black and moldy right in front of her. She was the happiest and most positive person I had ever known, and it was exhausting.

"We got to talking last night and thought maybe we could come down."

"What?" Lillian yelled, not liking that idea at all, and I agreed with her, that was an awful idea.

"I know you just got there, but you know how much we love family time. We don't have a date yet, but I was thinking it'd be fun to come down while you're there."

"I have a game in Charlotte on Monday," I blurted.

"We know," my dad said from off screen somewhere. "We will plan around your schedule. Just wanted to give you a heads up."

"Well that's exciting," Lillian offered, and I shot her a nasty glance. "Um Cruz was about to leave for work, and I need coffee."

"Oh yes, yes. You and your coffee," Gloria laughed. "Drink your water, too. Call me tonight!"

"Sure thing, Mom." Lillian sighed and said her goodbyes, then hung up. She turned to me with a cringe and covered her eyes with her hand.

"Why are they like this?" She moaned.

"You would know better than me."

"How am I supposed to stay with friends when they may show up at any given minute?"

"Why don't you tell them you have friends you want to stay with?" The answer seemed obvious.

"I met them online." She gave me a pointed look, and I nodded, knowing exactly what the problem was. Not only that, but I agreed with our parents on that one.

"Fuck that. Stay here."

"You know you don't want me here, Cruz."

I stood and started putting my sliders on and throwing a few things in my soccer bag that I would need at practice. "Yeah well, whatever."

She stood there silent as she watched me leave, and by the time I was in my car and driving toward the field, I was lost in old memories. Lillian wasn't my enemy, she never had been, but there were times I had to pretend she was, because being my enemy was safer than any other option.

Because of soccer, I never spent a lot of time at my dad's. It was always soccer weather in Miami so I played year round, and Dad knew how important my games were to me. But there were times he insisted that I get on a plane and attend a family function that they had planned. My mom always made sure I went, too. She worked a lot, wasn't married, and the small breaks she got from being a single parent were good for her.

The latest family function was a camping trip. I was sixteen years old, and my idea of outdoor fun was being on the beach, or the soccer field, not camping with my dad and two strangers. Yet, there I was, walking in the woods looking for something to start a fire with.

"Cruz!" My dad yelled through the trees. "We found some logs, let's roast hot dogs."

"Great," I mumbled.

It felt like Dad was trying too hard to have the big happy family he didn't get with my mom. But he didn't realize it was too late. I was almost a junior in high school, and Lillian was about to be a freshman. Not to mention, we weren't exactly raised together, or even had very much in common. I had a lot of independence, while Lillian barely got to brush her teeth by herself. I was athletic. Lillian kept her nose in her sketchbooks.

In fact, the only thing we had in common was how much we wanted to make our parents happy. Lillian and I both grinned and bore whatever they asked from us because they had both been through hell before meeting each other. I was glad Dad had Gloria, I just needed him to understand that I wasn't a baby. He couldn't start from scratch.

I took a deep breath and made my way to the clearing where our campsite was set up. Lillian was wearing her usual large hoodie, even though it was 100° outside, and there was a damn fire three feet away from her. Gloria was sticking hot dogs on a stick and handed one to Lillian before holding one up for me with a big smile.

I took a chair across the fire from Lillian and we all four quietly roasted our hot dogs. When I looked over the top of the fire, I saw Lillian's tired eyes and her pale skin. It made me wonder what her life was like when I wasn't around. But I never asked.

"How's the restaurant doing?" Dad asked me, making camp-fire conversation.

"Good," I nodded slowly. "Mom practically lives up there."

"You still helping her?" My dad beaded his eyes, warning me that my answer better be, 'Yes sir.'

"Not as much," I admitted, "Soccer takes up all my time."

Lillian rolled her eyes, and didn't even notice that I'd seen her. Dad had started to tell me how important family was, and to make sure I always helped my mom, but I was tuning him out.

Lillian's blue eyes finally found mine and I squinted at her, wondering what her problem was.

"Earth to Cruz," Dad laughed, getting my attention.

"What?"

"I said that you and Lillian need to walk the trail back to the car and grab the sleeping bags."

Lillian stood, instantly doing what she was told. "I can get them alone," she said, walking toward the trail, and out of sight.

My dad narrowed his eyes at me, and with one finger pointing toward the path, I knew I needed to go help Lillian, no matter what she said. I threw my arms in the air, but stood and walked slowly, in no hurry to catch up with her. But eventually I did, and before she saw me, she lifted her hoodie over her head.

I froze and hid, watching her wave her arms in the air to cool them off and tying the hoodie around her waist. When she kept walking, so did I, trying to stay quiet so I could keep watching her.

I knew I was acting like a creep, but I was an adolescent teenager who wanted to see what his step -sister was hiding under her sweater. My dad would have killed me, and I would never have lived down how disgusting it was that I leered at her when she didn't know.

A few steps from the car, she stopped quickly, and in response, I did as well, making a stick break underneath my feet. It was almost dark, but there was enough light for her to see me, and I raised my eyes at her as if I had been back there the whole time.

She stared at me for a solid minute until I couldn't take it anymore, and walked up closer to her. I reached around her and opened the car door, grabbing the sleeping bags with an angry tug.

Then I turned back to face her, and just in case she realized I had been lurking, I mumbled, "que asco," and kept walking back to the campsite. It took her nearly ten minutes to come back, and when she did, her hoodie was back on, and her eyes looked even more exhausted.

I hated myself, but it was better than my dad hating me for being so damn depraved.

Chapter Five

Lily

"Dang girl! I didn't know your parents were loaded! That place is nice."

"Yeah," I smiled into the camera after showing Angel around Cruz's apartment. "Just the one bedroom, but it's got a great view of the ocean."

It's not like I could show her Cruz's room. The door was shut and I wasn't crazy enough to peek my own head in, much less let her have a peek. She wanted to come over and see it personally, but I told her I was leaving for the day.

"So if you're going to the outlets in Little Havana, let's have lunch! I have to work tonight, but my shift doesn't start until five."

"Yes!" I was so excited to finally get to hug her. I intentionally chose an area she said she was near in hopes we could meet up. If I didn't go her way, she would eventually head my way, and until I figured out what to do about Cruz, it was safer to initiate the plans. "How about you pick a place, since you know the area. Text me the location and let's plan on meeting at one."

"Oh my God, Lily, this is insane! I wish Jackie wasn't working all day, but I know you two will meet soon."

"Oh we will. But for now, I need to get ready and head out. Wish me luck, hopefully there is a suit for these interviews with my name on it."

"Better you than me," she laughed. "I'll see you in a bit."

We hung up and I had a huge grin on my face. Even in my six years of college, I never felt like I connected with people the way Angel and I had. She was, without a doubt, my best friend. But it wasn't lost on me that I had never told Angel and Jackie my biggest secrets. It was intentional, because I had learned that those secrets changed the people around me. Before I confessed, I needed to meet them in person, and get closer to them. I just hoped that when the time came, they loved me enough to understand why I hadn't been upfront with them.

In the meantime, I had to mitigate the lies, because the more I told, the higher the chances I would lose the only friends I ever had. For example, I didn't really have to shop for a suit. My mom and I had gone together before I left home and I was already prepared for my interviews. But since I knew Angel worked at a restaurant near the outlets, it worked in my favor to come up with a reason to go over there.

By eleven-thirty, Angel texted me the address to a restaurant, and I searched up places that were around it. I wanted to give myself time to actually shop for a few minutes because it made me feel a little better about my fib.

Little Havana was on the west side of Miami, and by the time I got over there, I found an Old Navy and ran in to grab something–anything. I pushed the clearance rack around until I found a tank top that was marked down. Four dollars to prove I really was shopping, was all I could afford.

Once I checked out, I headed straight to the restaurant and immediately saw Angel bouncing on the sidewalk as I pulled into a parking space. She was squealing as if we were fourteen, and I cherished that moment. No one had ever been that happy to see me, especially when I was actually fourteen.

"Angel!" I screamed, getting from my car. I ran into her open arms and pushed the tears that wanted to fall as far down as I could. "This is crazy!"

She pushed me back from her hug to look at me and then pulled me into her arms again. "Girl. You're gorgeous, and taller than I thought you'd be. Hugging you is surreal."

When we finally separated, I gave her the same look she had given me and nodded. "You're shorter than I thought you'd be, and somehow we are the same height."

"But," she smiled and raised a finger toward me, "am I also gorgeous?"

"Oh please," I laughed. "You know damn well you make J-lo look like a gremlin."

Leading up to meeting one another, we joked around that the screen made us look different and we probably wouldn't recognize each other in person. *"I only look this gorgeous through a camera,"* Angel had joked with me. But she really was incredibly beautiful.

"Okay let's eat. You're going to love this place."

"Moros?" I read the sign. "Cuban?"

"Miami is crawling with amazing Cuban food. Moros is second best, but Jackie would kill me if we went to Tico's without her."

We got settled into a booth, and I let Angel order for me since she insisted I try the *pan con lechon*. It took us no time to start talking like we always did, and the fear I'd had of her not being real, was washed away as we connected face to face.

Our laughter was nonstop, and we shed a few tears as we talked about how much we had meant to one another over the past few months. When it was time to leave, I hated that I had to go back to Cruz's, and not home with her. But as we said our goodbyes, a quick text from my mom reminded me that I still had some secrets to handle.

Angel had started walking toward her own car when she stopped and turned back around. "I have a good idea!"

"I'm all ears," I smiled.

"I know Jackie and I both have to work tomorrow and Monday. Then on Tuesday, you have your first interview, right?" I nodded as her eyes gleamed with ideas. "But on Wednesday, let's do something fun."

"Yes! Let's do it. I'm all yours Wednesday."

"I'll get with Jackie and make the plans, you just be ready!"

"What should I wear?" I lifted my shoulders a little, being silly while pretending to be sexy. "I have a little black dress that I think you will adore."

"Ohh," she laughed. "And we will definitely find a reason to wear that. I say we call that your celebration dress for when you land one of these jobs. For Wednesday, let's go casual. No promises, yet, but I think I have an idea, and I want to surprise you."

My smile was hurting my face. I had never had a friend surprise me with anything. "You got a date."

We hugged one more time and I started my drive back to Cruz's house. I called my mom on the way, just to tell her I had been browsing the stores, and that she didn't have to worry about me. She even told me I sounded happy, and it made *her* happy to hear me so full of joy.

"It's Miami," I shrugged, even though she couldn't see me. "There isn't anything not to love." Thankfully, she kept our chat short and I was able to turn the music up for the rest of my drive. It helped me think and clear my head, and I felt the stress I always carried slowly fading.

By the time I got back to Cruz's place, I had decided that as soon as I knew about my job interviews, I would tell Angel more about me, the real Lillian Harris.

When I walked toward the elevator and made my way to the twelfth floor, I realized I had a strut that I hadn't had earlier that day. I felt confident, and didn't think there was anything that could ruin the day I had with Angel.

Then I opened the door to the apartment and saw Cruz. He was shirtless, with sweat dripping down his chest, and loose shorts hanging low on his waist. He had a backward baseball hat on and was barefoot. There was a woman next to him, quickly sliding a shirt over her head to cover a sports bra as they awkwardly saw me standing there.

"Oh, um," I tried to save myself and looked toward my bedroom door. "Sorry to interrupt. Um...I'm gonna..." Before I could finish my thought, I ran and shut the door tightly behind me, then leaned against it and slid down to the floor, trying to get my breathing under control.

It wasn't what I walked in on that had me close to hyperventilating, it was the image of Cruz that would probably forever be ingrained in my brain. The way he stood there with his sweaty, athletic body, his chest heaving, and the hat on backward. Cruz had always been attractive, and time had obviously been good to him, but it wasn't okay that I had thoughts and feelings about that, especially considering who he was.

Chapter Six

Cruz

I didn't know what Lillian was doing in her room, but she had been in there ever since she'd awkwardly run across the living room while avoiding eye contact. That moment was exactly why I didn't want her to stay with me. What she thought she saw, and what was actually going on, were two different things. And despite trying not to care, it bothered me that she assumed I would bring someone home to fuck in the living room, knowing she would be there.

I wasn't that big of a dick.

It had been three hours. My teammates and I were supposed to be meeting at a club, but all I could think about was knocking on Lillian's door and telling her about my friend Erin. I had even practiced subtle ways to tell her that Erin was into chicks, without making it seem like I was worried about what she thought.

Erin Rhodes was a fairly new friend, who I met through a teammate, Rhys Peyton. While he was trying to land his girl, Ash, I played the role of his wingman and entertained her best friend, Erin. I tried several times to get in Erin's pants, because she was a smoke show, but once I realized I wasn't her *type*, we clicked on a friend level. Ash and Erin both played soccer for Miami University, and Erin was getting ready to start pursuing her pro career. As her friend, she had asked me to help, which involved a few workouts and study sessions.

When Erin was leaving my place, she laughed, knowing what Lillian assumed, and knowing it would bother me. She even sent me a text later asking if it was all okay yet, and when I sent her a mad-face emoji, she just sent a crying-laughing one back to me.

"Um," I stood outside Lillian's door and held my hand in the air to knock. "Lillian?"

The door opened before I could even touch it and she looked at me with her big blue eyes.

"I ordered a pizza," I mumbled, then waved behind me toward the direction of the kitchen.

"Thanks," she nodded. "I'm not hungry, though."

Her stomach made a funny noise in the quiet space around us and I looked down, then back up. She looked mortified, and I couldn't help but crack a smile. "Sure."

"Okay," she shrugged. "Kind of hungry, but just trying to give you privacy."

"She left hours ago," I scoffed. "But the pizza just got here."

Walking away, I left her to decide to come eat, or not. I didn't really care. *Yes I did.* But I was glad that she knew Erin had left, and I was relieved when she started following me toward the kitchen. There were already plates on the bar, so I spun the boxes around to face her so she could grab what she wanted.

"I thought you said *a pizza.* Are you expecting company?" She asked as she sorted the seven boxes of cheesy goodness.

"I just didn't know what you would like," I shrugged, then took a bite of my own slice. "Ordered a little of everything."

The way her cheeks lifted up slightly made me fixate on her

lips for a minute. Her eyes were scanning over each box as she lifted the lid to see the contents. Once she had two pieces on her plate, she looked up, and caught me staring.

"Thanks," she whispered, shyly. "I was planning on leaving to grab something, but this is really nice."

I smirked and tried not to smile, I just couldn't help it. "Were you going to wait until I went to bed to be sure I wasn't fucking anyone in the living room?"

Her small smile fell, and my stomach twisted, afraid she wouldn't realize I was teasing her. She slid her tongue out and licked her lips as her cheeks reddened. I could tell her brain was turning over several responses before landing on one.

"I met with my friends today. They're great, and I know I can go stay there by the time you get back from New York."

"No," I snapped. "You're fine here. I was just kidding."

Her smile tried lifting again, but it fell just as quickly. "Like I said this morning, I know you don't want me here."

"Erin is gay," I blurted, making both of us stare at each other in confusion. *Why the fuck did I say that?*

"Oh. Well, okay. That changes...nothing really."

I nodded, agreeing with her. It changed nothing... *No wait.* "It means you don't have to leave."

"Who the hell is Erin?" She asked, her voice raising higher, clearly exasperated.

Only then did I realize that part of my conversation with her was happening in my head, and she had no idea what the hell I was talking about.

"The girl that was here," I explained. "I didn't fuck her. I'm helping her get ready to go pro. She would rather fuck you than me."

She had taken a bite of her pizza and was slowly chewing as she processed all the details I just laid out for her. When she swallowed, my eyes followed the movement of her neck, and the way she licked the grease off her lips. That reaction I was having to her was the exact reason I didn't want her there, while also being the same reason I wasn't going to let her leave. I didn't know how to act, but I knew it would make my life easier if I went ahead and figured us out. Especially since she might be moving to Miami.

Plus, we were already making more progress as adults than as teenagers. We were using whole sentences with one another.

"Okay, so," she started as she slid her remaining pizza away from her. "You don't want me here, but you don't think I should go to my friend's house, and Erin doesn't want to fuck you?"

"Not even a threesome," I shrugged. "She isn't into dick."

Okay that may have been unnecessary information.

It felt like forever before she responded, but I stayed quiet because I didn't know what else was going to come out of my mouth. Eventually, though, she busted out laughing. "I don't understand anything we're talking about, Cruz."

"Yeah well," I tried laughing with her, but my heart was beating too fast. "I'm just trying to tell you to stop trying to go stay with some stranger. Also, I don't bring women here, ever. So the odds of you seeing me fuck someone on that couch are zero."

She nodded, while still coming down from her hysteria, and rounded the counter, coming closer to me in the kitchen. I was still in my shorts, had no shirt on—my hat tossed onto the coffee table. She was in jean shorts and a tank top, and her hair was piled into a messy bun.

When she reached around me to grab a cup, I stayed still, feeling the heat from her skin barely skimming mine. Moving would have made it easier on her—and me—but some crazy part of me wondered if those awkward feelings were just one sided. *Was I testing her?*

She filled her cup with some water from the tap and drank it down while I watched her swallow. Then she refilled the same cup, and started walking toward her bedroom again.

"Where are you going?"

She turned around with another confused look on her face and tilted her head. "To bed?"

"So we're done talking?" *What the hell was I doing?* "Just like that?"

"Was there more? I think I got the basics. I'll stop trying to stay with my friends, you won't embarrass me by doing 'stuff' out in the open. I got it and I appreciate it. Promise."

"Then why are you going to bed?"

"Because it's nine-thirty."

"On a Saturday," I snorted. "Nine-thirty is early for any night of the week, unless you're seven."

"Yesterday was a long travel day. Then I drove all the way to Little Havana today. And I have spoken more words to you than ever before. I'm freaking exhausted."

Without another glance, she turned back toward her door and quietly shut it behind her. I was still in the exact spot I had been in since she joined me for pizza. My feet felt glued to the floor, and I started lifting them one at a time to make sure that feeling was all in my head.

Once I was able to make it back to my own room, I grabbed my phone and sent one of my teammates, Tripp Maddux, a quick text.

We still on for tonight?

Yeah. Meet you at Rosa Sky at ten?

Throwing my clothes on now.

I tossed my phone onto my bed and changed into jeans and a gray t-shirt that had a few buttons below the neckline. It was just enough to pass as "something nice" for a place like Rosa Sky. The thought to tap on Lillian's door and tell her I was leaving popped into my head, but I shook that idea off. I'd never had to tell anyone when I was leaving, and telling Lillian would just make me pissy again about her being in my space.

Dammit, I needed to get laid again. Apparently soccer practice and my workout with Erin wasn't enough to get over having a house guest. Turning back into my bedroom, I reached into my side drawer and grabbed a few condoms before heading back out. Three was probably overkill, but if I wanted to, I could have a use for all of them before I came home.

That should cure me.

Chapter Seven

Lily

Lying to everyone that breathed near me was exhausting, but I wasn't exactly tired.

Talking to Cruz, especially about him having sex with someone—or not—made me uncomfortable. There were too many questions on the tip of my tongue, like *"Why do you have your own place, but refuse to use it for intimate moments?"* Or, *"Have you ever had a threesome?"*

Not that I would know anything about any of it since I was still a freaking virgin. The closest I had ever come to having sex was with my college boyfriend. We were getting intimate one night, and asking him to be my first was an automatic *off* button for him. Admittedly, asking him may have ruined the moment, but I wanted him to know he was my first so he knew he was special.

Instead, he acted like I told him I was a serial killer and he was my next victim. No one in the history of getting dressed had ever gotten dressed so fast and left.

Obviously, I had never heard from him after that, which I chose to look at as a blessing in disguise because if he couldn't handle that, he wasn't going to be able to handle anything else about me. Plus, when I returned home for a few months to rest, Mom climbed into bed with me and we had a girl talk. It was a relief when I was able to honestly tell her I was a virgin. She didn't have to worry about me, and I promised her that night that I would wait for *the one.*

As soon as I landed a job and settled down, I figured I would join a dating app and start seeing who was out there for me. Maybe my 'one' was in Miami, waiting for me all along.

The slamming of the front door made me realize Cruz had probably left, so I crept out of my room to be sure. Like he had said, it was Saturday night in Miami, and that meant his plans were much different than mine. He was a superstar and I bet he loved going out, getting the attention from all the women that threw themselves at him.

It worked for me, because at least with him gone, I didn't have to hide and pretend to be asleep. I rummaged for some decaf coffee and sat on the balcony, soaking in the ocean breeze as I sipped from a mug that read, "I'm a keeper," with a soccer ball heart. *How very Cruz-like to have that on a coffee mug,* I laughed to myself.

The balcony was big, wrapping around the entire side of the building that faced the water. The other apartment on our floor must have had a balcony as well, but probably faced the bay, which most likely made it a little cheaper. *Geez, Lily.* Rolling my eyes, I stopped my silly thoughts before they ever got started. There was no way I would ever be able to afford something like Cruz had, and even if I could, living that close to him was not a good idea. The balcony was amazing, though, and I was going to make a point to soak in the view while I could.

With the moon, shining down and reflected over the water, it looked eerie and dangerous, yet serene and calming. It was a lot like Cruz and me, if I wanted to get deep, because despite how dangerous it felt being near him, he still felt calming in a way. We may not have gotten along, or even spoken to each other much, but he had still been around since I was twelve. His presence both scared, and comforted me.

By the time the decaf was gone, I was ready to go to sleep. It was close to one in the morning and I headed inside to clean my mug. When I got closer to the kitchen, I heard commotion in the hallway outside the apartment, and immediately assumed it was someone looking at the empty apartment.

But it was too late to shop for apartments, right? Then the handle on the front door started to shake, and panic settled into my stomach.

"What the–?" I set the mug on the counter and backed away, easing myself into the living room, but still with a view of the door. It had to be Cruz, but I couldn't imagine him having so much trouble getting into his own place.

Then the banging started, and my heart jumped into my throat. Grabbing my phone from the coffee table, I held it tight, ready to call 911 if I thought I needed to.

After several loud bangs, the door handle started to jiggle again and I pressed the nine on my phone's keypad. My mind was changing, it couldn't have been Cruz, and no one else should have been there, at least I didn't think so. His dad had a key, but our parents weren't here. They wouldn't just show up and scare the crap out of me, would they?

Maybe it was his mom?

I pressed a one into the keypad and held my breath, ready to finish dialing, when the door flew open with a loud thud. My phone flew from my hand as I screamed and backed away from a large figure that was walking toward me. The lights were off, but I could tell it wasn't Cruz. It was, however, a man's large frame.

The figure stopped near the wall, close to the bar that had all the pizza boxes on it, and started randomly hitting the walls.

It gave me a second to look around for my phone, hoping I could find it and finish that call that I should have made when the banging first started.

But I couldn't see it until the figure found what he was looking for and the lights came on. "Ah ha!"

"What do you want?" I yelled, hoping I sounded less afraid and more valiant.

The guy turned around and ran a hand through his hair before holding up both hands toward me. "You must be Cruz's sister. Fuck, sorry if I scared you."

"Who are you?" I demanded.

He looked at me like I was crazy for a minute, squinting his eyes like he didn't believe a word I said. But all I did was ask a simple question, and I squinted back at him, silently telling him that he owed me an answer.

"Um," the guy laughed then shook his head in defeat. "I'm Tripp Maddux. Cruz's teammate. The best midfielder in the league. Currently Cruz's knight in shining armor."

"Well, *Tripp Maddux,* what the hell are you doing here?" I ignored everything else about him and put my hands on my hips.

Tripp held up the key that he used to unlock the door, and I recognized it being the same set that Cruz had lying around earlier. "I brought your brother home."

I ignored his second attempt at telling me Cruz and I were siblings, and started walking closer to him. "Then where is he?"

Tripp held up a finger, asking me to wait a minute, and walked outside the door that he had left open when he barged in. He reached out, behind the wall, and when he started coming back inside, Cruz was wrapped under his arm.

"Oh my god!"

"Yeah, I've never seen him so fucked," Tripp laughed. "Dude was working out a lot of issues tonight."

"Is he drunk?"

Tripp smirked and then raised one eyebrow. "We don't normally Do-si-do like this after a night out. Trust me, he's definitely wasted."

"What are you gonna do with him?"

"I'm putting him in his bed and leaving. That's as far as our bromance goes."

I nodded and let Tripp lead Cruz into his bedroom. Cruz was awake and walking, but his eyes were glassy, and he was mumbling something about trying to score. I assumed he was just talking about soccer until Tripp came back into the living room laughing.

"Poor guy is still trying to score tonight. He's gonna be pissed when he wakes up tomorrow and realizes he struck out with the only girl he talked to."

Oh, *score*. Right.

"Well, um, thanks," I shrugged, not knowing the social protocol for saying goodbye to a stranger who brought your drunk step-brother home, and scared the shit out of his house guest in the process. It was a new situation for me.

"Do me a favor." Tripp stood in the doorway, about to leave, and looked back at me. "Go easy on him. He just wants to be a good brother."

"He isn't my brother," I finally said, not wanting Tripp to misunderstand our family dynamics.

"I know," he winked, then shut the door.

Walking quickly, I locked the door again, and then took a deep breath before restarting the search for my phone. It had slid under the couch when I threw it and I had to get on my hands and knees to reach it. I also silently thanked Cruz, or whoever cleaned his place, for doing a good job under the couch.

When I stood back up, I turned to head toward my room, but stopped when I saw Cruz standing near his bedroom door.

"Shit, you scared me," I screeched, putting a hand over my heart. I was going to need an EKG if the night kept going the way it was. "What are you doing up?"

"This is your fault," he slurred. "I was just trying to get lucky, let off some steam, and I came home with all three of my condoms."

"How is that my fault?"

Wait...Three?

"Because I don't have scoreless nights," he huffed. "I have lots of sex. But you stopped me."

"You said you don't bring anyone home with you. So how did I stop you?"

"That's hard to explain without getting grounded." He pouted like a kid.

"Grounded?"

"You heard me, *sis*." He may have been drunk, but he still snarled when he spoke.

"Goodnight," I snapped and started walking toward my door. I had no way of dealing with him while he was inebriated.

"Wait!" Cruz yelled. "Can you help me?"

I raised an eyebrow at him and crossed my arms, annoyed, and wishing he would just go to bed. "What?"

He waved me closer and I shuffled my feet in his direction. When I was only an arm length away, he reached out and pulled me against his chest and wrapped his arms around me in a tight hug. For just a few seconds, I forgot he was drunk, and was tempted to wrap my arms around him as well. It felt like a peace offering, or starting over.

Then he spoke.

"Can you help me find my room?"

Chapter Eight

Cruz

The first rule in my nightlife was to never go out and have more than two drinks. Any more than that was just asking for trouble. But the second I stepped into Rosa Sky, I threw all my rules over the edge of the high rise building we were on, and ordered three shots.

The headache I had, and my lack of memory, told me that I didn't stop after three. *No one ever does.* Placing that order was the equivalent of me saying, "Fuck it," and I didn't want to even speculate how much I ended up having.

I was curious how I got home, though.

Without moving, I reached for my phone on my nightstand where I always left it, but I came up empty after patting around a few times. Then I checked my jeans, hoping I found it in my pocket. Still, I came up empty.

"Fuck," I sighed, knowing I had to actually get up so I could start investigating how my night went. That would involve finding my phone, checking my bank account, looking at my camera roll, and then texting Tripp to fill in the hazy gaps.

Sitting up, I turned to hang my legs off the edge of my bed, but my right arm didn't come with me. I tried pulling it around, but it felt like it was numb, and had no feeling. Panic started to sink in and I turned around to see if I could wake my arm up. But when I did, I realized that not only was my arm asleep, but it was also attached to Lillian.

"What the fuck?" My words were so loud that her eyes popped open and she started moving, looking around my room like she was lost. When it finally sank in, she sat up and tried pulling her left arm away from me only to find out the same thing I just had.

"Take these handcuffs off," she croaked, almost in tears.

"How the hell did we get in handcuffs?"

She shook her head, disappointment radiating off her. "You came in drunk, and when Tripp left, you came out of your room and asked me to help you find your room."

Oh no.

"I walked you in here and you fell trying to take off your shirt."

I looked down and my shirt was still on, so I looked back to her and hoped she kept telling me the story–no matter how mortified I was.

"I told you to leave the shirt on and lay down so you did, but you held my hand and I fell down with you. When I started to get up, you handcuffed me and told me I wasn't allowed to go to my friend's house."

"Oh no," I groaned out loud that time. "Please God no."

"I looked for the key, but you passed out, and I gave up. Please Cruz, please, take them off of me *now*."

Wiping my freehand down my face, I groaned before reaching over to our joined wrists. I grabbed the cuff wrapped around her and pushed the release button on the side. It slid right open and her jaw dropped when she realized that no key was needed.

"These are from my Halloween costume two years ago," I confessed. "Not real."

"You mean I could have gotten out of here without a key?" Her voice was high as she climbed onto her knees. She had on a thin tank top that showed her nipples, and I had to lay back onto the bed and put both hands over my eyes to keep from embarrassing myself further.

"Just, go," I moaned.

She scrambled off the bed, then I heard the slamming of my bedroom door. Taking my hands to my temples, I watched as my fan circled on my ceiling, and hoped it was a sign that I was in a dream–or a nightmare. But vague memories started coming back to me, and I knew exactly why I ended up handcuffed to Lillian. I was scared to death she would leave. Whether I wanted her here, or not, I needed her to stay, and I knew I needed to apologize big time for the ass I turned into the night before.

My phone chimed with a text so I leaned up and started looking for it again, finding it clear across the room, cracked, and barely any battery left. Just enough to read the incoming text from Tripp.

You dead?

WTF?

You went hard.

Lillian told me you dragged my ass to bed.

She's fucking hot. We scared her a little, so she wasn't even thinking of how I could see her tits through her shirt.

Anger rose up in me, and I was tempted to throw my phone against the wall. But with only a few hours before I had to leave for New York, I stopped myself, knowing I wouldn't have time to replace it. Being a hot head wasn't normally my thing, but the guilt, and the anger, was almost too much for me to bear.

Everything okay after I left?

No, Tripp, it wasn't.

There was no reason to tell him the rest of the story because he would never let me live it down. Not after I spent all night talking about Lily, and how she always turned my life upside down without even meaning to. Then I vaguely remembered telling him I needed to fuck someone to forget her.

Oh fuck.

I groaned as I shuffled to my shower and turned it on cold. Without even taking my clothes off, I walked into the spray and let the water punish me for being so fucking off my game. Slapping my palms against the glass of the shower created an echo in the bathroom but the fact that the glass didn't shatter felt disappointing, and I was tempted to try again.

Slight movement out of the corner of my eye stopped me, and I glanced up toward the bathroom door. It was open, the way I had left it, but Lily was standing in the doorway. Her hair was wild, blond waves still messy from sleep, and still wearing her thin tank top and tiny shorts. Each of her hands were holding on to either side of the doorway and her legs were crossed as if she was about to take a step but decided against it.

We stared at one another as the water continued to beat across my chest, making my t-shirt cling to me. I waited for her to tell me why she was there, why she felt the need to come back into my room, much less why she was staring at me.

In my gut, I knew I was the one that deserved her ire, but just like when I was a kid, I got angry at her for no reason.

Giving her a snarl, I lifted my shirt away from my body and pulled it over my head, throwing it onto the tile floor. Her eyes got wider, but she never moved. Grabbing each side of the shower entrance wall, I mimicked her stance and leaned forward, tilting my head, daring her to tell me why the hell she was there.

She didn't back down though, she took two steps into the bathroom and put her hands on her hips, her own challenge being thrown between us. My head was pounding, and the memories that flashed back were making me wince internally. There was no way I could win a battle with her if it lasted too long.

"What?" I barked, urging her to get to the point and leave me alone so she didn't have to see me looking so weak.

"I thought you fell. I heard a loud bang."

My slap against the glass must have echoed through the whole fucking apartment. Her concern had me backing up into the shower and shaking my head, trying not to be upset. "I'm fine."

Her eyes gave me one more glance all over, and then she nodded, turning and walking from my bathroom. Reaching into my pocket, I pulled the three condoms I took with me out and tossed them through the open doorway and onto the bathroom floor with my shirt. Then I took my hands to my belt and started taking my jeans off.

My cock had hardened while I was having my stare down with Lillian, but I refused to acknowledge what that meant. Didn't mean I wasn't going to let myself feel the relief. My jeans were open in seconds and I fisted myself, secretly hoping she walked back in and saw how fucked up I was. She'd see it was her fault, and I wondered if she would feel the need to finish what she had unknowingly started.

"Stop," I growled at myself, not wanting to get off to her

image. But it was too late. Even with my head pounding, and my body weak, I painted the glass wall in front of me with my cum. The only upside was that maybe, just maybe, that would be enough to get me by until she was no longer staying with me, and no longer so tempting.

Chapter Nine

Lily

I may have been a virgin, but that didn't mean I didn't get turned on when I saw Cruz in the shower. Fully clothed was almost more erotic than had he been naked.

Before he realized I was there, he looked vulnerable. His guard was down, and I could almost see the regret in the way he was standing. Whether it was because he handcuffed us together, or because he drank too much, it didn't matter. He had acted out of character, and he was punishing himself for doing so.

Then when he pulled that soaked shirt over his head, I came close to clenching my thighs together.

By the time he came out of his room later, I was showered and dressed for the day. My mom had called, and I held the phone to my ear as I picked at the leftover pizza for breakfast.

"Yeah, Cruz is here," I told her as he looked up at me. He stood still, wearing loose soccer shorts and a t-shirt, his eyes wide with a little fear. "I know it's Sunday, but I think he has to leave." He had a bag over his shoulder, and he started walking again, dropping it near the door, before joining me in the kitchen. "And no, you can't speak to him."

Cruz huffed a little and I looked up to see him with half a smile on his face. He was relieved I was being a wall between him and my overprotective mother, especially after the morning he'd had. He grabbed a few slices of the pizza and placed them onto a plate, then popped them into the microwave.

"Let me call you tonight," I reasoned with her. "We can Facetime."

She was content with that idea and let me off the phone quickly, so I placed my phone down onto the counter and turned. Cruz was leaning his back against the counter on the other side of the kitchen. His hands were gripping the edges behind him and his fingers were tapping as he waited for his pizza to heat up.

"Whatever you do," he sighed, "don't go."

"I'm not," I shrugged, not really wanting to leave anymore. "You don't scare me."

"I don't want to scare you," he nodded. "So that's good."

"What time are you leaving?"

"In an hour or so." The microwave started beeping and he turned around to take his pizza out. Then he walked closer to me, and leaned his hip on the bar getting close enough for me to smell his shampoo. "Just enough time to apologize a million times."

"Stop," I smiled. "I'm actually glad you weren't alone last night. And your bed is pretty comfy."

He snorted and rolled his eyes. "I'll be home late tomorrow, maybe we can start over."

"Deal," I smiled. "Maybe we should pretend we just met."

"Ohhh that means you would be staying with a stranger, and your mother would fly here and beat my ass with her bare hands if she knew I let you stay with a stranger."

You are a stranger, I thought to myself.

"Well, what she doesn't know won't hurt her."

Cruz's head tilted and his smile came and went as he thought over my words. Then he nodded and took a bite of his pizza, temporarily ending our conversation. I cleaned up the mess I made while he ate, and when he brought his plate to the sink, I grabbed it and cleaned it as well.

"I have someone come by on Tuesdays. She cleans everything so just a heads up so she doesn't scare you."

"Won't you be back by then?"

"Yeah but we have another game Wednesday so I'll spend all afternoon Tuesday at the complex. I have meetings and stuff."

Putting the clean plate up in the cabinet, I nodded to myself, almost sad that I wasn't going to see much of him for a few days. His absence was supposed to make staying with him easier, but for some reason, I wanted him to be there more than I did yesterday.

Cruz grabbed my hand and led me to the couch, pulling me down next to him and our knees touched as we angled ourselves toward one another. "I, um..." he started to say, suddenly shy in a way I never knew he was capable of. "I never drink as much as I did last night. Things just got away from me."

There was no premeditated thought to me moving my hand to his hair. The longer strands on top were just flopped over and I wanted to touch it. Something to distract me as I thought of a reply. "We're good. If that is what this is about. I promise. It wasn't that bad, and now that I'm no longer cuffed to you, and can pee at my own freewill, it's kinda funny."

He smiled and grabbed my hand from his hair, holding it between us. "Good. And I trashed those cuffs. No reason to test temptation again."

Whether he meant to or not, I felt a flutter in my stomach again, and pulled my hands from his to create some separation. "Yeah, we wouldn't want that."

Or would we?

"What are you going to do while I'm gone?"

"Beach," I said with a dreamy sigh. "The beach, and then soaking up the evenings on your balcony. The view is incredible. All you're missing is something besides an old folding chair out there."

He laughed as he stood and flung his bag back over his shoulder. "I never spend enough time out there for more than that old chair."

"Well you should," I smiled at him. "It's breathtaking."

"I'll think about that," he nodded, then grabbed his keys and opened the door. "I know you have my cell number. Use it if you need me, or anything. And um, the game will be on the MLS network...if you like soccer."

"Thanks."

"Oh and, make yourself at home." Then he was gone.

My phone buzzed on the counter and I grabbed it as I made my way to the balcony, seeing Angel's name.

Jackie made plans for Wednesday! I'll send more details later!

Can't wait!

Looking out at the water, I knew I needed to be on the beach, so I didn't waste a lot of time getting my suit on and getting down there. I spent all day under a rented umbrella, reading a book and relaxing. It was the most relaxed I had been in a long time, and it made me think that Miami was actually going to be good for me.

I planned on doing the exact same thing on Monday, but an early sharp knock on the door changed those plans.

"Delivery," a guy yelled just as I put my eye to the peephole.

Quickly opening the door, I saw more than just the one

man. There were six of them, all wearing the same furniture delivery outfit. "Are you looking for the other apartment?" Maybe someone rented it out.

"I don't think so. Are you Lillian Harris?"

"Yes," I confirmed warily.

"A gentleman named Cruz Martin asked us to deliver these items and set them up."

"I don't know anything about that."

Just as I was going to ask them to leave, a text popped up on my phone. Luckily, it was a number I had already saved and knew exactly who it was.

> There's a delivery coming. Don't freak out, just let them in.

Chapter Ten

Cruz

I looked at my phone, waiting for a response from Lily, but it didn't come in before I had to head to the field to warm up. When I came back in, I checked my phone again, and smiled.

That was a laugh. One tiny gesture didn't change the fact that she would be ready to run the second she got that job. *Or I wouldn't be ready to throw her out.* That was just the nature of our relationship. Still, I wanted her to feel comfortable, and it was something I needed anyway.

"What are you reading?" Rhys asked, tapping my arm before sitting down next to me at his locker.

Rhys Peyton was the one guy I had to avoid for a while. He was our best player, but I may have teased him a *little* when he was trying to deny his feelings for Ash. If he knew what I sent Lily, he would have ammo to shoot at me for years.

"Just an email." That wasn't a complete lie, I had pulled my email up to confirm the delivery status.

"An email?" He asked unbelievingly. "From a girl?"

"No, just some shit I ordered." I put my phone up into my locker, and played off whatever Rhys saw on my face when he walked up. It was probably a little satisfaction at doing some-thing right for a change, but that's all it was, and Rhys didn't need details.

"Uh huh," he laughed but let it go. "How's your sister doing? She finally get in?"

"She's not my sister," I bit at him, only to see his face lit up like Christmas morning. "And stop trying to push my buttons."

"I didn't know there were buttons to push."

"Lily is a no-fly zone. You give me shit about anyone else, but Lily and I have a very strained relationship. The last thing I need is more reasons to try kicking her out of my place."

"So here's what I don't understand," Rhys leaned in, just as we were being called back to the field to start the match. "Why are you letting her stay with you if you don't want her there?"

"It's complicated," I sighed, standing up and starting my walk down the tunnel, toward the field. Rhys stayed beside me, listening, as if to tell me he wanted me to try explaining no matter how difficult it may be. "I don't want to disappoint my dad. She's always tried not to upset her mom. Together, they can make us do just about anything they want."

"I doubt not wanting your estranged step sister at your house would disappoint your dad," Rhys snorted.

"Lillian has always been an overprotected princess. If her mom gets upset, my dad will get upset, and they seem to think she is safer staying with 'family.'"

As we took the field, Rhys patted me on the back and shrugged, "Take it out on the field. She'll be gone soon."

We separated and jogged to our positions, getting ready for the first kick. I slid my keeper gloves on and started jumping in the goalie box, keeping loose while the referee set the ball. Then we were off, and I was in game mode, completely unattuned to anything that didn't involve the ball.

For most of the game, defense kept the ball away from our goal, and my night was almost quiet. But toward the end of the match, Charlotte FC got closer and closer to scoring. Their midfield got loose with the ball and drove toward me in the goal. He was wide open, and it was going to be me against him as soon as he decided to strike.

He tried to fake to my left, but when he kicked it toward my right side, I saw the shift and dove, blocking the ball from entering the goal. It would have been a good play if I had caught it, but it deflected, and went right back into the path of the Charlotte midfielder. He took another shot on goal before I could get back up, and tapped the ball into the other side of the net.

"Fuck," I sighed, knocking the grass off my shorts and getting ready for the reset.

Tripp took the kick off and sent it to Rhys, who passed it back to me. I pointed at our right wing, Luca, but kicked the ball toward Rhys instead. Charlotte wasn't fooled, but it was enough to get Tripp down the field and ready for Rhys to pass again.

When Tripp kicked toward the goal, their keeper stopped the score and punted the ball back to midfield. They drove hard, headed my way, and our defenders were overmatched. It was up to me, I had to stop them from scoring, because as much as tying sucked, losing was worse.

The same guy who scored earlier was nearing my goalie box and he faked right before moving left. He had no one to pass it to, so we were one on one, and his fakes weren't going to fool me.

He finally kicked, and the ball sailed toward the top left corner of the goal. I timed myself then launched my body as far as I could, grabbing the ball and curling it into my stomach to keep it from being rebounded. The whistle blew to signal the end of the game as my team grabbed me from the ground, and praised me for my stop. But I wasn't happy because we didn't win.

Even on the flight home, I stewed in my own self-hatred at letting Charlotte score on me the way they did. I didn't even tell my teammates goodbye, just walked to my car and drove home in silence, letting myself replay over and over again what I could have done differently, and how to prevent it from happening again.

It was late by the time I finally got home, and until I saw the pair of pink flip flops by the front door, it slipped my mind that I had a house guest. The fact that I had nearly forgotten Lily was there was indicative of how far into my own head I had gotten.

My heart sped up as my eyes roamed the empty apartment. It was nearly midnight and she had her interview the next day, so I figured she was asleep. Setting my bag by the door, I gingerly walked into the kitchen and pulled the refrigerator open. It was a habit, but I knew there was nothing to eat. If I didn't eat out, at the stadium, or at my mom's, I just didn't eat. But I had been too upset to eat after the game, and now that I was home, my stomach was growling.

Surprisingly, there was a bowl in the refrigerator with a note taped to the plastic that covered its contents.

*I saved you some dinner in case you're hungry.
Microwave two minutes for perfection.*

Peeking into the bowl, my mouth watered at the sight of the leek and potato soup. It was something her mother cooked often, and I never turned it down. Soup was comforting, and when I was in Brooksville to visit, it made me feel like I was actually part of their family.

Wonder if it was a coincidence? That she made it, or she knew I needed the comfort? Most likely a coincidence but I was going to take it and let it warm my soul that had gone cold on the field earlier that day. It was fucking delicious, exactly the way I remembered it being, and I fist pumped the air a little that Lily had learned the recipe.

There was already a lighter bounce in my step as I made my way to bed, but I stopped when I remembered everything I had delivered earlier, and decided to check it out first.

Right outside the door, I saw that a few lounge chairs, two rocking chairs, and a table had been set up perfectly to the left. Then I glanced to the right and saw the oversized chaise lounge and couch, with a coffee table and tabletop fire pit.

She told me I needed something out there, something to enjoy the space more, and spend more time soaking in the view. It looked good, and she was right, it was amazing having the space full of comfort. There was also a lot of satisfaction knowing I had arranged to get it there so quickly for her to enjoy.

Just when I was going to back up into the door and go to bed, my eyes glanced again at the chaise. There was a blanket pulled up to her chin so I barely noticed her at first, but Lily was sleeping soundly with a book laid in her hand.

It was Florida, "the sunshine state," which meant random

rain showers could pop up at any given moment, even if the radar was clear. The balcony was huge, she probably wouldn't get wet, but she may have gotten scared if lightning started popping over the water.

As high as we were, the wind was blowing, and despite the warm air, a chill came over me. I reached down to shake Lily awake, knowing I couldn't leave her out there, but she rolled over and ignored my attempt.

Instead of trying to wake her again, I slid my arms under her body and cradled her. Her head fell against my chest and her hand pulled at the fabric of my shirt instinctually. She was a feather in my arms, but my breathing still intensified.

I had an irrational urge to take her to my bed, and I even tried telling myself it was because she said it was comfortable. But I knew that wasn't the real reason. Just like always, I liked having her near me, even though I knew I shouldn't. She made me feel like a miscreant.

Shameful.

Depraved.

But it wasn't her fault. It never was. I may have had a hard time dealing with those feelings as a teenager, but as an adult, I trusted myself. We were starting over. And I could be a good big brother to her, the way my dad always wanted me to be.

Chapter Eleven

Lily

I was tucked in, warm, and smelling a lot like Cruz when I popped my eyes open the next morning. Whatever he showered or shaved with, was permeating my nose, and my smile was a reflex as I stretched.

Then reality hit me, and I sat up, taking in the fact that I was actually in my room, and really did smell like Cruz. Checking the time, I shuffled out of bed, noting that I had three hours before my interview, then cracked my door open. Cruz had clearly helped me to bed and for some reason, I expected that to make things awkward again.

Tip-toeing down the short hallway and past the living room, I got to the bathroom then closed myself in. It didn't take me long to brush my teeth and hair before I tried sneaking back to my room.

"*Buenos días.*" The sound of his voice took me by surprise.

With a hand over my heart, I looked around for Cruz and saw him shirtless with his feet up on the coffee table. A tablet was in his hand, and his hair looked as if he had just woken up. Damn he looked good. No one ever lived up to how hot Cruz Martin was, and not once had I ever tried denying it.

"Hey," I waved. "You're up early."

He flashed the screen of his tablet and smiled. "Studying the team we face tomorrow. No rest for the weary."

"What time did you get home?"

"Midnight."

I was nodding with my arms wrapped around my midsection, wishing I had the foresight to put a bra on before I went on my little adventure to the bathroom. But what did it matter? There wasn't a doubt in my mind that I was on that chaise lounge when I fell asleep. Cruz probably saw all of me then, as well.

"You moved me?" Asking seemed appropriate even though I knew the answer.

"Just in case it stormed."

"You could have woken me up."

"Oh I tried," he laughed. "You were dead to the world."

That was probably true. I had been so overwhelmed with the patio furniture showing up, and exhausted from watching Cruz's game, that I slept really hard. It was laughable that I even tried reading my book in the first place.

"Oh," he set his tablet aside and stood up, walking closer to me. "You probably make that soup better than your mom. Thanks for leaving me some."

"Yeah," I floundered with what else to say. I had almost forgotten I'd even made it.

After the furniture arrived, I no longer wanted to go to the beach, so I made a quick trip to the grocery store and gathered items for something I thought Cruz may like. All I could remember was the way he devoured my mom's soup.

"She taught me when I got older."

"Well it made you my favorite house guest of all time."

I was sure I was turning beet red, and my feet started moving toward my room to hide. Cruz was hard enough to deal with when he was grumpy, but seeing him smile and relaxed was not in my social skill set yet. *There was still too much to learn.*

"Thank you for the patio furniture. I spent all day soaking in the view, except when I watched your game."

"*Joder,*" he mumbled, sliding his hands into the pockets of his sweatpants. "So you saw?"

"You did great." My sincerity was real, but he still looked at me with disbelief.

"We needed a win."

"I don't get the details, but you only let one guy score. I was impressed."

He turned to head back to the couch, no longer looking as relaxed as he was moments before. Somehow, I figured that was my fault so I started to apologize, but his words made me seal my lips.

"I prefer to keep them scoreless."

What was I supposed to say? All I was trying to do was compliment him but it seemed to backfire. *That was my cue to escape.*

"Wait!" he turned back around and his hands reached out to stop me. "Can I treat you to dinner tonight?"

My jaw dropped. It sounded a lot like a date request, but since it was Cruz, that couldn't be right. *Could it?* "You don't have to take the 'starting fresh' thing so seriously."

"That's not..." he crossed his arms and tilted his head, eyeing me curiously. "What?"

"A date?" I said, foolishly. "Us getting along doesn't mean we have to date."

By the way his jaw dropped, I knew I had stuck my foot directly into my mouth. Why did I have to use the words that were in my head? Why couldn't I just be cool?

"No wait," I started to backtrack but he was already directly in front of me, looking down at me as if to gain the upper hand. "That came out wrong."

"I don't know if I'm upset that you think I asked you on a date, or that you thought I asked you on one, and turned me down."

All I could do was shake my head and back up toward the hallway and into my room. Cruz stayed still, watching me as I retreated, and I slammed the door shut hoping he was gone by the time I had to leave.

"Damnit Lillian," I scolded myself. "Why are you so weird?"

When I started getting ready, I applied a little make up, something I wasn't accustomed to wearing. It wasn't much, just enough to make me look alive–a skill that came in handy sometimes. My suit was well fitted, and my heels made the pants fall at just the right spot.

Two hours of pampering and I still hadn't heard Cruz leave. That meant I was going to have to face him one more time. At least with the outfit and pumps I felt a little less *mousy* and a little more like a *queen*.

Just as I made my way into the living room, Cruz was coming out of his bedroom. We both stopped, staring at one another like we had never seen each other before. He was wearing slacks and a button up shirt, nice shoes, with his hair slicked back. The button on his cuff was undone and he was trying to get it to fasten while his eyes stayed on me.

Walking closer to him, I grabbed his wrist, buttoning the cuff and letting my hand linger for a second in his. His fingers curled a little, almost holding my hand completely before he dropped it and nodded at me to say thank you.

When I turned to walk away, I rolled my eyes so he couldn't see my annoyance. How come the one time I felt like a goddess around him, he came out looking like he was about to teach a class on sex or something?

"You practice in that?" I blurted without meaning to.

I could hear his shoes following me on the tile as we walked toward the kitchen. The bottle I always carried hadn't been refilled in almost five days so I grabbed it and started running the tap.

"Practice today isn't physical, it's meetings and studying." He popped a coffee pod into the machine and placed a to-go cup underneath it before he turned around and finished speaking. "And the first thing I have to do is meet with my agent and a representative of Archer Athletics about my pending contract with them."

"Archer Athletics? Like the shoes?"

"Yeah," he smiled. "Among other things. I'm supposed to be in the running to be a part of their upcoming expansion to their new soccer line, but the details have been up in the air. We're meeting today to hash those out."

"That sounds amazing." I couldn't think of a better person for Archer Athletics to recruit to represent their brand. Cruz was good looking and talented. Not to mention a really good guy–once I stopped being mad at him for existing.

My water was full, and everything I needed to take to my interview was in my arms. Cruz had turned around to finish fixing his coffee then made his way to the door and opened it for me. "I'll walk out with you."

We got in the elevator and were both quiet, but when the doors opened and we started walking in different directions, Cruz stopped me. "About that date tonight?"

My head started shaking back and forth as embarrassment churned my stomach and threatened to spill out over the pavement. "I was just..."

"I'm kidding," he winked. "But I do want to treat you to dinner."

Licking my lips, I tried to think of a real reason to say no, but it wasn't like I could hang with my friends. Being alone in my room didn't sound good either.

"Yeah, okay."

Chapter Twelve

Cruz

"We'll be holding a dinner here in Miami on Friday," the representative from Archer Athletics was saying while I stared out the window of the office we were in. I had a great view of the field, and wished I was down there instead of all dressed up in a meeting. "You will need to be there. Bring a date."

That got my attention. "A date?"

"A date." He looked stern as he tapped a stack of papers on the table like a teacher about to grade them. "The executives take you more seriously when they think you are the commitment type. Mr. Archer pays attention to those small details."

"Commitment?" *Small* details?

"Not really a commitment," my agent, Silas, cut in and patted the back of my hand to calm me down. "It's just an image thing. Get a beautiful woman to escort you. People do it all the time. No one is going to ask you to marry her for the contract."

Leaning back in the chair, I was a little bit angry that they expected me to bring a date. It wouldn't be a problem to ask Erin, but I hated the idea anyway. At least with her, there was the added bonus that she wouldn't ask for more than a thank you.

"Fine," I agreed, already finding Erin's name in my phone.

"I'll email you any final details. Silas, Cruz, thank you so much for this meeting."

When we were left alone, Silas stood up and started laughing at my unfortunate situation. "You'll be okay. I'm sure a million women would love to hang out with you for a night. You always seem to find one to fuck around with."

"If everyone thinks I'm dating someone, the pool of available women to fuck around with will diminish."

"You poor, oversexed, superstar."

Hell, even I laughed at his sarcasm. I knew I was being ridiculous, I just hated being told what I should and shouldn't do when it came to women. Or any part of my personal life.

Silas left me alone at the big table and went off to his next meeting, which was what I should have done as well. We had a team meeting in five minutes, but there was something I had to do first.

Tapping on Erin's name, I brought up a new text thread.

> I have a thing and need a date.

> I'm almost ready to vomit waiting for you to suggest it be me.

> You know I don't want to do this at all. But Archer Athletics is requesting I have a date.

> Which night?

> Friday, 6 days from now.

> Let me check my schedule.

> Later.

I'm going back to sleep.

It's nearly noon.

If you can't understand that I don't give a fuck,
then I'm not sure you're the one for me.

Fine. Be lazy. Let me know, though. Okay?

She signed off with a thumbs up icon, which easily translated to "fuck you" so I started thinking of a backup plan.

Before heading down to my team meeting, I decided to call Deon, my cousin. He kind of owed me one, and it wouldn't hurt to see if he knew of someone that could help me out.

"Hey Cuz," he greeted. "You miss me?"

"You live across town," I laughed. "Am I supposed to miss you?"

"You moved to South Beach. Worlds apart, Cuz."

"Yeah well, I just talked to you yesterday. You said the same exact thing. How about you make my mom give you a day off and come hang at the beach."

"Nah," he laughed. "I'm close to that down payment on my car."

Deon could have asked me for the money and I would have given it to him. We were close enough that I wouldn't even ask for it back. But my mom's sister, my Aunt Roberta, made sure he worked his ass off for the things he wanted.

"Well, do you remember that favor I did for you?"

"Yeah..." he sounded worried and it made me want to laugh. "Am I going to regret it?"

"I have this thing for Archer Athletics, and I need a date."

"Who, me?"

"No you crazy motherfucker," I laughed. "But didn't you say you knew someone? Think she'd be up for a no strings, no commitment, no sex night out?"

He mumbled something in Spanish, but his voice was too low for me to make it out. It was easy to assume he thought I was crazy.

"I'll let you know," he said again. "But I gotta go, your mom is a slave driver."

"Give her my love. Tell her I'll call her tomorrow."

"Yeah, yeah," he said before hanging up.

Well, that didn't go as planned either, but it was all I could do for now. The next few hours were all about the next game, and that was where my focus needed to be. If I didn't keep Austin FC scoreless, Archer Athletics may not even want me at their event anyway.

It was six o'clock by the time I got home, and I noticed Lily's car in the parking garage. I practically bounced to the elevator and into the apartment, anxious to see how her interview went and surprise her with what I had planned for dinner. It was just the peace offering we needed.

"Lily?" I yelled, realizing I had, at some point, started thinking of her by her nickname again. One I was pretty sure only I used. "How'd it go?"

The apartment was quiet, so I peeked out onto the balcony but she wasn't there. The bathroom door was open and the light was off, so she wasn't in there either.

Hesitantly, I nudged her bedroom door open and found her sleeping on top of her made up bed, fully clothed in her pants suit and jacket. She had a blanket that I recognized from years ago wrapped in her arms like she was hugging it tightly. That blanket used to hang over the end of her bed, but I had once heard my dad tell her she shouldn't leave it there just because I was in town.

When I was sixteen, I would have thought that she was lame, or acting like a baby. Now that I was older, I wondered what the sentiment was to her. As I started to back out of her room to let her rest for another hour, I took one more glance at her. There was black under her eyes. Leaning in closer, I saw that it was her makeup, and had been smudged as if she had been crying.

"Lily?" I sat on the edge of the bed, putting my hand on her shoulder and nudging her so she woke up. "Lil? Are you okay?"

Her eyes blinked open until she realized that I was there, then she sat up quickly and squeezed the blanket to her stomach. "What're you doing?"

"Checking on you. You look like you have been crying. What's wrong?"

She wiped at her eyes as if she could hide the evidence but the damage had been done, and I needed to know why she was so upset. Maybe it was the "big brother" feeling finally coming out of me, but I wanted to beat the ass of whoever made her sad. And that was saying something, because I wasn't usually a fighter.

"I got offered the job," she nodded but refused to look up.

That wasn't what I asked. Putting my hand under her chin to lift her eyes to mine, I practically demanded she tell me more. "Why the tears?"

"Cruz," she sighed, "I really don't want to talk about this."

"I do," I gritted between my teeth, trying not to let her notice how worked up I was getting.

"Who do you think you are?" She snapped, pushing my hand away from her. "I don't have to tell you why I got upset, or anything for that matter."

"I'm asking because I care."

"No you don't! You have no idea what you're even talking about."

Fuck, she was making me angry. She had started to back up, scooting away from me on the bed, so I stood up and started pacing, running my fingers through my hair.

"All I asked was what upset you. Since you haven't even answered me, then you're right, I have no idea what I'm talking about."

"Can you please just leave me alone?" Tears were starting down her cheeks again as she spoke softly into her balled-up blanket.

"Dammit, Lil. Let me be your brother for once!"

Chapter Thirteen

Lily

I must have cried myself to sleep because I never would have risked Cruz seeing me so upset. Cleaning streaks of tears from my face had been as natural as eating for me, and the one time I let my guard down, Cruz saw.

"You're not my brother," I gritted at him, angry he spoke that word. He had *never* been my brother, and I hated when people tried to force the idea. He had been the only person I could ever count on to agree with me on that, and I recoiled at the thought of him suddenly changing his mind.

"What do you want from me?" he practically begged.

"I don't need a brother, I need a friend, and I thought that was where we were headed."

"We are!" He yelled, shaking his head. "Seeing you upset is making me crazy. Brother or friend, I don't know why I feel this way. Just tell me who made you cry."

"Please," I cried, begging him to leave it alone.

He beaded his eyes at me, his nostrils flaring in irritation. He was finally backing up toward the door, but I saw his fist flexing, and I shivered a little seeing him so upset. It made me want to tell him everything, not only because he seemed to actually care, but because I wanted to make him feel better as well. But before I opened my mouth, he turned to leave with a deep sigh of defeat.

"You win, Lil. Whatever makes you upset is your business. You don't need me acting like the brother or the friend I never was. But just remember, I'm not a kid either. So whenever you're ready, I promise to be whoever you need me to be."

He left, and my jaw was practically in my lap from the words he'd spoken, while also using my nickname. Knowing he cared so much about a few of my tears was making me want to cry all over again.

When I heard his bedroom door shut, I scrambled to my feet and down the hall to the bathroom. My face was blotchy and the black mascara that ran around my eyes almost made me look like I had been punched.

Geez, no wonder he looked so upset.

Before it got dark, I decided to walk the beach and get away from the apartment, so I cleaned up the best I could. When I walked into the living room, Cruz was standing in the kitchen with his phone up to his ear. He had changed into jeans and a t-shirt, with his hat turned backward and his sunglasses resting on the bill of the hat behind him.

"Dad," his eyes widened toward me as he spoke, making me pay attention. "She's been sleeping since I got home, so that is probably why you two haven't heard from her."

Shaking my head, I started to back away like they could hear me enter the room, but then at the last minute I made a run for it. Sliding on my flip flops, I darted toward the door, but Cruz's big arm wrapped around my waist and held me tight against him while he listened to his dad—and probably my mom—talk his ear off.

"Yeah Dad, listen, when she gets up, I'm sure she'll see the missed calls and check in. She's safe, though. No need to worry."

A few more minutes of him telling my mom that everything was fine and then he hung up the phone. He tossed it hard onto the counter, but didn't let his arm loosen around me. His breath was on my neck, and he mumbled something in Spanish like he always did when he was annoyed, or upset.

"Can you let me go?" I pushed on him, trying to get free.

"Can you tell me why you haven't checked in with those looney ass people we call our parents?"

"I was asleep."

"Gloria said you were supposed to call her on your way home from your interview, but you never did, so they called me."

"And you covered for me," I breathed heavily from how it felt being so close to him.

His nose went to my hair and close to my neck, his chest heaving as hard as mine. I let out a moan that made him jump a little and he backed away, letting his arm fall from my waist.

When I turned around, I could see chaos and distress in his eyes. He was looking off to the side, his jaw was tight, and I instinctively reached up to run my thumb over his cheek.

"Those two seem to think you need bubble wrap and goggles," he sighed, almost to himself. His hand went to mine and he moved it away from his face, but he still wasn't looking at me.

"They're looney, you said so yourself."

"It must be hereditary," he mumbled, finally looking at me.

My smile was weak, because I didn't know if he meant that for me, or for him. Not that it mattered. At the rate we were going, our parents were going to seem like they wrote a book on the art of sanity.

"I don't need bubble wrap," I huffed, a little petulant.

"No, you need a spanking," he growled.

That wasn't the threat he intended it to be, at least not according to my body. My legs clenched together, and I pressed my nails into my palms to distract me from the path my thoughts traveled.

Cruz noticed, because his eyes darkened and started running down my chest, my stomach, and then my legs. He shook his head, telling himself no, but I didn't hear him ask the question.

It was another few minutes of us silently facing off before he tilted his head up. "Ready for dinner?"

"What?" How did he expect us to enjoy dinner together after that?

"Did you forget we have a date?"

The look on my face must have been way more than confusion, but he rolled his eyes and grabbed his keys then pulled my hand. He guided me toward the door, and I didn't argue, or fight him, I was hungry, and despite our insanity, I wanted to spend more time with him.

When we were in the elevator, he was still holding my hand and he leaned over, nearly pressing his lips above my ear. "You don't scare me, Lily."

"Well you scare me," I admitted.

"I'm trying to change that."

"Not sure that's possible."

The elevator doors opened, and instead of pulling me forward, he held a hand out for me to go first. His other hand found the small of my back and he guided me toward his car, opening the door for me. I hesitated, and started to question what we were doing, but he leaned close again, his breath on my cheek. "Get in."

My knees practically gave out and I got in the passenger seat without another word. His car was a stick shift, some black, sporty, two-door BMW that suited him, without being too flashy. What *was* flashy were the veins in his forearms as he shifted us into reverse, and then into gear, as we left the parking garage. In fact, I could barely look at anything else until he slammed the brakes at a light and made me snap out of it.

We sped through the traffic of South Beach and away from the center of the city, past North Beach, and toward Bal Harbour. The music Cruz played was in Spanish, and I couldn't help but sway my shoulders a little with the beat while watching everything we passed, and reading every sign, soaking in the sights of a place I never knew existed. It was unbelievably gorgeous, well-kept, and serene. Even when it wasn't high-end shops and palm trees, the architecture, and the homes we passed, were unique in their characteristics and colors.

We pulled into an empty parking lot close to sundown and I followed Cruz's lead, getting out of the car. We were walking alongside the Ritz, which was the only place that I could see that may have served dinner.

But Cruz took my hand and led me behind the hotel, toward a long, rocky pier. It curved into the ocean, right next to the inlet where boats were pulling in and out of the choppy water. If it hadn't been for a few signs that other people had been there earlier, I would have assumed we were breaking the law. There were no sides or railings, and the wind seemed to blow harder and harder the closer we got to the end.

"What are we doing?" I finally asked, wondering why I blindly followed Cruz. It was eerie, being at the end of the pier, and looking back toward the land as if we were standing on the water itself.

"Dinner, remember?"

"Are we fishing with our hands?"

He gave me a look that told me I was ridiculous, but what else was there for us out there? We weren't going to be catching a boat, there was no way one could safely pull up along the rocks the way the waves were crashing on them.

"Sit," he instructed, then lowered himself down as well.

I crossed my legs like a butterfly while he stretched his out and leaned back on his arms. He took a few deep breaths of the sea air before he reached into his pocket and pulled out two candy bars.

"Dinner is served."

I started to scoff at him, thinking he was fucking with me on a new level. But then I glanced at the candy bar again, and I gasped at the memory it triggered.

"La Primada Baracoa," I croaked. "I haven't had one of these since I was, I don't know, seventeen?"

"Eighteen," he corrected. "Your jar was empty when I came for your graduation, so I refilled it one more time."

He was taking bites of his own candy, pieces of chocolate falling from his mouth as he pulled it away. His eyes were looking at the waves, the setting sun, the boats. They were roaming everywhere but at me, and I couldn't seem to look anywhere else but at him.

"You?" I finally asked in disbelief.

"Dad told me you ate them for dinner sometimes," he shrugged, like it was no big deal.

But it was a big deal, because La Primada Baracoa candies were not available on the shelf at every grocery store. They had to be bought at special places, and none of them were near Brooksville. Miami, however, had them at certain places, and my first taste of one was when Cruz had left a stash after his visit. Mom told me I could eat them because he wouldn't be around for another few months, and I fell in love.

I ripped the package open and sunk my teeth into the chocolate covered sugar. There was something about the chocolate used in a La Primada Baracoa, just like having a Cuban cup of coffee was so much richer. I had tried to find some online, but they were knock offs, and never quite the same as the ones I *thought* Cruz's dad kept in stock for me.

"Was it always you?" I hoped he knew what I meant, because those four words were hard enough to say.

"I brought as many as I could fit in my bag. After Dad told me you ate the ones I left, I figured you might want more."

"I..." My throat was tight, but I made sure to clear it before I tried speaking again. "I thought Ivan restocked them for when *you* came and I got to eat them after you left."

He smiled, but still didn't look at me. It took several more minutes of awkward silence before I scooted closer to him and wrapped my arms around his neck. He leaned up to keep from falling back and returned my hug, wrapping his arms tightly around me, and pressing his nose into my neck.

"I wish I had known."

"Why?"

"Maybe I wouldn't have dreaded your visits as much."

He pulled back and tucked the hair that was blowing around my face, behind my ear. "I dreaded my visits, so you had to dread them too."

Even though I felt like I should have been insulted, I still laughed and pulled away from him. "Was I that awful?"

"Was I?"

Chapter Fourteen

Cruz

After the sun had set, Lily and I made our way back home. I offered to stop and pick her something up for an actual dinner, but as I predicted, the candy had filled her up, since it was basically pure sugar. They were big, and she ate the whole thing. It may not have been the most nutritious dinner, but when I saw the two bars in my locker during the team meeting, the idea sparked.

My mom always had those candies at the checkout counter in her restaurant. When she ordered them, she made sure I had my own box, and I started saving them for my trips. There were a lot of reasons I didn't want to be near Lily, but I found some satisfaction in giving her that one small thing.

Instead of trying to impress Lily with a fancy dinner, candy and the sunset felt more her style. Not to mention I didn't need to impress her. She wasn't some girl I was trying to score with.

Once I asked her if I was that bad growing up, we stayed silent the rest of the night, with her never giving me an answer. Nor did I give her one. It was weird, because there was unspoken resentment between us when we were teens, and I hoped that was part of our past, for good.

The silence between us the rest of the night wasn't even awkward. It was somehow comfortable as the night air blew into the windows of my car and the music played.

When we got home, Lily started walking toward her room, straight to bed.

"Hey Lil?" She turned around, her eyes sunken in, and a forced smile on her face. "You never told me if you're going to take the job."

"I don't know," she shrugged. "I have two more interviews."

I bit my lip and nodded, expecting her to turn back around and head to bed, but she hesitated, and I could hear her taking a few deep breaths before she spoke. "Thanks for dinner."

"*Siempre, mi amor.*" Speaking English felt too vulnerable. I didn't trust myself to speak words I knew she could understand.

She nodded, then headed into her room, shutting her door quietly, while I made my way into my own room and fell onto my bed with an exasperated sigh. It was happening all over again. The same thing I was scared would happen the moment my dad asked if she could stay with me.

I was feeling things for her the way I always had, but could never explain. It made me resent her, and that wasn't something I wanted to do anymore.

But I couldn't actually spank her and watch her squirm either. *Fuck, I didn't mean to make her squirm in the first place.* Saying she needed to be spanked was coming from the way she pouted, and the fact that her mom was so overprotective. I doubt she ever got her ass spanked growing up, but I did. My dad beat manners and sense into me from ages five to eleven, making sure he didn't have to worry about the man I would become.

Maybe Gloria wouldn't worry all the time either if she had let Lily spread her wings and fuck up every once in a while. Our punishments were our lessons.

Picking up my phone, I decided I needed to learn a lesson of my own. No more thinking about Lily and watching her rub her legs together. There was a definite cure, and I knew Tripp would be up for being my wingman.

"What's going on?" He answered, sounding almost worried.

"Did I do something wrong?" I laughed.

"Just didn't expect to hear from you tonight. You left the locker room in a hurry earlier."

I sat up and twisted my neck around, hoping the tension eased its way out of my body. "I needed to hit you up before you made other plans."

"Big game tomorrow," he sighed. "I'm not going out tonight so that you can avoid your sister."

"I'm talking about after the game tomorrow. Mangos. It's walking distance from the house, and they do dinner and a show on Wednesdays. Oh, and she isn't my goddamn sister."

"Yeah, yeah," Trip laughed again. "I'm in though. Win or lose, I need to get out."

As I headed out for the game the next day, I noticed Lily on the balcony reading a book. The smartest thing I could have done was just leave. No goodbyes necessary. But I had yet to learn any lessons when it came to her, and I stupidly walked out to check on her.

"Good morning," she chirped happily, like she hadn't stayed up all night thinking of ways we could get grounded for life by our parents if we touched one another.

Because I had.

"It's noon, Lil."

"If you just woke up, then it's morning for you."

"I've been up for a bit," I admitted, leaving out the part about how I was lying in bed and stroking my dick because of the previously mentioned ways my adult self could still get grounded. Just because I couldn't touch her didn't mean my imagination got the memo, and my dick definitely didn't give a fuck. "I just wanted to tell you I'm headed out. You gonna tune in?"

"Oh, sorry," she shrugged. "I actually made plans with my friends today."

Oh yeah, she had *friends*.

"I'm headed out after the game, with Tripp." *Why was I telling her all this?*

"I'll hide the handcuffs," she teased, making me have to turn around before she caught me blushing.

"I'll be good," I mumbled, facing the ocean and pretending like it was the first time I had ever seen it.

"No one said you had to be good," she laughed. "But don't forget that if you're not, we are considering spankings now."

I whipped my head around, but she was looking down at her book again, like she hadn't just gone there. She thought she was cute, and damnit, she was.

"Not sure what my friends have in store for me, so don't wait up for me, either."

"Be good," I managed to get out in a low growl that only made her laugh.

Tripp was going to have to keep me on task, because I was already thinking of new plans that involved tracking Lily's phone and finding her after my game. I was very aware that I sounded no better than her mom, probably worse, but I didn't even know these friends of hers. What if they were drug dealers? Or peed in pools? What if they didn't tip their waitresses, or, oh fuck... what if they were the kind of girls I was planning to score with later? The kind that would suck my dick just because I asked them to?

"How well do you know these girls?" My voice was cool and calm while my eyes were boring into her with a million other unasked questions.

"You're not my mother. Don't act like it." Her eyes were hidden behind her sunglasses, but I thought I saw them roll before she answered me.

"Don't be too trusting," I warned her.

"You're not my father, either," she sighed.

"Lil, just... be good," I repeated.

"And you're not my brother," she tsked.

Holding my hands up, I surrendered, knowing I overstepped. She may have been from a small town, and a little naive, but she wasn't a child. Just like Dad and Gloria, I had to back off.

"I gotta go," I bit out, holding back the urge to drag her with me and throw her in the suite seats next to the bench. "Have fun tonight. Extra condoms are in my side drawer if you need them."

Lily just shook her head at me, not even giving my offer the hell it deserved. But I was going to do a quick inventory, and if I was missing one later, then... then nothing. She could do whatever she wanted.

She pulled her book back up and smiled, quietly saying, "Later."

I stared down at her, watching her read for a minute. She had the upper hand without even knowing it, and I was buzzing with anxiety. Then I realized she must have not been as cool as she was letting on, either. Because she had her head in her book for way too long, and never flipped the page. She was fake reading while I stood there like an idiot.

"Okay," I finally took a step, trying to think of one more thing to say that could explain why I hadn't left yet. "Um..."

Her eyes came back up, and through her dark lenses, her stare made me shake a little. She had no idea she was affecting me the way she was, but it wouldn't be long before she realized she had so much power, and I couldn't let her figure that out.

"You have to turn the pages to read," I mumbled, then headed inside. I walked across the apartment and out the door, finally feeling like a badass, and like I turned the tables.

Psh, I told her.

But as I climbed in my car and started driving toward the stadium, I realized that all I did was show her my hand. I was paying more attention than I should have been, and I just tattled on myself.

Chapter Fifteen

Lily

"Look at your tan!" Angel squealed when she saw me. "I see you love Miami as much as it loves you."

"The balcony and the beach have been my friends." I lifted my sunglasses and waggled my eyes at her, making her laugh.

I had once again avoided her coming to Cruz's apartment by telling her, when she called, that I was taking a casual stroll down the oceanfront in South Beach. She told me she would pick me up and then we could grab Jackie from work.

We were driving through traffic listening to Camila Cabello, and singing along, as if she was giving us a private concert in the car. Never in my life had I had a friend that I could hang out with like that. Someone willing to sing at the top of their lungs to old songs, laughing and carefree. If I had given myself a second to think too hard, I would have been annoyingly emotional.

"Jackie's so excited to finally meet you," Angel yelled over the music.

I clapped my hands, unable to voice how excited I was to

finally meet Jackie. Angel and I had always been closer, and kept in touch more, but Jackie had been a vital part of our girls' Facetime nights. Plus, Angel said she was the one that created this night for us. She wanted to show me what summers in Miami were all about.

We drove up to an old restaurant whose name I could barely read because the sign was so weathered. There were a lot of cars in the parking lot, so the locals knew where they were, and that was all that mattered. Angel sent Jackie a text that we had arrived and within minutes, she was bouncing out of the door.

I climbed out of the passenger seat and ran to her, hugging her like I did Angel when we first met. Jackie was receptive, and hugged me back, but I definitely got a different vibe from her than I did Angel.

"Geez," Jackie laughed, making me spin around. "The flowery top is very Smalltown, Carolina of you."

It felt like a backhanded insult, but I didn't let it bother me too long. She and I were going to be good friends, and I was going to have to learn that not everyone expressed themselves the same way I did.

"You look gorgeous," I said to Jackie, motioning toward her tight, shredded jeans, and the strappy top she wore that barely covered her boobs. She wore high heels, and had on a face full of makeup that I wouldn't have been able to duplicate to save my life. Her hair hung down her back, and her nails were long, painted bright pink.

Thankfully, Angel merged my plain flowery top and jean shorts with Jackie's sexy look by falling somewhere in between. Angel wore less makeup and a less revealing top, but had tight jeans. Her nails were done to perfection, and I thought that maybe after some time, I would learn how to be sexy and hot the way they were.

We all climbed in the car and I took the backseat. Jackie spoke to Angel about her day at work, mostly complaining because she wasn't supposed to work at all. She mentioned people I didn't know, but it sounded like a mess I was thankful not to be in. I did feel a tad left out, but it was stupid of me to feel anything but thankful to have them, so I sat in the backseat with a smile and enjoyed the scenery.

"Almost there," Jackie clapped, looking back, and finally speaking to me.

"Where?" I laughed, holding my hands open. All I knew was that we had left the city and driven fifteen minutes north. But nothing looked special, or abnormal, and I had to assume our hot Miami summer was going to start at the strip mall next to us. "Shopping?"

I tried to look excited, because I wanted them to think I loved shopping, but I didn't have money to shop. Of course, that would be what I got for lying to Angel about needing to shop on the first day I met her. She probably thought it was my favorite pastime.

"No," Angel laughed. "It's up here a little."

"So why is this such a big secret?"

"Honestly," Jackie laughed, looking back at me. "I was kind of scared you wouldn't want to come. This doesn't seem like your type of thing."

"That makes me extra nervous," I admitted, while still trying to look relaxed.

Angel turned into a huge parking lot and I looked ahead to see where we were.

"Oh no," I gasped.

"Told ya she would hate it," Jackie groaned.

"I don't hate it," I cringed, knowing I wasn't being completely honest. "I just never imagined, of all places, you'd want to go to a soccer game."

"The Miami Inferno are everything right now," Angel explained. She pulled up a ticket to show someone, and they motioned for her to keep driving until she found a parking spot. "I think you'll love it."

"I scored us some amazing seats." Jackie tossed her hair as she climbed from the car, feeling good about herself. "I kind of know one of the players."

"She's also close to scoring with said player," Angel laughed, making Jackie waggle her eyes a little.

I repeated in my head that everything was fine. There was no way Cruz would even know I was there. In fact, maybe it would be fun. I didn't hate soccer, I just usually avoided it because of Cruz. Since we were friends, maybe I could learn to love it.

Then we got past the gate, and there was a huge picture of Cruz on a feather flag banner. The magnitude of the realization that flashed before me was intense. Cruz was famous, his face was on flags. People were walking all over the place with his name on their backs.

I knew he was a pro, and what it meant to be a pro, but to me, he was Ivan's son who was always perfect, and too good to talk to me when we were kids.

And the same guy who carried me to bed the other night, bought me seven pizzas, and handcuffed himself to me so I wouldn't leave while he slept.

"Holy shit," I mumbled.

People were taking pictures with each flag, and Jackie gave me her phone, asking me to take a picture of her and Cruz.

"Cruz?"

"She's been crushing on him for a while," Angel laughed, watching Jackie stop next to Cruz's flag. She looked my way, and made a sexy pose, while she waited for me to take the picture. "Do we look good together or what?"

"Um," I barely made a sound. "Um..."

Angel grabbed the phone from my hand and snapped Jackie's picture. She had to because I didn't want to take the picture. I didn't want her having a crush on Cruz.

Or doing anything with him.

"You okay?" Angel asked.

"Yeah, I just. Wow. Look at all the people."

What else was I going to say? *"Hey guess what? Cruz is actually my stepbrother and I can't be here because ever since I saw him in the shower fully clothed, I've been fluttering in my lady parts. And he wants to spank me, no biggie."*

Ugh. Plus, I had already told too many lies to hide that secret, and because Jackie had a crush on Cruz, my reasons for those lies were as solid as ever. I wasn't even sure Jackie liked me, but I knew if I told her about Cruz, she'd be my BFFF—best fake friend forever.

One day, I would have to tell them, but that wasn't going to be until after I knew they loved me for me, and not because of who I knew, or what I had been through. That didn't have to be then and there. I had time, and I planned on trying to enjoy the game regardless of the lies I was sitting on.

But once Jackie led us to our seats, that plan fled as quickly as it came. There was no way Cruz wouldn't see me sitting right behind the bench, in the front row. If I was lucky, he would avoid eye contact, and be too embarrassed to acknowledge me in public. *That was actually very likely.*

No it wasn't. He seemed to be trying hard to be my friend. If he saw me, he may wave and...dang it, I had to confess before they found out another way.

"Hey," I sighed. "There's something I–"

"Here he comes," Jackie squealed. *Oh right, she kinda knows him.*

Looking out to the field where the team was warming up, I

saw Cruz walking with number seventeen, who I knew was Rhys Peyton after watching the game on Monday. Cruz was taking his gloves off and looking down at his feet while Rhys talked about something with his arms animatedly waving around. They were headed toward the bench that was directly in front of us. And by bench, I meant a dugout, where the team sat protected from the elements and the fans during the game.

But it was close, and if Jackie so much as waved at him, he would see me. I had to get the truth out fast, and ask for forgiveness later.

"Wait," I started again, but Jackie had started talking as well.

"He told Deon he would come say hi." She was somehow whispering and squealing at the same time.

"What? Why?"

"Deon is Cruz's cousin, and he has a huge crush on me," Jackie smirked. "I'd never waste my time with him except for the fact that, *hello*, Cruz Martin is his cousin. He got me these tickets when I ran my hand down his chest and made promises I won't keep. Then he told me he would ask Cruz to come say hi when I grabbed his junk."

My heart sank, and I wanted to go home. Not because of Cruz, but because of Jackie. Her words were everything I was afraid of when I made friends. She used Deon to get to Cruz. She led him on, and made him think they had a chance. She'd do it to me as well.

The only thing stopping me from standing up and calling a rideshare home was Angel, and the nasty look on her face at Jackie's words. She was clearly upset as well, and I wanted to stay for her.

"Cruz?" Jackie yelled, when he got closer, waving at him like she was working the street corner. Rhys didn't look up, just jogged ahead of Cruz, who slowed down and looked toward us.

Jackie was by far the most noticeable, waving her hand while simultaneously making her boobs pop out of her shirt. *Real talent.*

"Hey," he smiled, jumping on a railing to get higher, then reaching his hand out to shake hers. Shoving my back against my seat, I tried to hide. "You must be Deon's friends."

I thought she knew him?

"Jackie," she purred, leaning forward and blocking his view of me even more. "Deon and I are good friends. I've heard a lot about you, so it's good to put a face to a name."

Oh barf. She knew exactly what Cruz looked like, and she and Deon were *not* friends. He just didn't know it yet. Angel was sitting down as well, letting Jackie have her moment, but when Cruz spoke again, unexpected jealousy flared up inside of me.

"So did he mention the thing on Friday?"

Jackie sucked in a sharp breath, taken by surprise at Cruz's words. "He said something, but I hadn't checked my schedule. What did you have in mind?"

"I'll, uh, get your number from him." I could hear the hesitation in Cruz's voice. Something had been lost in translation, and made him wary. *Good boy, Cruz.*

"I'll get yours from him, just in case," Jackie giggled as she leaned over and pushed her hair back.

When she did, Cruz's eyes caught a glimpse of me and he did a double take. His mouth fell open, and he started to speak, but I silently pleaded with him to go away. With the way Jackie was acting, maybe it would have been better to ask him to save me, but I still didn't want to risk Angel hating me too.

He didn't look away, but he jumped down from the railing and back pedaled toward the field, keeping his eyes on mine. Just like every other time our eyes locked, my heart sped up and my palms started to sweat. The way his nostrils flared and he licked his lips made me feel like he wasn't seeing Jackie at all.

Finally, he turned and started jogging back onto the field. Somehow, Jackie had no idea Cruz had just stared a hole into my heart, but Angel was eyeing me strangely, so I shrugged like I was just as clueless as she was.

Chapter Sixteen

Cruz

Lily was at my game.

The favor I did for Deon ended up being tickets for her friends. He even asked me to say hi to them because he thought it'd get him laid with one of them. *It better not have been Lily, because I would beat his ass.*

Jackie, on the other hand, was exactly what I didn't need in my life. She tried to act a certain way, but I had seen that game so many times that it made me uncomfortable, and I was ready to run away from them. I even made a mental note to warn Deon not to give her my number. That was pretty much a standard code among us, but I was going to double down and be sure he understood.

When I caught Lily's eye, though, I wanted to go back up on the rail and ask her what she was doing. Excitement made its way through me that she was at my game at the same time I registered the fear in her eyes.

She looked sick. Scared. It became very clear that she didn't want me saying a word to her. I had to surmise that it was because she hadn't told her friends about me. That hurt more than it should have, considering I didn't blame her.

As I backed away, not wanting to cause any trouble, I couldn't stop looking at her. She was in *my* seats, but I didn't give them to her myself, and I felt like I should have.

When I finally turned away, all I felt was pissed and bothered. I walked out toward my spot in the goal and realized my head wasn't even in the game at all. It was in the stands with her, hoping she saw all the emotions on my face before I had to turn away.

"Hey," Tripp yelled at me while I put my gloves back on. "What the fuck is wrong with you?"

"What makes you think anything is wrong?" *Was I that transparent? Was I wearing the wrong shirt?*

"Well, for starters, you always laugh and jump around, then tell us it's going to be another scoreless night for whoever we are playing."

"I'm not in the mood to be cocky."

"And the second thing, I saw your sis..." I cut my eyes up at him, making sure he knew before he even kept talking that he needed to reroute whatever noun he was about to use. "Your *roommate* in the stands. You didn't seem happy to see her."

"I didn't invite her," I snapped at him. "She's here with friends."

"And?"

"If I wanted her here, I would have invited her." *I should have invited her. I should have told Deon I'd help him get laid another way.*

"Not sure how I feel about this new and improved Cruz Martin," Tripp laughed with sarcasm as Rhys ran up to join us.

"Hey, what's your deal?" Rhys asked, not realizing Tripp had just asked the same thing.

"Nothing!" I yelled, looking down at my shirt to make sure I wasn't wearing one that said, "In a mood to be rude." Then I considered getting one made just so those fuckers could be warned to leave me alone.

Tripp may have let me get away with shrugging him off, but Rhys was the leader of the team and he didn't let anything slide. Grabbing my shoulder, he turned me back around and made me face him. Right there in front of all the fans and players—and Lily—he leaned down and spoke low.

"It's a mindfuck, isn't it? You can barely think straight, and you want to punch someone because it's the only emotion you can process?"

All I could do was look at him with my eyes beaded, and nose scrunched up. We both knew what he was talking about, but I thought playing dumb was the better option.

"Show her why you're a pro, and worry about why you care later. Got it?"

Slapping my gloved hands together, I turned away from him and walked toward the goal. I jumped around, warming my body up and letting go of everything but the game. There was a reason Rhys was the captain. He was right, I was a pro, and I got there because I knew how to focus and play my game. Despite outside noise and feelings about Lily being at the game, I knew I was capable of zoning in on what was important.

The whistle blew and I watched as Rhys and Tripp passed the ball around for a while. They were dominating, which made my job easy. Most of the first half was spent on the other side of the field, and when the ball was kicked out of bounds, I took glances at Lily, just to feed that defiant side of me that even soccer couldn't cure.

She was standing and clapping. Pretty sure I even saw her high-five a stranger when Tripp scored a goal. The girls next to her were sitting, and I could tell the one in the middle, the one I asked my cousin to help me get a date with, was not as excited to be there.

The third one was more animated, definitely happy to be there, but she wasn't standing with Lily. She seemed torn between indifference and excitement, like she was trying to be a chameleon in that odd group of friends.

A corner kick by Rhys got headed by Austin FC, and with a lucky break, their midfielder raced toward me with no other defender nearby. He was going to take a shot on the goal, and for the first time all night, I was going to be challenged.

He broke left, then right, and before our best defender, Otto, could catch up to him, he took aim at the top right corner of the goal. I jumped and dove, skimming the ball with the tips of my fingers and kept it from getting in. But just like the last game, I couldn't hold on, and Austin FC was there for the rebound.

Otto was finally there, though, and kicked the ball toward the crowd. It was a close one, too close, and I looked up wondering what Lily would think if I couldn't keep Austin FC scoreless when they were supposed to be a cakewalk.

"Fuck!" I yelled, mostly at myself.

"Let it go," Rhys hollered back as he lined up for the throw in.

Everything was moving at a quick pace, and the ball was being kicked back down toward the other goal before I had time to tell Rhys to mind his own business. The ball stayed down on that end of the field until the whistle blew for half time, and I jogged ahead of Rhys, not wanting anymore of his dumb words of wisdom.

Lily and her friends were right above our bench so I kept my head lowered, and tried not to look as I went down the few steps. But right at the last second, my eyes shot up and connected with hers. They were big and bright as always, and the smile on her face, and the way she held her hands together against her chest, made mine almost explode.

It may have finally been time to admit that I had issues when it came to Lily. Ones that I constantly thought I could control, and never seemed to get a grip on. She would always be the girl that looked like an angel from heaven, but would send me straight to hell.

Or to the timeout chair in the corner of my dad's living room.

"Good block," Tripp tapped me on the shoulder as I sat at my locker.

I gave him a nod to say thanks, but kept my mouth closed as I unwrapped the tape around my ankles for no good reason. Then I trudged toward the trainer for them to wrap them again. It pissed them off to have to redo it, but it was an excuse, not to have to speak to anyone else during the half.

When we made our way back to the field, I did some warm ups near our bench like I always did, and fought like hell not to look up at Lily again. But of course, I had control issues, and that didn't last. I just had to know if she was still there, if she was watching me. But I wasn't going to make it obvious.

Tripp kicked the ball my way and I decided to act like I missed it. He started to call me out because I never would've missed that kick, but his words turned into a laugh when he saw me glance up towards Lily.

She was still there, still looking at me, and her eyes were still bright from everything going on around her. Her friends were no longer there, and she was sitting alone, which allowed me to slow down, and take a minute to lock eyes with her again with a smile.

Her returning smile made me feel like I was a kid again, and walking her down the aisle behind our parents after their wedding. I always pretended I hated that moment in my life, but I felt like a prince that day.

Lily gave me a shy wave and turned bright red, like she

wasn't sure she should be waving. To avoid drawing attention to myself, I didn't wave back, just gave her a wink.

When I saw her friends coming back to their seats with bags in their hands, I knew our moment was over, and I had to turn away. But not before I saw them handing Lily an Inferno jersey. She held it up and smiled, with the back of it facing me, so I could see the name and number of who it was before she started putting it on.

Maddux, number five.

Lily was excited and thankful, just like I would have expected her to be, when given a gift. She wrapped her arms around her friend and then slid them into the jersey. She put it over her head, covering her flowery ruffle top, then her friend pulled her own jersey out.

Peyton, number seventeen.

I didn't have to see the back of Jackie's jersey to know that it said Martin, number one, on the back of it. It shouldn't have bothered me because thousands of fans wore my jersey, but when it came to those three girls, I wanted my name on Lily's back.

"Time to focus," Tripp yelled, completely oblivious that I was going to rip his jersey up later, and burn it in my sink.

Until then, we had to get back to business and unless we scored a few more goals, I knew the outcome of the game was riding on my shoulders. I jogged into position and tried to forget about who was watching me. I tried Rhys' method, using my adrenaline and anger to fuel my game.

It must have worked, because every ball kicked my way was denied, and with two minutes left, I knew it was going to be a win. Nothing could get past me when I pictured the ball being Tripp's head and Lily wearing his fucking jersey.

After the game ended, the news media pulled me aside and asked for an interview right in front of our bench. I looked up and smiled, thinking I would see Lily watching, but all I saw was the back of her head and her dumb jersey. She was leaving, and the magic of having her there was gone. Answering the questions as quickly as I could, I made my way to the locker room.

Rhys kept smirking at me while he changed, and I wanted to shove my shorts into his face. I was well aware that I got lucky. Had it been a more competitive game, my distractions would have cost us.

Chapter Seventeen

Lily

It may not have been how I imagined my night going, but the high from watching Cruz play was bizarre. It was an excitement I never envisioned when we first pulled up to the stadium. I just wish Angel and Jackie could have known why I was so exhilarated.

When they finally caught on that I was turning into a hard-core fan right before their eyes, I played it off by mumbling Tripp Maddux's name. It was all I could think on a dime, since I had met him the night he brought Cruz home. He was easy to remember, and easy to spot as he ran down the middle of the field.

"Did you love it?" Jackie squealed as we made our way back to the restaurant where she left her car.

"I did!" I smiled. "Thank you both again, for my jersey."

"You gotta have a favorite player," Jackie winked at me. She was assuming because I said Tripp's name that I had the same crush on him that she did Cruz. And I was going to let her believe it. For some reason, she seemed to like me more once she thought I was looking at the game with the same goggles she was.

"Peyton is your favorite?" I asked Angel.

"Probably," she shrugged. "He's the best in the whole dang league."

"And kinda hot?" I teased.

"Well, duh. But choosing a favorite player based on looks is Jackie's thing."

Jackie shrugged, having no shame in the truth.

We laughed, and things got easier from then on. What started out as being a very uncomfortable night for me ended on a high note, and I was once again thankful for Angel, and even Jackie.

After dropping Jackie off, Angel and I started heading back to South Beach.

"I want to come up and see your place," Angel suggested, making me panic.

"It's still early," I teased, even though I would have killed to go to bed. "Want to grab a drink first?" I didn't drink, but I could pretend to drink.

Her face grimaced like she was reliving a bad night with a bottle of tequila. "We can walk down the strip and see what kind of trouble we can get ourselves into, but I may not drink anything but diet coke."

I loved her.

"Sure," I shrugged, not really knowing what I was agreeing to. Honestly, the word *strip* made me uneasy. Where I was from, that meant you lost your clothes. But if I had to strip to keep Angel from realizing I was staying with Cruz Martin, then I was glad I wore my red panties.

Knowing how hard Jackie was crushing on him had convinced me that keeping that secret was vital. Especially until I got to know more about her. The whole night was hot and cold with her, and while I was ultimately thankful for her friendship, I couldn't forget how uneasy she made me feel when she first got in the car. And I definitely didn't want her using me the way she did Cruz's cousin. I hated that continuing to lie to Angel was a side effect of that fear.

So," I tried being detached with my tone. "How did Jackie get our tickets again?"

"She used to work with Cruz Martin's cousin, which makes her think she knows Cruz, himself," she laughed. "It's the first time she's asked for tickets, and he came through. Poor guy, though. Not sure Jackie will stop at just tickets, now."

My return laugh was fake, and I had to force myself not to voice my concerns. The crazy thing was, Cruz seemed to think he and Jackie were supposed to have plans. Jackie was taken off guard by that, but then acting all night like Cruz was already hers.

There were so many lies, and so much miscommunication, and I seemed to be the only one that could see it all. Of course, I was the one doing most of the lying, so I shut myself up.

Angel parked along the sidewalk near all the bars in South Beach. She pointed at a sign lit up that said, Ignite, and took my hand as we jogged across the street.

"It's Wednesday so the crowds are somewhat manageable." She had to be kidding, because there were people everywhere. Probably more than were in my entire home town.

We got lucky and found two empty stools at Ignite, an outdoor bar that faced the main sidewalk. It was perfect for people watching while we chatted.

Angel ordered two colas and I pulled the maps app up on my phone, trying to gauge how far I was from Cruz's apartment so I had a plan for getting back.

"Are you lost?" Angel teased.

"Just checking what's all around here."

"Everything is around here," she nudged me. "I hate that I don't make it out here very often anymore."

"Did you used to spend more time in South Beach?"

"Yeah," Angel snorted. "Every weekend. We would go to the beach all day, then shower in one of those outdoor showers, change into club clothes and hop to all these places down the strip."

"You're still young, why stop?"

"College," she started ticking off on her fingers. "Work. Bills. Money. Life."

Angel was two years older than I was, but started college after I did. She took more time to know what she wanted to do, but she was still young. Though, I got what she meant. We all had to grow up at some point.

"I never lived the night life," I admitted. "My vibe was a little more *loner*. Probably still is."

"You told me stories about some of the parties you went to in college."

"Those are *literally* my only stories," I laughed. "I'm a sad situation."

"Well I love you the way you are."

I beamed at her words and took a sip of my cola. "So how did you and Jackie meet again?"

"We worked together. She and I have both waited tables, and became roommates when I decided to start college. It's easier to pay the bills when I only have to pay half so that the other half can go toward school."

Jackie and Angel were the same age and they seemed like the perfect roommates when we would Facetime. But seeing them in person was changing my mind. They were so different.

"You know," Angel leaned in close to me with a smile. "Once you move here, we can get a three bedroom and all be together."

My legs started bouncing, once again excited for the friends I never thought I would have. "I can't wait!"

"In the meantime, you can just stay in my room with me. When the lease is up, we can get a bigger place. I'll even start looking around."

"I'll *cheers* to that." Lifting my cola, I held it up to hers.

She clicked her glass on mine and we fell into conversions about her dad, who was in jail, and her mom who wanted nothing to do with her. It made me thankful for Ivan and Mom in a way I had never considered. I never really knew my birth father, but Ivan had been good to me and treated me as if I was his own. More importantly, he had been good to my mom.

When it was my turn to talk, I did my best to be honest. It was easy since Cruz was rarely around. Plus, I stayed on fairly easy and boring topics, such as the times Ivan would take me to a movie, or Mom would ask me to help her cook dinner. I left out the parts where I struggled, and the days they spent trying to keep me strong and moving forward. And not once did I mention having a step brother.

After a few colas, I decided to cave and let Angel drive me back to Cruz's. Walking alone that late seemed daunting, and like an all-around bad idea.

Just before we crossed the road back to her car, people started screaming and running. Angel stopped to look at what was happening, but I felt like we should have been running too. The small town girl in me figured if they were running, they had a good reason, and I didn't want to be the one left behind.

"Probably a celebrity sighting," Angel shrugged.

"Who?" My first guess, based on the crowd, was Taylor Swift, and I was too curious to see if I was right to stand still. Angel and I both walked closer to where the crowd was gathering, and I peeked around until I spotted the "celeb."

"Oh geez," I moaned at the same time Angel squealed.

"It's Cruz Martin and Tripp Maddox. Let's go get a picture with them and make Jackie jealous."

As fun as that sounded, I was shaking my head no, and walking toward the car as quickly as possible. Angel caught up and grabbed my arm, turning me back around and leading me toward them.

"No," I whined. "I'm not interested in seeing them again."

"Again? Girl, seeing them at the game doesn't count!"

Does it count if one of them handcuffed themselves to you?

"I don't want to be a fangirl," I said adamantly.

"I thought you told Jackie you thought Tripp was cute! You two bonded over being fangirls. What if he's single and sees you in his jersey, then wants to marry you and give you his cute babies and million dollar condos?"

If I hadn't been trying to retreat so fast, I would have laughed at how quickly she escalated.

"I was just trying to connect with her," I confessed, skipping the part about having Tripp's babies. "I just wanted her to like me."

Angel's excited face fell, and her shoulders sagged. Her back was to the commotion so she didn't see a woman throw her arms around Cruz and kiss him. He wrapped an arm around her waist and whispered something in her ear that made her laugh, and turn bright red. Then he escorted that woman into a nearby club.

Wrapping her arms around me, Angel rocked back and forth then pushed back to look in my eyes. "I get it. You're afraid if we send her pics of us with Cruz, she'll get jealous and kinda hate us."

Well, I hadn't thought of that, but I nodded because it made sense.

"You're right," Angel sighed. "She'd probably not want to talk to us for a week."

"And I don't want to lose her friendship before I even feel like I have it."

"You're a better friend than both of us, because you are the only thing stopping me from saying, 'screw Jackie,' and running over there. Especially after we didn't get a chance to talk to him at all at the game."

No, I wasn't a better friend. I was a liar. No better than Jackie using her friend to get to Cruz. We both sucked, just in different ways.

"I don't feel too well," I grabbed my stomach. "Maybe too much cola." *Or too much shame.*

"I'll drop you off at home," Angel smiled softly.

We drove the two miles down toward Cruz's condo, but I stopped her a few buildings away. "It's this one," I lied again, as Angel pulled off to the side to let me out.

She grabbed my hand and pulled, forcing me to look at her before I got out of the car, but I could barely look her in the eye. "We are so lucky to have you in our lives. Jackie is hard to get along with sometimes, but you are the kind of friend she needs in her life. Same with me. Love you girl."

I leaned across to hug her awkwardly, and then cried. "Love you back."

"Keep me posted on those interviews. I bet you get them all, and get to choose where you want to be. We will celebrate next week when I get time off again."

Shoving the door open and climbing from the car, I started walking into the random building that wasn't Cruz's, just so I could keep up my lies. When I was sure Angel had pulled away, I left the building and walked down the sidewalk, tears soaking my face.

Maybe lying wasn't worth all the pain.

Chapter Eighteen

Cruz

"*Estoy lista, Papacito. Déjame mamar tu bicho.*"

"*Siempre.*"

Fuck, that was a lie. Not only did I not want to be with whatever her name was, but I didn't want to be out at all. I wanted to track Lily down and rip Tripp's jersey off her, then nail mine to her skin.

Not sure why I even agreed to a repeat with last week's fuck. She was just there, and I was desperate to feel something other than *anything* I was feeling for Lily.

"Let's go," I decided, grabbing her hand and pulling her toward the back of Mangos where I knew we could fuck in private.

She giggled, and pressed her tits into my arm as we walked. When I pushed her against a wall, I turned my head away, avoiding kissing her on the mouth. Grabbing onto her tits over the tight dress she was wearing, I closed my eyes, and willed my dick to get hard.

But it didn't. I just kept seeing Lily's bright eyes, and Tripp's jersey covering her body. Just like I knew she would from the day my dad called, she broke me, and I wasn't sure how many random fucks it would take to forget her again.

"*Ahora, Papacito,*" she moaned, knowing that a club fuck had to be quick.

"*No puedo,*" I mumbled, before backing away.

"Are you kidding me?" It was the first time she used English and her voice was loud and shrill. She was pissed, and I guess I couldn't blame her since I made promises, and couldn't follow through. Not until Lily was out of my life again.

"Nine more scoreless nights," I groaned, but no one was around to hear me anymore. I rested my forehead on the wall and resisted the urge to bang it until I was unconscious.

When I felt like I had my bearings again, I made my way back to the table, but I immediately stopped when I saw who was sitting in my seat with Tripp.

What the fuck?

Slowly I approached the table and narrowed my eyes. "Hunter Ward?"

"You two know each other?" Tripp asked as Hunter stood up.

"Sorta," I mumbled, then cleared my throat. "Coach Crazy? Right?"

Hunter smirked but I could tell he was annoyed. He was the assistant coach for the girls' college team that Erin played on, and all the girls thought he was a tad crazy. Erin told me they were calling him Coach Crazy behind his back, but it wasn't much of a secret.

"Hunter and I played against each other in college, then with each other in Lexington League One," Tripp explained.

"Just came to say hi," Hunter added.

Hunter had tried going pro, but I hadn't realized he had made it to League One. That was one step away from the MLS. The way Erin described it, Hunter barely made it out of college.

But then again, she admitted to not knowing much about him. He had been keeping himself a mystery, which was why they all thought he was crazy.

What I did know was that Hunter had taken a leave of absence from the team after their tournament win a few weeks ago. I expected him to be in a straightjacket somewhere working his problems out. Definitely not in one of the hottest clubs in Miami on a random Wednesday night.

"Is this a coincidence?"

"It's easy to run into people when I spend every night out like this."

"Sounds pathetic," I goaded him, knowing I was no better. I prowled every club in Miami, every chance I got, looking for something, or someone, to lose myself in for a while.

"You should know." He leaned over the table, pleasantries forgotten.

Tripp stood up and pushed us away from each other, thinking we were close to a fight. We weren't, because I wasn't sticking around for one.

"I gotta go," I told Tripp. "You two have fun."

Tripp didn't even question me. He knew I wasn't gone long enough to fuck that girl, and he knew why. After the way I acted on the field, he knew exactly why I had to get out of there. So he nodded, and then tilted his head toward the door.

"See you at practice."

"Yep," I nodded and walked out.

Tripp and I had a car service drop us off, but I chose to walk the two miles home. The sidewalk ran all the way down next to the ocean—a route I took often—and it always relaxed me.

When I walked through the door, I was almost back to my normal self. Then Lily walked out of the bathroom in nothing but a towel and I had to hold onto the counter to keep my knees from letting me down.

"Fuck, Lil," I groaned.

She didn't see me, and she wasn't expecting me, which was made obvious by her scream hitting decibels that would have made the Air Force jealous. Without thinking of what I was doing, I ran to her and put my hands on her shoulders.

"Hey, it's okay. *Cálmate*, Lil." I pulled her against me and wrapped my arms around her, waiting for her to realize it was okay.

"You have to stop coming in so late," she cried. "You're scaring the shit out of me."

That was the first time I ever heard her use a swear word, and only because she couldn't see me, I smiled, enjoying the odd way it rolled off her tongue. My hand pressed gently to the back of her head, my fingers tangling in her wet hair. Her mouth was against my shoulder and I could feel the warmth of her breaths as she began to calm down.

"Shhh," I added, wanting to soothe her. *"Lo siento."*

"Actually," she pushed at my chest. "It's not that late. Why are you here?"

She was trying to back away, but I kept hold of her arms. The towel was threatening to drop, so she held it up tight and narrowed her eyes at me, waiting for my answer.

"I live here."

"I saw you go into that bar a few blocks down a few hours ago. Shouldn't you be getting lucky, or drinking too much?"

"You saw me?"

"Angel and I were at Ignite. We saw you and Tripp crossing the street to get there. You wrapped your arm around some girl, and I assumed I'd be alone for most of the night, and then handcuffed to you sometime after two in the morning."

Profanity and humor? Mix that with her earlier wit and charm and I wasn't going to be able to resist her too much longer. She was speaking my language, and in a wet towel, making my dick take notice.

"I don't think my nights will be the same while you're here." I was admitting that to both her and myself.

"What did *I* do?"

"The same thing you've always done."

"I haven't—" She cut herself off, remembering that she was in a towel and my hands were still on her. She backed up further making my hands fall, then just to fuck with her, my eyes went down her body and back up to her face. "I better get dressed."

"Hey wait. You gonna tell me how you ended up at my game?"

"Wasn't it obvious? Apparently my friends are friends with your cousin." She sighed, then turned around and headed back into the hall. "Let me get dressed."

She was going to come back because the conversation wasn't over, so while she changed, I decided to do the same. Then I poured two glasses of wine and took them to the balcony to wait. It was almost midnight, and the way the moon shone over the ocean was intoxicating. The wind blew at my t shirt and shorts, my hair was wild, and as I leaned on the railing and looked down the sidewalk I had just walked down to get home, I felt content and peaceful. Like I was exactly where I should have been.

Chapter Nineteen

Lily

I didn't expect Cruz to come home so early, and was planning to read a book on the balcony until I couldn't hold my eyes open anymore. Maybe have some decaf and soak in the sound of the ocean below.

Instead, Cruz was on the balcony waiting for me, and had poured us each a glass of wine, setting them on a table between the two loungers. Even though I didn't drink, I didn't want to tell him that, so when I opened the door and he motioned for me to take one of the stems, I graciously accepted with a smile.

We sat quietly on the loungers, and I crossed my legs, carefully holding the glass so I didn't spill the wine. Then I looked up to him and smiled, biting the side of my lip shyly.

"Well, cheers!" He lifted his glass and waited for me to tap mine against it. As I did, our eyes locked and I brought the wine to my lips knowing I shouldn't have. One taste wasn't going to hurt, though, at least I hoped it wouldn't.

Tilting my glass up, I sipped just enough to touch my tongue. There was no telling what alcohol would do to my body since I wasn't a seasoned drinker, but I knew after seeing Cruz come in the other night with Tripp that it would treat me to times worse. I needed to start talking before he expected me to drink more.

"Great game tonight."

"The worst game of my career," Cruz groaned, leaning back on his lounger. His legs were crossed at the ankles, his glass was being held in his lap, and his head was turned toward me while he spoke.

"But you kept them scoreless, just like you wanted. Right?"

"It wasn't so much that I kept them scoreless, as it was that my team did a good job of keeping the ball on the other end of the field." His eyes flicked around a few times, like he was still debating on something else he wanted to say, then they landed back on me as he shrugged. "Once I saw you in the stands, it was all I could think about."

My cheeks felt warm and my hand went to my forehead checking for a fever I knew I didn't have. I'm sure he didn't mean for his words to sound so sweet, it was probably more of an annoyance for him. But knowing that I had some sort of effect on him was enough to make me shift in my chair, and my mind to start racing.

"I saw you twice tonight when I least expected. I guess maybe Miami is a small world after all." It was supposed to be a joke, but my delivery was off and the only thing funny about my words was how strained they were when I said them out loud.

"I guess it's safe to assume that your friends have no idea that you know me."

"My friends have no idea," I confirmed. "And I know that sounds awful, to lie to them like that. I really don't want to hurt you, either, but I'm trying to start a new life. Something fresh. I don't want friendships based on who I know."

I expected him to understand and to agree with me, but his smile seemed sad, and his nod didn't feel approving. He leaned back on the chair and took another sip of this wine. His eyes were on the moon and I heard him take a few deep breaths. It felt like forever, but he eventually turned his head back to face me.

"Are you ashamed of me?"

My mouth dropped open and my eyes widened. I was shaking my head *no* because I wasn't ashamed of him. Maybe I was ashamed, but it was only at myself for the lies I had been telling.

Before I could respond, his lips quirked up, and I could tell he was trying to suppress a laugh. "I'm just kidding, Lil. You're doing the right thing. You don't even know those girls very well, and they're already using Deon the same way."

Pushing my shoulders back, I scoffed at him, ready to defend my friends. For some strange reason, it was important to me that he approved, and liked my friends, but he wasn't wrong. At least not about Jackie. She admitted to using Deon to get to Cruz, and I recoiled at her words on the spot. I was just glad Cruz had realized it without me having to tell him. I had already been a shitty friend, I didn't want to tack on bad mouthing Jackie to the catalog of wrongs I had committed.

"Speaking of my friends. Jackie is under the impression you're going to call her. What was that all about?"

"I have a thing Friday night and need a date. When Deon called for the tickets for a few girls, I thought maybe he knew one of them well enough to play the part for one night."

"I don't think Jackie would mind playing the part for more than one night."

"I caught on to that," he grimaced. "Not sure I can handle that while trying to land the Archer Athletics contract. Plus, when I called Deon about not giving her my number, he seemed relieved, like he half-ass told her the plan because he's into her himself. I wouldn't do him like that. He should have said something to begin with."

"Did you tell him she was using him?"

"No," he sighed. "It would sound shitty coming from me directly. He may not even believe me. But he'll figure it out, he's smarter than he's acting right now."

Taking another fake sip of my wine, I processed everything he said. Cruz was smart, and caring. Add that to good looking, athletic, and charming, and I was shocked he was even single. It didn't make sense–unless it was intentional.

"Why not go solo?"

"Because my advisor for Archer Athletics told me the head honchos will take my commitment more seriously if I present that I'm capable of commitment in their faces."

Suddenly, my lies didn't feel so bad. Not because Cruz's was worse, but because it seemed as though we all fibbed a little when we had to. My lies started as lying by omission, but then there were the residual lies in order to keep the questions from being asked.

Which reminded me...

"Before I forget, thank you."

"For what?"

"For not calling me out. I saw the recognition in your eyes fade when you realized I didn't want them knowing I knew you. You played the part, and just...thank you. I promise I'm not ashamed of you," I laughed, "but I've lived in your shadow long enough."

"What?" He sat up and set his wine down, so I set mine down as well and turned in my chair so I was facing him. "Why would you say that?"

"Because it's true?" I laughed again, only to realize he wasn't laughing with me. He was seriously confused.

"How did you live in my shadow when I didn't even live with you?"

"Oh come on." I threw my hands in the air and shook my

head. "All your dad did was tell everyone what a great soccer player you were. My mom was just as bad. You may not have been there, but I lived with you."

"What about you?" He was no longer relaxed. His feet were on the ground, his legs bouncing, and his hands were holding on tight to the edge of the lounger. "Always the princess. I couldn't even call to talk to my dad without him mentioning how special you were. It was like he married your mom and adopted you as his very own princess."

"Princess?" I would have stood in shock, but there wasn't enough room between the loungers with his legs taking up the foot and a half of space between us. "You mean overprotected? Don't get me wrong, I'm thankful for Ivan being in my life, but he wasn't my dad and I wasn't his little princess. He served my mother, and ever since..." I trailed off, not sure I wanted to finish my thought.

"Ever since what?"

Popping my jaw, a nervous tick I had picked up when I was younger, I started running my fingers along a small scar on my leg that I got when I fell off my bike. "Um..."

"You're doing that thing," Cruz pointed. "Your jaw and the way you rub that scar. Just talk to me."

"Ever since my dad died," I blurted, skimming right over how he had picked up on my tells and remembered them after all the time that had passed.

"You think your mom was overprotective because your dad died?"

I shrugged, knowing the answer, and not wanting to say it. "Can we talk about something else?"

"No," he huffed and laid back on his lounger. "I cannot believe you thought you lived in my shadow when in reality, I lived in yours."

"Maybe our realities were just different. Doesn't make either one of us wrong."

"Sometimes it felt like my dad found a replacement kid."

"No," I shook my head adamantly as a tear found its way down my cheek. "All he did was brag on you. Both of them did. 'Cruz is varsity' or 'My son got a scholarship.' The day you signed with Miami I had to drive home from college just to attend your celebration dinner."

"I didn't have a celebration dinner."

"I know!" I shouted, hoping he saw the irony. "You weren't there! But I was. Mom and Ivan took me to a local restaurant where they could brag on you as people passed our table to say hello. They were proud, Cruz, don't get me wrong. It was boastful in a way that I knew they were just so dang proud of you. But it made me feel like I was always going to be second rate. The girl who took six years to graduate with a four year degree. The girl who loved to draw but never drew anything worthy enough to be considered an artist."

The tears were streaming down my face in full force, and Cruz had moved to my lounger as I rambled. He pulled me closer to him, and held me against his chest as I cried my truth.

"I had no idea," he whispered.

"It's not your fault." I sniffed. "You gave them a lot of reasons to be proud. I just wish I could do the same."

"What about being here? Getting your dream job? They are proud of you."

"They are," I nodded against his t shirt, thankful that it absorbed my tears. "I know they are. But I have to call home three times a day. I've never had real friends. I've never even..."

I stopped again, definitely not admitting to him that I had never even had sex. But of course, Cruz didn't let anything go.

"Never even..." he pulled me back so I was forced to look at his face. He reminded me of his dad, the way he beaded his eyes at me as he waited for my confession. Ivan would never punish me, he let my mom do that, but he would make me confess to him when I was in trouble. It had been his way of helping us both, because he took the news, and then eased it to my mom carefully instead of her being hit over the head with bad news. Not that I did much wrong, but even the small things were serious to Gloria Martin.

"I've never had a relationship."

"Like a boyfriend?"

"Like…um…anything." The way his eyes widened made me start to back away but he pulled me back against him and held me tight enough that I couldn't move. He didn't speak, just processed my words while trying to soothe me.

It felt like hours, but it was probably only minutes before he found his voice. "I don't believe you."

Chapter Twenty

Cruz

There was no way someone as gorgeous as Lillian Harris made it to twenty-four and still hadn't had... anything. I knew Gloria was overprotective, but she couldn't spend every night in Lil's bed. She couldn't have prevented Lil from doing whatever, or whomever, she wanted. Not unless Lil was a goody two-shoes.

And she wasn't.

She may have been extra cautious and careful when it came to her mom, but she had friends no one knew about, wasn't truthful about her job interview the other day, and didn't call to check in when she was supposed to. It may not have seemed like a lot for an adult woman, but the signs of rebellion were there. Lil was capable of feeling things her mother probably didn't think she knew the definition for. I saw it in her eyes a few times, the way she looked at me, especially the way she reacted when I said I was going to spank her.

"How can you not believe me?"

"You've been known to lie," I teased, hoping she confessed. "I won't tell Mom and Dad, ya know?"

"I had a boyfriend in college," she blurted. "He was

supposed to be my first. But I opened my big mouth and spilled my guts to him. Scared him away, and I never heard from him again."

"What could you have possibly said to scare him away?"

"That my first time was going to be special because it was with him."

"He left because of that?" My arms got tighter around Lil. Some protective side of me came out, and I was thinking of looking the guy up and paying him a visit. I surmised that wouldn't make me much better than Gloria when it came to 'Lil the Princess,' but it wasn't like I chose to feel that way. "You still waiting for someone special?"

What are you doing, Cruz?

"Just waiting on life to finally begin," she sighed.

The tears had stopped, and I could tell she was starting to get tired. It was the perfect chance to end the conversation. But did I do that? Not really. My mouth just kept thinking of things to say that would probably get me in trouble.

"You owe me." I pushed her up and held her by the arms, looking into her eyes.

"Owe you?"

"For pretending I didn't know you at the game. First time in a while I had someone in the stands, and I had to act like we were strangers."

She rolled her eyes, knowing I was being intentionally dramatic, but a small smile played on her lips. "Then I guess I owe you one."

"Be my date Friday for the Archer Athletics dinner."

"Excuse me?"

"We've been on a date before. Did you forget dinner by the water already?" I stood and started pacing the tile in front of her lounger, making a scene at how devastated I was. "I slaved over a hot stove for hours for you, and you don't even remember."

"So I tell you a huge secret about being a virgin, and you decide I need to be your date? Do you hear how creepy that sounds, Cruz?"

I stopped and rested my chin on my hand, thinking about her logic. "It sounds perfect to me. I need someone that won't fall in love with me and expect sex afterward. You hate me, and my shadows, and you won't beg me for sex."

"Well," she laughed. "You do make a very valid point."

"So you'll go?"

"You do realize that being a virgin isn't the same as being a nun, right?"

"Are you saying if I take you, you'll beg me for sex?"

"What? No!" She stood up and huffed, placing her hands on her hips. "I just mean that your reasoning isn't sound."

"That's true, Sister Lily." She immediately got my joke and narrowed her eyes at me, fighting a laugh.

"And what if someone takes a picture and there is some headline that reads, 'Cruz Martin dates his sister!'"

"They'd never believe it, I'm not Catholic!" I argued back, making that laugh finally burst out of her chest. Fuck it felt good to be the one making her so damn happy. It could easily become my newest addiction.

"You know what I mean," she sighed with a lingering smile.

"You're not my sister," I eased closer to her, getting back to being serious for a minute. "How many times have we said that? Plus, no reporters will be there. This is an exclusive dinner, and we will introduce you as my date. No one will question anything. It's perfect."

"I don't even know what I'd wear to a dinner like that."

"I will give you my credit card tomorrow and you can buy whatever you want to wear. Shoes. Outfit. Jewelry. Whatever. Please?" I poked my lip out and laced my fingers together in front of my chin as if I was praying, and trying really hard to resist calling her Mother Teresa.

"Fine," she sighed. "But if we end up on the internet, our parents will kick your ass. Not mine. Because you will make sure of it. Ya got me?"

"Cross my heart," I assured her, adding *The Sign of the Cross* just for good measure.

"And stop that," she pointed at me, laughing.

Licking my lips, I winked at her and suppressed my grin so hard it hurt my cheeks. She stood up and eyed me one more time, before turning toward the door. "We've overshared enough for one night. I'm going to bed."

"Night, honey," I teased.

I expected her to shoot me a look, some warning that I better not make it worse for her now that she's agreed to be my date Friday. But instead, she kept her back to me and slid the door open with a sigh. "It's Miss Harris to you."

"Sí señorita."

She shook her head but kept walking in and toward her bedroom. I decided to lay back on the lounger and finish my glass of wine–and hers–before turning in. There was no way I was going to sleep, as keyed up as I was.

Spending the night talking to Lil gave me a high, and the blood in my body was pumping. It felt good knowing she was helping me Friday, but I felt equally as good knowing where we stood, and that I could make her laugh so hard.

Never in a million years did I expect her to say she lived in my shadow. Dad was always proud of me, and her mom was always treating her like a delicate flower. Combined, they tried to force a family dynamic between us, but all they did was cause us to resent one another. I didn't blame them for navigating waters they weren't sure how to navigate, but I wondered how

Lil and I would have been with one another if our parents were different toward us.

Would we have grown up closer? Would I have gone back to Dad's more often than I did?

Would I consider her my sister?

Probably not.

Getting a hard-on for her wasn't exactly very *brotherly* of me. Then again, my sixteen-year-old self would beat off to images of Velma Dinkley, and Lunchlady Doris if that was all that was available. My judgment was lacking back then.

Maybe it still was.

Taking Lil with me on Friday was a bigger risk than I would ever admit to her. I didn't lie to her when I said there wouldn't be reporters, but that didn't mean someone wouldn't post us on social media. I should've let her off the hook and called her friend, Jackie. That was still a risk, but it seemed to be a much smaller one. That kind of risk was one I knew how to navigate.

Lil wasn't someone I was willing to hurt. Not ever. Even when we were younger, I never would have hurt her, and I would have killed anyone that tried. Now I was the one at risk of hurting her.

I pulled out my phone and made a quick note to call my lawyer and my agent before taking Lil to the event. They knew that whomever I took on Friday was going to be a fake date, so I needed their help keeping Lil off the social media radar. That was at least something, and I felt better knowing I was taking a few precautions.

Because the only other thing I could do was not take her, and now that she had agreed, I was looking forward to it more than ever. No matter how bad it may have been, I wanted to spend time with her.

I wanted to fake it with her.

Chapter Twenty One

Lily

After coffee and Facetiming with my mom, I stood in the kitchen contemplating breakfast. Cruz had been up for a while, but kept to himself while I did my morning routines. But once he was sure my mom was no longer on the phone, he tossed his credit card onto the counter and tapped it to make sure I saw.

"They said it was dressy, but not formal. Buy whatever. If you need... I don't know. Just use that, okay? Have fun. Wait, should I go with you? I feel like I should go with you."

"You want to spend your only day off in a department store?"

"I will if you need me to."

After our talk last night, I wouldn't have minded spending more time with him. Then again, I didn't *need* to spend more time with him. Pretending to be his date was going to be hard enough.

"No, I better go alone." I swiped his credit card from under his finger and smiled. "But this will make the afternoon way more fun for me."

"Don't hold back, Lil." His words could've come across as being pompous and flashy, but he had a serious look on his face.

"I'm not really even sure what I need. Just an outfit I guess. All I brought with me was clothes for the interviews."

"Just remember you're the one doing me a favor, so have fun. Get whatever."

"I better get to it then." I waved his credit card in the air. "It's gonna take me a while to get to Dolphin Mall."

"There are one million shops right here on South Beach. You don't need to drive all the way to Dolphin Mall. Besides, isn't that mall an outlet?"

"I like shopping at outlets. My mom and I would spend a full day at outlet malls getting ready for each new school year when I was growing up."

"My mom and I did something similar, but instead of going to outlets, we would spend the whole day at the flea market. That's where I would get all my things." The memory made him smile. "But that's not the point. The point is that the card has no limit on it, and I've given you free rein to swipe it as many times as you want. Don't worry about the cost, Lil. Stay here in South Beach and don't fight the traffic."

I shook my head and looked down at my feet as I shuffled toward my bedroom. I knew Cruz wasn't Richard Gere, and I wasn't Julia Roberts, but it sure felt like if I got turned away from a posh boutique here in South Beach, I'd be able to go back with an arm full of bags and tell them they made a big mistake.

Putting on some comfortable leggings and a tank top, I got ready for what felt like war. It might not have been the best shopping attire, but it was all anyone around here wore when they weren't in their bathing suits, and I wanted to blend in as much as possible. I grabbed my sunglasses and my bag to finish the look then cut back across the living room and toward the kitchen. Cruz was fixing himself a sandwich, which was not something he could've done had I not gone shopping for groceries.

"Maybe while I'm out I should use this to stock up your fridge," I joked. He stopped what he was doing and looked up at me, like I had just discovered the molecular structure of DNA.

"I don't know why I didn't think of that before. I've never worried about food, but you staying here should have made me worry about it. Just keep that card. Use it for whatever. Better yet, I'll have them send me one in your name."

"Whoa," I snorted. "I was just kidding. Stop trying to make me spend your money."

"You're helping me. Not just tomorrow night, but it's been nice having food here at home. There's no reason I shouldn't foot the bill for that."

All I could do was shake my head and change the subject. "Well, wish me luck." I took a few more steps towards the front door. "If your dad calls, I told my mom I was window shopping to get out for a while. I wasn't in the mood to explain our fake date."

Cruz had a mouthful of his sandwich and was nodding, trying to swallow it down before he responded. "Pretty sure my dad would try to ground me like I was a kid if he knew I was taking you as my date to a sponsorship dinner."

Every shop and boutique I went into was overwhelmingly posh. I felt so out of sorts and wasn't even sure how to properly shop at places that didn't have racks of clothes with price tags that I could flip through.

Instead, these places had nine mannequins, fully dressed in

outfits, and if I liked one of the outfits they would bring me that outfit in my size. Even knowing I was using Cruz's card, I still wanted to know how much I was spending. But I was too scared to ask. As much as I loved the movie Pretty Woman, I didn't want to live it.

After a few hours of failed attempts, I walked into a place called Sean Lala. The girl behind the counter must've seen my resignation because she walked toward me with her arms stretched out like she was going to give me a hug. She settled for grabbing my shoulders and tilting her head as she asked, "Tell me what you need girl. I got you."

"I'm going to a...*thing* tomorrow night," I sighed. "I need something dressy but not formal and I'm really tired of shopping."

"What kind of *thing*? A dinner? A party? A sporting event?

How did I explain to her that she was right on all three accounts? It was a party that was serving dinner about sporting stuff.

"Yes."

"Which one?" she laughed.

"Yes," I repeated, "those all sound about right. It's a dinner party about sports stuff." I hoped she didn't ask for more details because even though she was a stranger, I didn't want to tell her where I was going, just in case she was one of Cruz Martin's major female fans.

"Okay, so this is how we stage our floor, but we have a ton of options in the back. Take a seat and let me bring you some things."

I sat down and nodded, too tired and over it, to care what she brought me. She was the friendliest person I had spoken to all day, and even if everything she brought me made me cringe, I was already more comfortable at Sean Lala than I had been all day.

"What's your name?" She asked, as she pulled a measuring tape from a drawer.

"Lillian. You?"

"Simone." She reached her hand out to shake and I smiled again, thankful for Simone's easy nature. She took a few quick measurements around my body, and then disappeared for fifteen minutes. When she came back she was pushing a rack full of more than a dozen outfits, none of which were on the main floor of the shop.

I wonder if all the places are like this? Not that it mattered, because until Simone, no one had offered to help me get that far and I hadn't been savvy enough to ask for them to bring me some choices.

"Let's do this girl," she clapped. "We have to get you ready for the complicated ball tomorrow night."

She held up several different outfits, all of which I loved. They suited me. It was like she could tell that I wasn't the kind of girl to wear bright colors and flashy clothes.

After I picked a few of my favorites out, she put me in a dressing room, and then took a seat in the chair I had been in. "I'll be right here. I want to see them all. Do a fashion show for me."

For the next hour, I had the best time trying on some of the most gorgeous yet subtle outfits I had ever seen in my life. Simone was more than a sales clerk, she was like having a friend with me. She ooh'd and ahh'd over everything I tried on, but was also honest when something wasn't working.

By the time we were done, I had the perfect outfit for the 'dinner party sporting event.' I also had matching shoes and a new clutch I could carry because according to Simone, my big, bulky bag would cover too much of the expensive fabric.

As she rang everything up at the register, I started bouncing on my heels, worried about how much it would cost. As nice as

Simone was, I had been too afraid to ask so I was just going for it and hoped and prayed it wasn't thousands of dollars. Cruz may have said not to worry about it but I didn't want him to think that I was taking advantage of him being so kind.

Then another thought crossed my mind.

I pulled the credit card out that Cruz gave me and looked at the name on it.

Sebastian Martin.

I was relieved that it didn't say Cruz Martin. I knew Cruz was really his mother's last name and Martin was his father's last name. He had never gone by Sebastian so the girl shouldn't know who's card I really had. Not unless she was a fanatic.

"Your total is $750.84."

That's it? It was still more than I could ever afford, but way less than I feared.

I slid her the fancy black card and she looked at it and smiled. "Let me guess, your boyfriend is footing the bill?"

Not really.

"Is it that obvious?"

"Girlfriends are my favorite clients."

"Well, you're one of my favorites too, Simone. Thank you for being so nice to me. I wish I had come here first."

Simone handed me a card and gave me a sincere smile. "Here's my number if you need anything. Just let me know."

Before I left, Simone rounded the counter and gave me a hug wishing me a good time. She never got nosy and asked where I was going, and I just kept letting her believe that I really was a girlfriend. Because for the sake of the event, that's exactly what I was.

I walked a few blocks back to my car feeling like the weight of the world had been lifted off my shoulders. I had an outfit, a great time, and I really was looking forward to whatever Friday night held.

Chapter Twenty-Two

Cruz

It was supposed to be a day off, but I had work to do. Which was the main reason I didn't fight to go shopping with Lil. Not that I loved shopping, but I thought maybe it would be more fun for her if we both went. Had I not had to run through the game plan for Sunday's game, I would've gone with her.

Instead, I spent all afternoon on my iPad and TV, watching old games and footage. I also took some time to call my mom, who was the hardest working woman I knew.

Both of my parents were born and raised in Miami, but my mom had deep Cuban roots and knew how to make the best Cuban food anyone had ever tasted. Cooking was her life. Being a chef and owning a restaurant was her dream.

My dad's parents were from Puerto Rico. Both of them moved to Miami to go to college, and set my dad on the same path. He became an engineer who fell in love with his waitress. They got married and had me, but it was never going to work. Mom wasn't just the waitress, she was the owner, and she was married to Tico—the name of her restaurant.

Thankfully, she and dad had remained friends, and I always had access to both parents. Even when Dad was offered a job in Brooksville, to take over a supervisor role at a mechanical engineering plant, he and my mom discussed the move before he left. They made sure I would still be able to see them both.

After he met Gloria, my dad always made sure my mother and I were included in his life. The best part about Gloria was that she understood and supported that relationship. In fact, the only thing I didn't like about their marriage was Lily. I hated that I was forced to be someone to her that I wasn't, and I never understood Dad's insistence that I make it work with her.

"How's Lillian?" my mom asked as I heard pots and pans being moved around the kitchen.

"She's...good."

"You hesitated," she yelled. "What's wrong?"

The one secret my mom and I had from my dad was how much I didn't like being around Lily. I think she understood *why* without me having to tell her, though. She would give me pep talks before I flew up to their house, and then tell me how good I did when I got home. They were loaded conversations with no real details.

"Nothing's wrong," I sighed. "In fact, it's great. I kind of like having her around without Dad and Gloria pressuring us to be one big happy family."

"Well, that's not what I expected you to say."

"Well, it's not what I expected to feel."

She laughed, but let the subject go. We ended up making plans for her to come to a game before the end of the season, and I warned her that Dad and Gloria were thinking of coming to town.

I got off the phone with her just as Lil came in from shopping. It surprised me that she only had one bag. For some reason, I expected her to come in with bags from several different places.

"So how'd it go?" I stood from the couch and started walking toward her, shoving my hands in the back pockets of my jeans.

"I got something." She held up the bag. "I hope it works, and I hope you don't mind that I got the shoes and a bag to match."

"Of course I don't mind, that's what I wanted you to do. Can I see it?"

"No way," she waved her hand in the air, making sure I didn't dare ask again. "If it isn't gonna work, I'm not going back out there. You'll have to see it right before we leave. That way it either works, or I don't have to go." She had a small smirk on her face and a gleam in her eye. She wasn't gonna let me see what she picked out, and she knew it was a tease.

"Fair enough. I'm sure it's going to be perfect. We can't really mess this up, and it should be an easy night."

"Here's your card." She slid the black metal across the bar in the kitchen and I pushed it back her way.

"Hang onto it, remember?"

"Oh yeah... *Sebastian.* I'll hang onto it but don't expect me to use it unless you want me to pick up the tab for dinner tonight."

"Dinner tonight would be a date before our date," I laughed.

"I'm starving. I haven't eaten all day, and it would be rude of me not to ask you to come since I'm going to use your fancy card to pay for it."

I walked over near my room where I had haphazardly discarded my shoes, eyeing her while I pulled them on. "So where are we going?"

She tapped the card onto her chin, acting like she was thinking really hard, and then asked, "Where is somewhere expensive and that I can also go dressed like this?"

"I don't know of anywhere in Miami that you can't go dressed in leggings. It's the best part of South Florida life."

"Then give me an idea where to take you."

I grabbed my keys and my wallet from the bar and then grabbed her hand. She dropped the bag that had her outfit in it, and left it on the kitchen floor as I dragged her back out the door. "I know just the place."

"Is this going to involve La Primada Baracoa's again? Because I wouldn't be mad about that."

"No *señorita*. This will be an actual dinner."

We left South Beach and drove towards Tico's after I sent my mom a quick text letting her know I was bringing Lil for dinner. She assured me we would have the best table in the place.

When we pulled up, Lil's eyes widened as she got out of the car and shut her door. She looked up at the building knowing exactly where she was.

"Your mom's place?" she said, but somehow also made it a question.

"Yep. This is where I worked growing up. My mom's second child, and the main love of her life. She's worked so hard, and I'm so proud of her. Tico was my grandpa's nickname."

"Do you still help her out around here?"

"Nah. I tried to wait tables a few years ago when she needed an extra server, but people were learning who I was at that time and it wasn't very much help."

Guiding her by the small of her back, I opened the door and nodded to the hostess. She showed us to the table my mom had saved for us in the back where I could dine without fans noticing me too much.

Lil and I sat in the booth facing one another, but her eyes went above my head, and I rolled my eyes, already knowing what she was looking at. "It looks like your mom is very proud of *you*, as well. There's a whole wall with pictures of you and one of your jerseys is framed."

"Maybe we should switch sides, because that's actually embarrassing."

The way she laughed made me change my mind instantly because I wanted more of her laughter. "I think it looks amazing and if it makes you squirm, that makes it even better."

"So all of a sudden, you like to see me squirm?"

"No, I've always liked to see you squirm."

We smiled at each other, our eyes connecting across the table. For a moment, it was completely quiet, and all I could think about was making her squirm again, as well. I couldn't look away from the gorgeous woman Lillian had turned into, especially when she looked so happy.

It seemed like every time I went to my dad's, she was unhappy. My dad would say she was just a teenager, but it always felt like there was more to it than that. If I had had the guts, I would've asked her myself. I didn't go to her school, but I used to picture myself showing up and finding whoever it was that made her unhappy. Of course, I never admitted that to anyone, and a part of me knew she was so unhappy just because I was there, no matter how many times Dad assured me that it was just a phase.

Looking at her years later, maybe it was a phase. Or maybe it was because we were actually talking and getting along. It made her smile. It made *me* smile. I almost regretted all the years I spent not trying to make her smile when I had the chance.

"Hi, how are you doing this evening–" The waitress cut herself off when I looked up at her.

I didn't recognize the waitress. It'd been a couple of months since I had been to Tico's, and Mom was always hiring new people. But she recognized me and started backing away with her hand over her mouth.

"You're, you're, you're..." she gasped.

"Hey," I raise my hand awkwardly, half waving, and half trying to get her to stay quiet. "Is my mom around?"

She nodded while she kept her hand over her mouth and then turned to walk away quickly. I would prefer my mom be our server for the night. Plus, I wanted her to meet Lil.

Lil watched the waitress walk away with amusement on her face. She didn't think I saw, but she snorted and shook her head, not believing the response the waitress had to who I was.

"I will have you know," I leaned across the table, "I'm kind of a big deal around here."

She leaned forward and met me halfway across the table before glancing over my head again, and then back into my eyes. "I know. It's literally written on the wall."

We both laughed and fell back into our seats right as my mom came around the corner.

"Hi, I'm Mariana. Cruz's mother. You are Lillian, and I am so happy to finally meet you."

Lillian slid from her booth and surprisingly didn't shake my mom's hand. She wrapped her arms around her neck and squeezed, making my mom close her eyes while she hugged her back.

"I know exactly who you are, Ms. Cruz. Ivan always sang your praises."

"But Cruz didn't sing my praises?" She asked, her accent sounding strong. She had her hands on her hips, giving me a side eye with a smirk on her face.

"It's only been a week that we've actually spoken more than two words to each other."

"Well, you're all grown up and gorgeous. I've only ever seen pictures of you."

"Same to you. So gorgeous, but only ever seen pictures of you."

Shit, Lil was quite the charmer, making my mom smile and blush.

Once Lily was back in her seat, my mom told me she would bring us something special, and that there was no need to order. I asked Lily if that was okay first, and of course she smiled and nodded with excitement.

"I feel like meeting your mom is like meeting someone famous," Lily blushed after Mom left our table. "I've seen pictures of her, and heard stories, but seeing her in real life is such a treat."

It wasn't very often someone was more amazed at meeting my mom than they were me, and it honestly felt really good. My mom was a rockstar, and I loved that Lily jumped up and treated her like one.

While we waited for food, our conversation was casual, mostly talking about what to expect at our dinner. She wouldn't have to do much other than stay close to me. I would treat her like any other date, and it would be fine. I didn't want her to stress. I wanted her to have fun.

We also talked about college. She told me about how becoming an art broker wasn't exactly her dream job, and I wondered if that was why she cried the day she got the offer. But I didn't ask her because I told her she could come to me with that story if she wanted to tell it.

"You used to draw all the time. Do you still draw?"

"Nonstop. I draw everything."

"I kind of draw. I mean, I write on my goal post, sometimes," I laughed and shrugged. "Not to brag but I wrote, 'Keep them Scoreless' the other night and I did."

"An artist in the making. Do you do that a lot? Write on your goal?"

"Actually, I do," I swallowed, realizing I was telling her something I hadn't told anyone before. "Mostly just my way of manifesting."

"I need to manifest the art of making a living being an artist in this country. Unfortunately, the art business thrives on buying and selling, and I can't afford to be a struggling artist while I wait on my big break."

"Is that why it took you six years in college?" I teased, but she was already shaking her head.

"I always knew I was going to go the broker route. But life is crazy sometimes. Things change. I had some problems in college, some hurdles I had to get over, but it's definitely not something I want to talk about."

I understood, not wanting to talk about things, especially with me, but I reached my hand across the table and took hers, using my thumb to rub her knuckles. "There's a lot you don't like to talk about. But like I said the other day, I can be your friend. I can listen." There was more I wanted to say, but my mom interrupted us with two plates of *ropa vieja*.

"Here we are," she said joyfully as she placed them in front of us. I pulled my hand from Lil's and sat back, trying not to feel uncomfortable with the fact that my mom probably thought there was more to that than there actually was.

While Lily was looking at her plate, I looked up at my mom, who beaded her eyes at me quickly to let me know she saw us holding hands. I just gave her a slight shake of my head, hoping she understood it wasn't what she thought.

When Lily looked up, my mom transformed her face back to a smile and told her how *ropa vieja* was my favorite. She waited while Lily took a bite, and when Lil's eyes got big and she moaned, my mom gave her shoulder a squeeze. "I knew you'd love it."

After Mom left, Lily and I chose to stuff our faces instead of talking. But my phone buzzed in my pocket and I checked it to see that my mom couldn't even wait for me to leave before she had to say something.

> Be careful, Lillian means a lot to your father.
> Don't you dare treat her like someone you can
> fuck around with.

I couldn't ignore the text so I lifted a finger, letting Lil know I needed to respond.

> It's not like that Mom. She got emotional over
> telling me about college. Trust me I've never
> held the hand of a girl I want to fuck around
> with. Stop worrying.

Before I could even slip my phone back in my pocket, a new text from her popped up.

> I just needed to be sure, because even from
> across the restaurant, I could tell that look you
> gave her was not brotherly, or friendly.

She was right, it wasn't. Because Lil and I weren't that. My mom knew better than to say that to me, but she did anyway, and I got irritated. It wouldn't do me any good to respond to her, so I tucked the phone away.

For the rest of dinner, Lily and I laughed as we swapped stories about our parents. When the original waitress cleared our plates, Lily lifted a finger and informed her that she would like the check.

The poor girl's eyes widened as I suppressed a laugh. Everyone knew my mom didn't charge me for food. She never had and she never would, no matter that I could afford it ten times over.

Eventually, the girl just nodded and agreed, but I knew that check would never see our table. Except when she finally did come back, she put a bill down and slid it towards Lily.

What the hell?

Lily whipped out my credit card and laughed before placing it on top of the check. "I told you I was buying dinner."

"But you're using my card." The waitress grabbed the payment and walked off with it as Lily leaned on her hands and batted her eyelashes at me.

"It's a lot of fun, Sebastian."

I got caught in her eyes again, biting my bottom lip and running my thumb along my jaw to distract myself.

Mom brought the check back herself, and gave my credit card back to Lily as if it was hers. "I like your style," she winked, making Lily's smile even brighter.

We stood to leave and Mom walked us towards the door, looping her arm through Lil's. "You're welcome here anytime, Lillian. You're part of the family."

"Thank you, Ms. Cruz."

"You can call me *mamá*."

No she couldn't because that would be almost as bad as our parents being married. Why couldn't everyone stop with the happy little family shit?

Lily didn't respond, just leaned in to hug my mom goodbye. Then my mom turned around to face me. "I'll see you at your game next week. I love you."

I gave my mom a hug and then I grabbed Lily's hand and walked her to my car. Mom was watching, and I was sure I was going to get another text message as soon as I got home. But I couldn't help it. I opened the door for Lily and waited for her to get in before I shut the door and rounded the front of my car. When I chanced a look at my mom, she wasn't looking at me the way she did in the restaurant. She had a smile on her face, and I gave her a small wave before I climbed into the driver's side.

My mom always saw something, and we never actually talked about it, so when we got home and I had no text messages on my phone, I knew she had decided that once again, when it came to Lily and me, it was what it was.

Chapter Twenty Three

Lily

Meeting Cruz's mother was a high I wasn't prepared for. It felt so meaningful in a way that I didn't expect. My mother married her ex-husband. Her son used to be someone that I hated being around. Yet, she was warm, and made me feel so welcome.

I instantly loved her.

Cruz was quiet on the drive home, and when we walked in the front door, we each made our way across the apartment to our own rooms.

Instead of going to sleep, I decided to sketch, and I started with what I could remember of the details of Tico's. The signs, the shape of the windows, and the lighting. When I finished the drawing, I put the date at the bottom, knowing it was always going to be a special day.

I flipped through some of the pages of my sketch pad and looked at my recent sketches. Like I told Cruz, I still sketched all the time, but I mostly stuck to the memories I wanted to keep. Moments that meant something to me.

Just a week in Miami, I already had more of those moments than I did my entire last two years of college. I looked at one that

I'd drawn of Angel after we'd first met, and how pretty I thought she was in person. She seemed so perfect, with a big smile and dark hair that fell perfectly at her shoulders. Not one strand felt out of place.

Then there was a picture of *La Primada Baracoa* Bars on the old pier. And one of the outside of the art studio I interviewed at a few days before. The rest were sketches of Cruz. Him at his game, the way he leaned against the bar in the kitchen when he ate his sandwich, and the two of us in his bed, handcuffed together.

My heart started beating faster as I looked at the image I'd drawn. It was how I imagined us while we were sleeping. Cruz had his arm thrown over his head, and the one handcuffed to me was on my thigh. Maybe that wasn't how it really was, because Cruz was already awake when I woke up, but I couldn't change the way I pictured it inside my head.

Even if it did cross a few lines, I couldn't picture us any other way.

Closing my sketch pad, I tucked it under my pillow and tried to get my heart rate down. It was just like me, to get worked up over something so seemingly innocent as a touch to my leg. But I was innocent, and I didn't want to be. I felt so much, was needy, and anxious to know what it was like to have that moment with someone. It had to be the only reason I was so affected by Cruz.

I groaned and turned over, mad that I couldn't seem to control thoughts, and fell asleep thinking about how inappropriate I wanted to be with my step brother.

"Lil. Wake up."

I turned my head away from the noise—which sounded a lot like Cruz. Plus he was the only one that called me Lil.

"Lil?" I heard again. "You've slept all day."

No I hadn't. It may have been late when I finally fell asleep, but that was a mere fifteen minutes ago. I had a lot more sleep to get through.

"*Levántate y brilla, señorita.*"

I smiled, loving that he was still calling me that, even though he said it as a joke. Peeking my eyes open, I saw that the sun was shining brightly into my room, and that meant I had been asleep longer than the predicted fifteen minutes.

Flipping back over to face Cruz, I smiled up at him. "What time is it?"

"Two."

"What?" I yelled, sitting up and checking the clock.

"You've been asleep all day. Late night?" He held up my sketchbook that had moved from under my pillow as I slept.

Grabbing the book, I bent over the side of the bed to stuff it into my bag. There wasn't anything too embarrassing, but my drawings were private. Someone looking at them without asking would feel like a violation of some sort.

"I just picked it up off the bed, Lil. I didn't look."

"I'm not worried if you looked," I lied. "Sketching is just kinda private. Like having a diary."

"It doesn't look like the same one you used to draw in."

"I go through a new book every few years," I shrugged. "I'm sure the one you remember is tucked away in a box back at Mom and Ivan's house."

His smile was soft as he stared into space, reflecting on whatever memory I jogged for him. Then the look was gone just as quickly as it appeared.

"A car is picking us up in four hours. Just didn't know how much time you needed, or if you wanted to eat or anything."

Sliding past him, I got out of bed and stood. He stayed sitting on the edge and lifted his hands toward me before stopping himself and tucking them under his legs. Letting him know I saw him, I tilted my head, and in a very brazen act for me, bit my lip and smiled. I wouldn't have minded if he grabbed my hips and held me in front of him.

Was it wrong? Probably. *But was it really?*

"I made food," he mumbled, then looked toward the door. Before I could ask what he made or respond, he stood up and left my room.

I did a little twirl, hoping that my small attempt to flirt affected him the way he walked around affecting me. Even though nothing would ever come of flirting with him, it boosted my self-esteem knowing I could. One day, I would be a single woman in Miami, and learning how to flirt was going to be a necessity.

When I went out to eat whatever Cruz made, he was gone. There was a note on the bar that said he had gone out for a run, and beside it was a bowl of boxed mac n' cheese. I took the wrapper off the bowl and dove in since it was still pretty warm.

I hadn't seen a box of mac n' cheese in the cabinets, and I didn't take Cruz for being a big mac n' cheese eater. But it was a favorite of mine growing up, and I wondered if he remembered the same way he remembered the *La Primada Baracoa* Bars. Was he being intentional?

"Of course he is," I whispered to myself. "You're doing him a favor today."

Finishing up my lunch, I went straight into a hot shower and started getting ready for our night out. It wasn't going to take me all day to get ready, but I was going to pretend it did to avoid having to leave my room. Cruz didn't scare me, but the mac n' cheese made me mushy, and it was better to keep my distance until it was time to *pretend*.

When he came in from his run, he didn't knock on my door, he sent me a text.

> Gonna lay down for a bit then get ready. We need to walk downstairs right at six.

I sent him a thumbs up, and went back to a new sketch I was doing. It was a bowl of pasta, and around the edges were random pieces that had been flung out of the bowl. It didn't mean much to me in the beginning, but as I looked at it more, I felt like my emotions were the pieces scattered all over the place. The more time I spent around Cruz, the harder it was to keep those emotions in my little bowl.

Chapter Twenty Four

Cruz

Avoiding Lil until it was time to leave was my only option, because I was a weak little shit. I had almost grabbed her by the waist and pulled her to me. Almost made her straddle my lap so I could kiss the cute look she gave me off her face.

I was fucked.

Hoping to get more control of myself, I went for a long run, and then came home and beat off in the shower. I fell face first into my bed and slept for an hour, and by the time we had to leave for the Archer Athletics event, I felt a little better.

I dressed like the advisor told me to dress—slacks with a dress shirt, no jacket, no tie. The event was dressy, but not formal. Adjusting the watch on my wrist and tapping my shiny dress shoes on the tile proved how anxious I was as I waited for Lil to come out of her room. There were sounds of movement but I hadn't messaged her, or knocked on the door since I had already told her what time we had to leave.

At 5:55, her door cracked open, and I looked up to see her walking casually towards the kitchen where I was leaning on the bar. My eyes went straight to her feet because her heels were clicking. Fuck, I was almost afraid to look higher because just looking at her feet was making my dick twitch.

Slowly, I moved my eyes to her body and saw she was wearing a jumpsuit with flowy pants and a V that dipped down low between her breasts. There were only two thin straps that went up over her shoulders and around her neck, keeping the fabric up over her tits.

And she definitely wasn't wearing a bra.

Her hair was up in a ponytail, yet it looked sexy and stylish, slicked back and high on top of her head. I could see shiny earrings dangling from her ears, almost to her neck. Her lips were bright red, and when I finally landed on her eyes, I realized she had somehow made them bluer and brighter.

She nervously adjusted a small clutch in her hand before stopping in front of me and giving me a heart stopping smile. "Ready when you are."

I didn't talk, I didn't even move. My jaw was almost on the floor, and if I had been a cartoon, my tongue would've rolled out and my eyes would have popped from my head.

"Cruz?" she asked. "What's wrong?"

"I don't know, Lil." My chest was heaving, I wanted to reach out and touch her skin. I wanted to run my finger right down the V that dipped between her tits.

"Do you need to sit down?" She was so innocent, completely unaware that I had just decided I was done doing the right thing–at least for the night. I could just tell myself it was all pretend and it would be alright that my cock got hard for her.

"You look so fucking beautiful," I told her honestly. "I mean you always look beautiful but seeing you all dressed up for me is making it hard to want to leave."

Looking down, her cheeks pinked from my words. "You look

really good too. I'm so used to seeing you in soccer clothes or jeans."

We stared at one another for a few beats until my phone rang in my pocket. Pulling it out, I looked down to see a number I didn't recognize, but already knew who it was.

"That's the driver. Let's head downstairs."

My hand fell on the small of her back as I opened the door, letting her go first and leading her to the elevator like she had no idea where it was. When we were in the lift, I still didn't drop my hand, and squeezed the side of her waist, pulling her closer to me.

We exited out the double doors to the lobby where a black SUV was waiting for us. The driver instantly recognized me, and tipped his hat before opening the back door.

As we drove off, Lil's hands began to fidget, so I took them in mine and squeezed, making her look up at me.

"I'm nervous," she whispered.

"Me too. But probably not for the same reason you are, though."

"Why're you nervous?"

"Just worried I won't be able to fake this date."

She nodded as if she knew what I was talking about, but she had no idea. She probably thought that I wasn't going to be able to pretend to date her, but I was really just scared that the line was too blurry for me to even notice it was there at all.

The drive was about thirty minutes through the grueling Miami traffic, but eventually we pulled into the hotel where the dinner was taking place. When we climbed from the car, I grabbed Lil's hand and she held on tight to mine as I led her toward the main room. There were already a ton of people there, and once I stepped through the door, I became everyone's target.

My name was being called from every direction. People

were coming up and shaking my hand, and I was trying to introduce Lily as we went, wanting to include her in every aspect of the evening. To her credit, she was only overwhelmed for the first ten minutes, but as the night went on, she played her role perfectly. She smiled and held onto my arm, then leaned into me almost without thinking. When someone would ask her about me, she would smile and look into my eyes.

There was no story for our ruse. We didn't discuss any questions that may have been asked. But Lil seemed to have all the right answers.

"We met about twelve years ago," she said, and bit her lip. "We were so young with so many crazy emotions. It just wasn't our time yet. But we're all grown up now, reunited, and it's finally our turn to be who we want to be, despite what anyone else may think."

I believed every word she said and wanted her to say more. But I was also relieved when the topic of our relationship moved on, and we started discussing ways I would be representing Archer Athletics. That was why we were there, that was the safe topic.

"I need to use the ladies room, I'll be right back." Lil whispered quietly into my ear as we walked away from a group of people.

Had the head of the Archer Athletics campaign not been making his way up next to me at that very moment, I would've insisted I follow her. Not for any other reason than the fact that I didn't want to be away from her.

"Cruz Martin, in the flesh," Mr. Archer said as he raised his hand up to shake mine.

"Mr. Archer, it's good to finally meet you."

"Likewise. I've been watching you work the room with a beautiful woman on your arm."

"Lil is amazing." Those words were so easy because they

were true, and I looked off towards the door to see if she was coming back yet.

"I always found value in a man that can commit to one woman. Do you think she's the one?"

"She's always been the one," I said softly, as if I was telling myself more than I was telling him.

"Well, I bet you two make a great team. My wife and I have been married for forty-seven years, not sure where I'd be without her."

Mr. Archer may have been happily married and pushing seventy years old, but each woman that passed us giggled and waved at him, then he returned their admiration with a wink. Was it his silver hair, or his deep pockets, that made everyone bat their eyelashes at him?

"Is she here tonight, sir?"

"She didn't come down to Miami with me this time. She had a weekend planned with the grandkids, and I couldn't blame her. If I had a choice that's where I'd be too," he winked.

When I finally saw Lily walking back, I walked away from Mr. Archer to meet her halfway and took her hand, kissing her knuckles and giving her another smile.

"I missed you." I knew it was corny, but I really did miss her.

"I was only gone for ten minutes."

"I just missed you," I said deeper and lower, then led her toward Mr. Archer, who was watching, and waiting for us to return.

"There she is," he crooned, his arms up for a hug that Lily didn't seem to want to give him. She did, but I could tell she was uncomfortable, so I pulled her back into my arms, hoping to ease that awkward moment.

"Lillian, I would like you to meet Mr. Archer."

"Mr. Archer, so nice to meet you."

Fuck she was perfect, so poised and classy. She was unimpressed and professional at the same time, and I knew I had made the right decision by bringing her with me.

For another few minutes Mr. Archer, Lily, and I talked about Archer Athletics.

"Mr. Archer?" A short, redheaded woman approached him from behind. "Dinner will be served in a few minutes. Can we ask you to say a few words beforehand?"

"Of course," he cleared his throat and fixed his tie. "Tell me where to go."

She pointed to the front of the room, taking him away. It was the first time Lil and I had been alone since the night began.

"Are you okay?" she asked with concern, rubbing her hand on my back.

Smiling as I looked down at my feet, like I always did, I took a moment before I turned and faced her. Lifting my hand to her neck, I rubbed my thumb along her cheekbone in a caress. "You're amazing."

She shrugged it off, and gave me half a smile. "It doesn't really feel like I'm pretending, Cruz. I'm just being honest when I speak. That's what you told me to do."

"Your honesty is perfect. Your truth is perfect." She blushed and tried to move her head, but my hand was holding her in place as I stepped forward to get closer to her until there was no distance between us.

It felt like I should kiss her, but that was probably more than our fake date could handle. The lines were already being stomped on. Did I have it in me to stay on my side?

Chapter Twenty Five

Lily

The night was surprisingly easy. Being with Cruz was easy. But maybe that's because we weren't lying to anyone other than the fact that we weren't really a couple, so that helped with the ease of it all.

People were mingling around us, but it felt like we were completely alone. It felt like if it had been a real date, it would have been the moment Cruz would kiss me.

I took my hand to his, the one he had wrapped around my neck, and I held it close to me. I wanted to somehow tell him I was wanting him to kiss me without having to say the words because I wasn't brave enough for that.

But then I saw his jaw tik a little and his hand fell from my neck. He backed up a few feet from me, and finally turned his eyes from mine. I didn't know what else to say. I didn't know what to do. He seemed angry, and I was instantly glad that he didn't give in to kissing me the way I hoped he would. Not if the mere thought made his mood change so abruptly.

After a minute, he grabbed my hand and gently escorted me to our seat at the table for dinner. He ran a finger across my back, casually taking his seat beside me, sending chills through me. It was a complete contrast to his mood, and I had to remind myself that it was confusing because it was fake.

When dinner ended, I decided I needed air, but I also needed some space from Cruz for a minute, so I excused myself and headed to the large balcony. No one else was out there, but I moved to the corner where I couldn't be seen from the big windows of the ballroom. I took several deep breaths and twisted my fingers around one another as I looked out over the city.

"Miss Harris?" The deep, familiar voice behind me made me jump but I pasted on a smile before I turned around. Mr. Archer had his hands in his pockets, casually walking towards me in the corner. "Is everything all right?"

Trying not to ruin our ruse by hiding, I gave him an awkward smile and quickly tried to think of some reason I was out there alone. By the time he was right in front of me, I still didn't have anything to say so I shrugged.

"Events like these can be overwhelming," he winked. "That's why I came out here."

"Yeah." Good point. *Why didn't I think of that?* "I just needed a breather."

"And Cruz is quite social. A charmer. It's probably pretty exhausting trying to keep up with him."

"I'll be supportive in any way I can be," I told him truthfully. "He's worth a few conversations with strangers."

Mr. Archer's eyes twinkled a little, and he pulled one of his hands from his pocket and pointed it at me. "You sound like a keeper."

"Technically Cruz is a keeper," I laughed, then realized how lame that sounded. "You know, like a goalie?" *Fuck, that made it worse.* "Thank you."

Despite the fact that I was incredibly awkward, Mr. Archer smirked at me as he eyed me with questions swirling in his eyes.

It felt like a pivotal moment for Cruz, and I didn't want to screw up his contract because his "girlfriend" was an idiot. So I rerouted and decided flattery was a better idea.

"You are very smart, Mr. Archer. This new line of athletic gear focused on soccer that your company is doing is unbelievable. Congratulations. You really have an eye and a heart for athletes."

There was a moment that I thought I went too far. That my flattery was overdone and sounded incredibly fake. But then he leaned closer to me with a wicked smile on his face, seemingly buying everything I was selling.

"You must be very smart as well. Can I tell you a secret?"

I leaned in and nodded. "Of course."

"I know you're not really Cruz's girlfriend." He couldn't see my face because his lips were so close to my ear but my eyes widened and my heart picked up its pace.

"Wha–?" I started to ask before I felt his lips below my ear, creating a trail towards my mouth. I tried to pull back, but there was nothing behind me except for a wall, and I was trapped as he continued running his lips to mine.

In an attempt to push him away, I took my hands to his chest, but he was too formidable. A laugh escaped his mouth and before his lips covered mine, he said, "It's okay. Remember? I told you I know it's not real."

"It's not," I pushed him again.

His mouth smothered my words and he slipped his tongue between my teeth as I started to scream. But all the noises I made were muffled by the wind on the balcony and the way he was using his strength to push his lips against mine.

Tears began running down my cheeks as I continued to push his chest. I was so close to the edge of the balcony and it seemed like my only way out was to just go over. But we were too high up and I didn't have a death wish.

His tongue was circling my mouth, tasting my teeth, and then truly, I started to gag. His hand found my chin, and I prepared for him to hold me tighter. But before he could get a grip, he was gone.

My eyes were so blurry from the tears that I couldn't see where he had gone, but when I wiped my eyes, I saw Cruz. He had Mr. Archer pinned against the balcony rail with his hand around his throat. It looked like Cruz had punched him based on the blood I saw trickling down Mr. Archer's face.

"Who the fuck do you think you are?" Cruz yelled.

"Oh please," Mr. Archer laughed despite being dominated and in a precarious position. "I knew she was only here as arm candy for you. Women who are that fake only care about one thing."

Cruz pulled him away from the edge of the balcony and landed another punch to the side of his face, making him fall down. Then he hovered over the top of him as a crowd started to come out from the commotion.

"There's nothing fake about my relationship with Lily. Touch my girl again and I won't settle for a punch to your face. I'll throw you over the side of that balcony."

Cruz looked up where I was still huddled in the corner then lifted his hand up. "Come here, baby," he said to me with a calm look in his eye. As a few people started tending to Mr. Archer, I pushed from the wall and ran into Cruz's arms. A few people were yelling that security needed to be called, but Cruz's only attention was on me.

"I'm so sorry," he whispered as he guided me toward the door.

"I hope this was worth losing your contract," Mr. Archer yelled. He was on his feet, flanked by two other people that worked with him.

"You can accept that black eye as me officially pulling my name from contention."

Cruz placed a hand on the small of my back, guiding me through the crowd that had gathered. When he put his phone up to his ear, he said a few things in Spanish before putting it back in his pocket. I knew enough to know he had called for our car, and it was waiting by the time we got out the door of the lobby.

Cruz didn't wait for the driver to open the door. He jerked it open himself and gently guided me in before climbing in behind me and slamming the door shut. He said a few things in Spanish to our driver and then pulled me across the backseat so that I was almost in his lap as we drove away.

"Oh my God, Lil. I'm so sorry. I'm so fucking sorry." His words were pained, such a contrast from who he was moments before when he spoke to Mr. Archer.

"No, I'm sorry," I managed to get out, nearly choking on the words. But with one look from Cruz, I stopped saying anymore and just let the tears fall down my face again.

"Don't." His forehead fell to mine and his hand stroked the side of my face.

"He said he knew it was pretend," I cried. It didn't rationalize his actions, but I hoped Cruz knew I was just trying to explain why Mr. Archer even attempted to kiss me in the first place. But Cruz just shook his head and held my eyes with his.

"Nothing about tonight was pretend."

Chapter Twenty Six

Cruz

The rest of the car ride was quiet, and I held Lil close to me as her tears kept slowly falling. It took everything I had to not go back and get in a few more punches on Archer. If it hadn't been for Lil needing to get home safely, and my need to be with her, I would have.

After getting back to the apartment, she started walking towards her room, and I stopped in the kitchen. Leaning on the bar with my head down, I took deep breaths, trying to compose myself until the click of her heels stopped.

They started clicking again, coming back toward me, getting closer each time. Picking my head up, I watched each of her strides until my gaze traveled up her body and locked onto her face. She had streaks of mascara running down, black lines across her perfect cheeks. But her chin was high, and her eyes looked as though they were more concerned about me than herself.

When she was directly in front of me, I stood up straight and waited for whatever she had come back to say.

"Thank you."

It didn't feel like I deserved her thanks, but I knew why she said it. If it hadn't been more for me asking her to be my date, she wouldn't have been in that position. But I didn't make that argument with her. Licking my lips, I nodded and accepted her words, keeping my eyes locked on hers.

"Tell me how to fix it."

"I just wanna brush my teeth and get the taste of him out of my mouth." Her shiver was a little exaggerated and she tried smiling as if it was a joke. But that was just for my benefit, so I grabbed her hand, pulling her back toward me.

"Let me take it away."

Her head tilted in question, so I pulled her closer and lowered my voice while running my thumb over her lips. "Let me kiss you, Lil. Let me take away what he did. My lips. My taste. My tongue."

Her sharp intake of breath and the way her bottom lip trembled a little made me think that asking her that was a stupid idea, but I didn't want her thinking of him. She didn't say no, though, and she didn't back away when I moved in closer.

With my lips an inch from hers, I stopped and gave her one more chance to tell me no, because I may have wanted to kiss her, but I wouldn't be like Archer and take it without her consent.

She gave me a small nod, but all that came out of her mouth was another moan, which I smothered as I closed the gap between us and pressed my lips to hers.

My hands went to her neck, my eyes were closed, and I pressed my body against hers. Lily's hands grabbed onto my biceps and I felt her melt against me as her mouth opened slightly. Taking that opening, I slid my tongue between her teeth while tilting my head and intensifying the kiss.

The moment I started losing control was the moment she

gained clarity, and pushed at my arms to make me move back. My chest was heaving, and I opened my eyes to look at her, worried I had misread her body language from the beginning.

"You don't have to do this," she whispered with her eyes still closed. "Don't kiss me because you feel guilty."

"I'm not," I growled, making her eyes pop open. "I'm kissing you because the thought of someone else's mouth on yours makes me sick. I don't want you thinking of what happened, I want you thinking of me. *My* kiss."

"I want you to kiss me because you want to," she spoke so quietly, so shyly.

"I've wanted to kiss you since I was fourteen," I confessed.

She searched for the lie in my eyes, but she wasn't going to find it, because I had never been more serious than I was at that moment.

"You hated me."

"I hated how you made me feel. And when I got older, I hated that I couldn't have you. And now, I hate that you're sleeping across the apartment, and I'm supposed to act like none of those feelings ever existed."

"You hated me," she repeated, only with less conviction.

She was going to have to mull that over while I kissed her again, because I was done resisting her. We may not have been able to be forever, but we could have that moment, that kiss.

My lips found hers again and her arms wrapped around my neck as I lifted her from the ground, onto the counter, and got between her legs.

"Is this okay?" She asked against my lips.

"It feels okay to me." I wrapped both my hands behind her neck and pulled her closer so there was no more room to ask questions. She was holding on tight to my shoulders, and clawing at me, urging me to keep going despite whatever was going on inside her head.

Every instinct in my body told me to rip her clothes off and use my mouth to taste every part of her while I could. But she had told me how inexperienced she was and I didn't feel like the right guy to take away anything she coveted. It was easy to forget, in that moment of passion, that she may have been waiting for someone who was going to be with her forever.

Maybe even marriage.

With that in mind, I pulled back and my hands fell to her hips to keep her still. My eyes locked with hers and I watched as her chest heaved. She looked scared, but not because I had been kissing her, but because I wasn't kissing her anymore.

"You're...you...I mean." I didn't know what to say to explain to her why I had to stop so suddenly, but she knew, and I could see embarrassment flash across her face as her head dipped down. "Don't do that." I told her as I took my hand to her chin to force her eyes back on me. "If I keep kissing you, I won't be able to stop myself."

"Don't stop yourself," she whispered so low I was practically reading her lips.

"Where's the line, Lil?"

"Remember? We crossed it about ten minutes ago. Please don't stop. I want to feel everything with you."

Maybe it was because I'd had a week of scoreless nights and I was eager to end that streak. Or maybe it was because I wanted to be the first person that touched her.

"We're going to be in so much trouble," I finally said before nipping at her lips again. "Time out may last forever."

"What they don't know won't hurt them," she shrugged, breaking the last shred of willpower I had.

She took her hands up my chest and to the opening of my shirt, slowly exposing my chest as she undid each button. For being inexperienced, she was bolder than I imagined. It was like she knew what she wanted, was finally getting it, and wasn't going to let blurry lines stop her.

My lips moved to her cheek, and then to her neck as my fingers traced a line up her arms to the straps holding on the thin material that covered her tits. I pulled the straps down and she lowered her arms so that the fabric fell. She didn't have a bra on, and her nipples were so hard that I imagined them cutting my hands as I squeezed her.

"Is this what you want, *Señorita?* "

"I've waited so long to be touched like this."

As she finished the last word, I pinched her nipple and then placed my mouth over the sting to ease the spark of pain. She leaned back, her arms on the counter, and watched as I played with her and tasted her.

When I glanced up, she was biting her bottom lip, and her eyes were so heated that she looked like a completely different person. Still Lily, but so turned on and intense that I completely forgot who she was to me, and how innocent she was.

It no longer mattered.

"Lean all the way back, baby." She did, and I took the new angle to reach the rest of her jumpsuit and pull it down. Once it fell to the floor, I took her legs and wrapped them around my waist. All that was between my skin and her pussy was a tiny thong and I had to press my cock against the cabinet just to ease how hard I was pulsing.

As I leaned over to kiss her, she reached for my shirt and tried to finish undoing the buttons but my patience was too thin. Reaching my hands up, I ripped the rest of them off and discarded my shirt onto the floor.

I leaned back down over her, my stomach bare, and I could feel how wet she was through the thin fabric of her thong. I moved a finger under the fabric of her thong and pulled it away, just slightly as my knuckle grazed the lips of her pussy.

"You're so wet for me."

"It's not the first time," she said with her teeth gritted, trying to move against my finger. "It's just the first time you've known about it."

"Oh fuck," I whispered, her words making me tear the rest of the fabric from her body.

I ran a finger through her folds and looked down at her trying to gauge every reaction she gave me. I wanted to learn everything about what she liked and what she wanted. If she had thought about us like that before, I wanted to make the reality even better than she imagined. There had been plenty of times I had fucked my own hand—and other women—to the image of her behind my closed eyes. The real thing was already better, even with my dick still in my pants.

The heels of her tall pumps came up to the edge of the counter, and she pushed her pussy up, bravely encouraging my fingers to touch her harder. But I had never been with a virgin, and I was scared that I was going to hurt her if I went too fast and too rough. Suppressing every base instinct I had, all that mattered was that she was okay.

Flattening my hand over her lower stomach to hold her down, I stroked her clit with my thumb. Our eyes were locked as I teased her, pressing harder with each pass until eventually she couldn't keep her eyes from closing.

Without warning her, I leaned down and took my tongue between the folds of her pussy and that one touch made her start shaking. She was already coming, and I was mesmerized by how easy it was. Her cum covered my lips as I tried to push my tongue inside of her as far as I could, not wanting her to ever come down from the ecstasy I just gave her. But her hands were on my head and she was pushing me away as she tried to back up and create room between us.

I looked up, worried that she was already having regrets. My chest started to ache because no matter how wrong it was, I would never regret making her come. Now that I knew how she tasted, I never wanted to stop, either.

Chapter Twenty Seven

Lily

His chest was heaving and his arms were out at his sides. The neat locks he had slicked back for the dinner were now a mess on top of his head. His lips glistened in the soft light, coated with my cum, and he didn't even attempt to wipe it away. That, along with the way his dress slacks were hanging on his trim waist, a patch of hair leading down where I couldn't see, was making my mouth water.

But his eyes were beady and scared.

Without hesitation, I wrapped my arms around him and breathed into his neck. "If you kept touching me, I think my heart may have literally exploded."

"That's the point," he growled, returning my hold and encasing me in his arms. "I want to make you come as many times as I can.

Shaking my head was the only way I could tell him that I wasn't gonna be able to take it. At least not until I explained to him how my heart was feeling. And not until I knew that he was getting as much pleasure from us being together as I was.

As sheepish as I was to be so inexperienced, I knew that whatever I said wouldn't have Cruz running away from me. Not because of who I was to him, but because of who he was as a person.

"Can I touch you?" I asked quietly.

He grabbed a fist full of my hair and pulled me back so that he could look down at my face. "Another first for you?"

Nodding, I felt the heat in my cheeks return, but I kept his eyes locked with mine so he knew that I meant it.

Without warning, he reached underneath me and picked me up, forcing the wetness he had created between my legs to rub against his stomach as he carried me towards his bedroom. When he placed me on the bed, he backed away and started to unbuckle his belt. "Get on your knees, Lil. Stay on the bed but get on your knees."

"Should I be on the floor?" I asked, doing the geometry in my head and not feeling like the angles were going to work for what I had in mind.

His slight smirk told me he found me a little funny, but he started shaking his head as his pants fell to his ankles, and he stepped out of them along with his shoes. His underwear was tight and I could see the outline of his dick, hard and confined. It made me forget all about angles and logistics so I popped onto my knees like he had told me to and licked my lips.

When he got to the edge of the bed, he knelt down, so that we were face to face and kissed me hard as he gradually pushed me back farther onto his bed. Once I was exactly where he wanted me, he grabbed a handful of my hair and pulled my lips from his, forcing me onto my hands so that my mouth was lined up with his cock.

Neither one of us moved. If he was waiting for me to reach out and lower his underwear, then he was going to be waiting a few more minutes because I didn't quite have the nerve. But while he waited, he pushed my face and rubbed himself on my parted lips.

"Take my cock out, Lil." He was getting more demanding, pulling on my hair a little more. "If you don't, I'll come right here, right now, and the only taste you'll get will be whatever you can suck out of the fabric of my boxers."

That made me move, and I reached up, pulling the band down just enough to free him. Then I wrapped my hand around the base realizing it was the first time I had ever touched a man that way. I wanted to look at him and feel him. His skin was so soft but at the same time it was like I was touching a steel pole. It may have been my first time, but I wasn't an idiot. Men got hard, and the word *hard* was used for a reason. But I didn't realize how hard he would actually be, or how strong he would feel even though I was the one holding onto him.

"Take your time," he whispered, seeming to be a little calmer now that I was touching him.

"I... I... don't really know what to do," I confessed, my eyes looking up at him with humility as my hand fell from him back down to the bed.

"Do whatever you want. It's yours, Lil. I promise, as long as you're touching me, it's gonna feel so fucking good."

"I'd be less self-conscious if you would teach me."

"I've never sucked a dick before," he smirked, running his thumb over my cheek.

"But you've had it done, right? Tell me what you liked. Talk me through it."

He hissed a few words in Spanish, so low I couldn't even try to decipher what he was saying, but I knew it wasn't bad. He was coming to terms with the fact that he was about to teach me how to suck his dick.

"Open your mouth," he finally commanded in English.

Staying still, I did as he said and waited for my next instruction. He took his hand from my head and held on to himself, pushing his cock down and swiping the tip along my lips. "Take your tongue out and taste me."

I licked him innocently, barely even touching him, but he hissed, running his other hand down his face trying to find control.

"Take your tongue all over me. Everywhere, Lil. Drench me."

I started to lick the underside of him from base to tip, then rolled my tongue around the topside to get him wet like he told me to. But while he was hissing and moaning at my touch, he was also shaking his head.

"Wetter, baby. Make it sloppy."

Making sure I had more saliva, I started coating him again, as he looked down and watched my mouth. "That's it."

Once he was satisfied, he grabbed my hand and had me hold the base of his cock again, where he had just been holding himself. "You're going to need this, because I'm not going to fit all the way in."

"I want to—"

"No," he cut me off. "Sheath those teeth and start stroking me with your lips."

After a few strokes, I went down farther, as low as I could before gagging. He shook his head at me and tugged my hair, pulling me off of him. He lowered his face to mine and growled, "No," before kissing me quickly and straightening back up.

"Use your hand to stroke where your mouth can't reach," he instructed. "Try to use the same pressure. Don't fucking hurt yourself."

Going up and down on him, I did as he said, waiting for him to give me more instructions. But they never came. His head fell back and his mouth fell open. He was grunting and I could tell he was trying not to pump himself, trying to let me have the control. But he was losing the battle with every swipe I took.

My pussy started to throb again, getting off on seeing how weak he was in my hands. I knew that it would bring him pleasure but I had no idea how needy it would make me in return.

Without meaning to, my hips started to move, practically humping the air. If both of my hands weren't serving a purpose, I would have touched myself to feel some kind of relief.

When Cruz looked down at me again and saw me move, his eyes beaded at me and his nose scrunched up. *Was I doing something wrong?* It shouldn't have been about *me* so maybe he was pissed off, but I couldn't help myself. It was like I had lost complete control over my own body.

"That's it baby," he spoke, making me realize his face wasn't a snarl. It was just contorting from how turned on he was, and apparently, I was adding to that with every movement of my hips. "Who's dick are you fucking, Lil? Who are those hips moving for?"

I groaned around him and realized the vibration of my mouth only added to his pleasure. Instead of moving my body, I tried to give him all of my focus, but he leaned over me and grabbed my ass, making me move again the way I just had been.

"Keep fucking moving," he growled. "We played pretend tonight, right? Pretend I'm under your pussy and touching you just the way you like. Pretend you're riding my fingers and grinding your clit on my thumb."

I moaned again, his words making me feel dirty and carnal and his hands making my ass move up and down. Nothing mattered anymore. Only pleasing each other and there was nothing that felt embarrassing or wrong about moving however he wanted me to move. Whatever made him happy was what I wanted to do.

Then, he slapped a hand across my backside, making me scream, his cock suppressing the noise. When he slapped me again, pleasure ripped through my body and I started coming, the vibration being just enough to tip me over the edge.

"I told you that you needed a spanking," Cruz hissed as I continued to come. "Scream for me. Scream around my cock."

He pumped his hips gently as I felt his cum coating my tongue. His growl didn't sound human, his body was tense, and my heart started to skip a few beats as his eyes refocused with mine.

Biting his lip, he tapped my chin with two fingers. "Swallow."

Once I did, he pulled from my mouth, making the leftover saliva slide down my chin. He leaned down and licked it up, then closed his mouth over mine in a searing kiss. I wanted to pull away, my mouth too dirty for him to be tasting, but he kept me close and laid me down, hovering over the top of me.

"That was..." he shook his head, not able to finish his thought.

"I didn't mean to, ya know," I shrugged, feeling a little nervous now that it was over.

"That was the sexiest thing I've ever seen." He kissed me again, then lowered himself next to me, pulling me to rest in his arms on his chest.

"Did I do okay...with my mouth?"

He looked down and only then did *he* realize I was feeling confused and worried. He turned us each onto our sides, facing one another and stroked the hair from my face. "That was the best I've ever had, Lil. You're fucking perfect."

The smile on my face was relief mixed with satisfaction. I didn't know if he was telling the truth, but he really did seem happy and content. He laid back down and pulled me onto his chest again, lightly running his fingers up and down my back.

At some point, he covered us up, and we fell asleep together, making my heart feel way more than it had earlier.

Chapter Twenty Eight

Cruz

"Holy shit!" Rhys whistled as I walked in for practice the next day. "I'm assuming the girl you took to that dinner was just the girl to get you out of your scoreless streak."

"A week isn't a streak," I pushed at him before taking my seat in front of my locker.

"It is for you," he huffed. "In fact, it's a long ass streak."

Not even Rhys' brutal honesty could bring me down from the high I felt when I woke up with Lil still in my arms. She had moaned a little as I slid out from under her then her eyes had popped open while I was getting dressed. I sat down on the side of the bed before I left and kissed her again, assuring her that everything was fine.

Better than fine.

I wanted to do everything all over again with her. Lil's mouth was better than any pussy I ever had and though I knew I couldn't fuck her, I think we both knew there was plenty of other ways we could spend time together.

Like she said, the line was already crossed. There was no

going back and I couldn't see any reason we couldn't keep finding pleasure with each other. It wasn't like we were actually related. Other than our parents flipping the fuck out, there was nothing wrong with us being together. And again, like Lil said, what they didn't know wouldn't hurt them.

But to assure it stayed between us, that meant I wasn't telling a soul. Not even Rhys. So if he thought the girl from the game was the one I was with, then so be it.

"I guess this means your sis...I mean the girl that is staying with you, is no longer making that dick hard?"

"Never was," I scoffed.

"Fucking liar," Tripp laughed as he came up behind me and sat on my other side. "Last I saw, you were sprinting back home to that pussy."

"Stop!" I warned him, not wanting to hear him, or anyone, talk about Lil's pussy–which was now *my* pussy, and fuck him for talking about anything that was *mine*.

"Whoa," his hands flew up in surrender, seeing how serious I was. "Just giving you a hard time. Don't dish it out if you can't take it."

Rhys was laughing, probably finding the irony that I always knew was coming. But I chose to ignore them both before I tossed their lockers around and stomped off like a toddler. It felt good to be back at practice, and with another game on Sunday, I knew I had to stop thinking about Lil and start thinking about stopping the goals I knew St. Louis United was going to try getting past me.

Knowing that I could refocus on Lil when I was done made practice fly by, and I left before I even took a shower, anxious to get back home and see how she was feeling. Also anxious to get away from the guys before they started in on me again.

When I walked into my apartment, my heart started racing.

I could smell food, the balcony door was open creating a warm breeze, and I could hear Lil's soft voice echoing from somewhere.

I crept toward the balcony, focusing on the fact that she was talking to her mom on the phone.

"The next interview is Monday, then another one Tuesday. Then I'll head back until I decide, so you and Ivan don't need to come. Not this time." A few moments of quiet while Gloria spoke and then Lil sighed. "I don't know if I want the offer they made. It's not... I don't know." I could tell she was talking about her first interview. The one that upset her and I didn't know why. I knew it was wrong, but I wanted to listen to her and find out more.

"Everything else is good. I even made a few friends." I didn't like her friends, but maybe that was because she felt the need to lie to them. Real friends didn't make you feel that way. "One of them has a crush on Cruz, though, so pretty sure she will hate me by the time she finds out I know him and have been staying with him." She didn't say it, but I knew she was thinking, *"And sucked his cock."*

"Cruz is good," she continued. "Keeps to himself." *Not anymore.* "Yes, he is keeping an eye on me, I promise." I needed to stop listening in, and save her. I could tell she was getting annoyed and if Gloria mentioned that I was her brother, she may bail on the "unbrotherly" things I wanted to do with her later.

Walking out, I saw her eyes pop wider in surprise, but I held my finger up to tell her to be quiet. Luckily, she wasn't on Face-Time so there was no danger in Gloria knowing I was there because of Lil's reaction.

Gloria must have been saying a lot, because Lil had been quiet for a full minute as I made my way in front of her and lowered myself to my knees. She was on a chair with her legs up over the side, but once I was in position, I pulled her legs around, pushing them open, and placed them on my shoulders.

Her breathing was getting ragged and her eyes somehow got wider as she realized my intention. But she didn't stop me. She gave her mom an, *"Uh huh,"* to acknowledge she was listening but then sealed her lips shut and watched as I ran my mouth from her knee to the top of her thighs.

She was wearing loose fitting shorts and when pushed to the side, I had easy access to her pussy. I could tell just by grazing her with a finger that she was already getting wet as she watched me kiss her.

"Mo..om?" Her voice wavered and I smiled, reveling in what I was doing to her. I couldn't help it. She had just mentioned that she was leaving after Tuesday. There was no reason to not fill the next few days with as much temptation and tests that we could handle.

"Mom?" She said again, louder and sterner. "I need to get some water and lay down."

As Gloria responded, I swiped my tongue against her pussy and she squirmed. "I promise I'm fine. Just started getting too hot and I need to..." I shoved my tongue inside of her and her free hand pushed the back of my head, keeping me where I was. She hung up without another word and her phone dropped to the tile of the balcony, probably cracking the screen.

"You can't..." She started to speak, but I bit at her clit and made her catch her breath again, her words trailing off.

"Yes I can," I laughed against her, then started rubbing my tongue back and forth to build up her tension.

"Cruz," she moaned, making me grab my own cock through my shorts and press against my hand. I was a dirty fucking mess from practice, and already knew I would be fucking my own hand in the shower, but if she kept up those moans, I would probably come in my shorts before I even left the balcony.

"Go ahead and come," I told her. "I'll do it again later, then again after that. We don't have to stop until you have to leave."

I pushed two fingers inside of her, momentarily forgetting that she had never had anything, or anyone inside of her before. I was too rough, and I started to pull back out as I cussed myself under my breath.

"Keep them there," she moaned. "It feels so good."

I did as she asked, but kept my movements slower and less aggressive than I originally planned. My tongue laid flat against her clit and she started to shake. Her groan was loud but not so loud that I couldn't hear her phone ringing over and over again from where she had dropped it.

There was no doubt it was Gloria. Poor Lil was going to have some explaining to do, but as her orgasm crested and I tasted her sweetness on my tongue, I couldn't find it in me to care.

When I pulled back and her eyes refocused, I smiled up at her and made a show of licking my fingers. "I'm home," I winked. "You probably need to change your shorts."

The phone rang again before she could respond and she jumped up and pushed at my shoulders. "Now I have to go lie to her," Lil practically yelled. "As if I'm not doing enough of that already."

She stomped off and glanced back as I stayed on my knees and leaned back on my legs. She tried looking angry but I could see the twinkle in her eye before she put the phone to her ear and answered yet another incoming call.

"Mom! So sorry! I dropped my phone and couldn't reach it." As she turned away, she stuck her tongue out at me as if she really was my sister and we were kids again. "Everything is fine. I promise. Just exhausted from trying to reach my phone."

Her words drifted off and I stood up ready to head to the shower. Before I even started the water I was already stroking myself. I shed my clothes and started to step into the warm shower but with my back turned, it was Lil's turn to sneak up on me, and her gasp told me she saw exactly what I didn't want her to see.

Chapter Twenty Nine

Lily

I didn't bother changing my shorts, just assured my mom everything was fine and then got off the phone properly. I shouldn't have hung up on her, but I had no choice. Cruz came home from practice and went straight back to the way things were the night before.

Not that I was complaining because I had been looking forward to more of it myself. But I didn't realize he would come straight in and take his mouth between my legs, not giving a shit that I was on the phone with my mom.

I started to breathe hard just thinking about it and put a hand over my heart trying to calm myself down, but then I heard the shower turn on and I decided to surprise him the same way he did me.

Walking straight into his bathroom, I didn't bother knocking. He was just climbing into the shower, completely naked with his back to me. If he could come in and be so bold, then so could I.

Stepping closer, my eyes focused on a mark on his lower hip, and I gasped. He heard me and turned around, immediately recoiling knowing exactly what I saw.

Closing the gap between us with a few steps, I turned his body back around and he complied. He licked his lips and lowered his face, clearly afraid of what I was going to think, but not trying to hide.

Reaching out, I ran my hand over the mark that was about two inches big and so familiar I was shaking with disbelief.

A tattoo

A lily.

"I drew this," I whispered. "This is mine."

There was no response, just more heavy breathing as he watched me run my fingers over his skin and let me process what I already knew.

"I found your drawings. I looked through your book while you were gone with your mom one day. You drew a lily, and I was the only one that called you Lily."

For a while, he was. I hated that nickname. It made me feel like I was two. My mother named me Lillian and never intended for me to be a Lily, so I insisted that I was always referred to as Lillian.

But not with Cruz. I wouldn't correct him and no one else ever did either. Sometimes, I think he knew it bothered me and did it on purpose, but then it became something I secretly held close to me.

When I was at college, I referred to myself as Lily just to see if it translated. If it was the name or Cruz that made it feel so special. It was definitely Cruz, but for people like Angel, that was all they knew. It had become a part of who I was now.

"It was my favorite," Cruz started to explain. "I kept that picture on my phone for a long time and when I turned eighteen, I got it put on my body by an artist in San Francisco. I flew out there for him to do it because his hand seemed to have the same touch as yours did when you drew it. Please don't be mad."

I didn't think *mad* was the right word. Yeah, I felt a little violated because that drawing was a secret expression of feelings I was having at that time. It was my first flower, and even though I tried several different flowers to see how they made me feel, it was always the lily that felt more complete.

"What else did you see?"

He turned around to face me, his cock still noticeably hard. "I didn't get far, I promise. Just a few flowers."

He bit his lip and grabbed a towel as I nodded, then started wrapping it around his waist to cover himself up. "I promise that was all I saw. When I heard your mom's car drive up, I flipped back to the lily and took a picture of it and then shoved it back under the mattress where you hid it.

"That was private, Cruz. To me they weren't just flowers. It was my private thoughts."

"Did you think of me? It felt like it was for me."

When I looked back into his eyes, I nodded, making him nod back with heat.

"You never thought I'd see it."

"No," he smirked, not laughing but clearly seeing the irony. "I intentionally put it somewhere no one would ever see it."

"Were you ever going to show me?"

"No," he replied again, his answer being painfully truthful. "I never expected you to see that part of my body."

"I came in here to return the favor."

His hand skimmed the side of my cheek and he smiled. "I'm not upset about that. Just hope you can forgive me for being too nosy when I was younger."

"I cannot believe you had it turned into a tattoo. That seems crazy."

"When it comes to you, I've always been crazy. It's been 12 years since our parents got married and I don't think anything has changed when it comes to how crazy you make me."

"Tattoos are forever."

"I wanted that drawing to be forever."

"Can I see it again?"

He slowly turned around and then dropped the towel, giving me a view of the tattoo. I couldn't believe it had been there for nearly eight years. And the details he'd made sure were there, were incredible.

"It was there last time I saw you then? At my graduation?"

"Yeah, it was there."

I started tracing it with my finger and goosebumps formed on his skin under my touch. My shock outweighed my anger, and I started to melt as the image of him standing with my parents at my graduation came flashing back to me.

He wore khaki pants with a polo shirt. So plain and simple, but underneath that fabric had been a secret he thought he would take to his grave. Yet there we were.

Naked.

In his bathroom.

His dick still hard as I skimmed my fingers over his skin.

"I want more," I whispered, suddenly feeling like Cruz and I could share anything.

"More of what?" he asked. "Just name it."

If he thought he had to make this up to me, he didn't. His invasion of my privacy somehow made me trust him, and I wanted more of *everything*.

"What is it, baby?" he asked again. "Tell me what you want."

My heart skipped a beat every time he called me baby. *Señorita* was a joke, but when he called me baby, he didn't even realize what he was doing, and I loved that it was uncalculated.

"Before I leave, and things go back to normal, will you...?"

"Anything," he urged me to keep going, running a hand through my hair.

"Will you, um, cross all the lines with me?"

He paused, clearly surprised but he knew exactly what I meant. "All of them?"

"I want it to be you," I confessed.

He started shaking his head, but his eyes told me he wanted to say yes. "You've been waiting for the right person. I can't be the one that takes that from you."

"I've been waiting for someone who won't run when I ask questions, or tell them how inexperienced I am. I've been waiting for someone who cares about me enough not to hurt me. I've been waiting for a moment where I don't have anyone breathing down my neck because of how worried they are about me."

My last words nearly choked me as I tried to stop myself from crying. Cruz didn't understand, and he never would, but he knew what I was saying was the truth.

Still, I thought he would keep saying no, and turn me down. He took his hands to the sides of my cheeks, his thumbs rubbed the top of my cheekbones where a few tears had spilled down.

"Okay," he whispered, then kissed me.

It took me a minute to realize that he had agreed, but when it finally sunk in, I returned his kiss and laced my arms around his neck. He lifted me up, and I wrapped my legs around him, and then he backed into the shower, hot water stinging my skin as we continued to deepen our kiss.

With our lips still connected, he set me on my feet and pushed my shorts down, then trailed his hands under my shirt, pulling away from my lips only long enough to take it off. His hands roamed my body and I did the same to him, wanting to touch every muscle and dip he had.

When he finally pulled back from my mouth, he reached out for a bottle of body wash and rubbed it in his hands. He started putting it around his chest, and I took the loofah that hung on a hook and started rubbing his body with it. He moaned and turned around so I started scrubbing his back, savoring the feeling of caring for him.

As I placed a kiss on his shoulder, he grabbed his cock and started stroking himself fast and hard.

"Don't," I jumped. "I thought..."

"Not this one," he groaned. "It's too late for this one. I'll never be able to give you what you deserve."

It took me a minute to realize what he meant, but when he started stroking himself again, it clicked. *He was too far gone.*

"Wait," I said again, making him groan, as his hand stopped.

With the water hitting his back, I got down on my knees and took my hand up the inside of his thighs. His knees buckled and I licked my lips before I did what he told me to do and make it wet and sloppy, then using my hand for whatever I couldn't take.

I started sucking on him harder than I did the night before. I was braver, and dare I say more experienced? I felt more confident in what I was doing and as long as my teeth didn't get in the way, I knew that my mouth was bringing him nothing but pleasure.

Cruz decided to teach me something new and grabbed my free hand from his leg, putting it underneath his balls. My palm covered him as my finger skimmed his perineum. It felt extra naughty to touch him there, but I stroked him with two fingers while I continued to work him with my mouth.

Then he grabbed onto the back of my head and I felt his cum start coating my tongue. Instead of being told to swallow, I did it on my own and then went back on him as if I could get more.

"Fuck no," he laughed and pulled me up by my arms. "You can't bring me to my knees yet, I need those for tomorrow's game."

"I want to come," I blurted as my hand skimmed his bare chest.

"To the game? Or like, in my bed?"

Shoving his chest playfully, I laughed. "Both. But I meant your game. Alone. I wanna cheer for you without being worried about my friends knowing who you are to me."

"Who am I to you?"

"The same person you've always been," I smiled. "*Not* my brother."

He laughed, then pressed his lips to mine. "You're damn right I'm not."

By the time we managed to get out of the shower, I could smell the dinner I had in the oven, and I started to panic that I had let it go too far. Completely naked, I ran across the apartment into the kitchen to open the oven and took the dish out, setting it on top of the oven. Cruz had thrown on some shorts and was walking slowly from the other room and running a hand through his wet hair.

"Oh hell yeah. You're naked and pulling food out of the oven. I'm not sure there's a bigger turn on."

"Don't touch it." I pointed and then ran past him to my room to put clothes on. I may have asked Cruz to be my first but I knew it wasn't gonna happen right then. I hoped it happened naturally, maybe the next time we touched one another or after his game.

I wasn't in a rush. As long as we both knew the line between us was officially erased, it would happen eventually.

Chapter Thirty

Cruz

There was something special about having Lil in the stands, cheering for me. She was in the exact seat she was in before, but she had no one around her. She did, however, have her Tripp Maddux jersey on, and I hated myself for forgetting that I was supposed to burn it. It just seemed like since that night, every moment I spent with her, I hadn't been thinking of Tripp at all.

Much less his jersey.

Lily joked about it the night before while we ate the best chicken and rice I ever had. She tried to explain that she didn't have a Cruz Martin jersey, so she was going to have to wear her Maddux one.

When the game was nearing the end, I kept thinking about how much fun it was going to be ripping that jersey off of her when we got home. And now that we were no longer tip-toeing around our attraction to one another, I really did intend on ripping that fucking shirt.

The St Louis midfielder had closed in around the goal and I refocused on the game. He kicked but it was an easy stop for me and I quickly punted it back into play. I glanced up at Lily, who was cheering for me as if I had made the game winning save in the championship game. I smirked at her and shook my head, trying not to let everyone in the world see how she was affecting me. So I schooled my face and made it through the last two minutes of the game before the whistle blew.

Jogging toward the middle of the field, rain started coming down as I congratulated my teammates. We all ran toward the tunnel to escape, but before disappearing, I gave Lily a little wink, and then raced to get changed out of my uniform. She was supposed to meet me outside the locker room and it wasn't going to take her long to get there.

Before the rest of the guys could even finish their congratulations and interviews, I headed toward the exit, making sure I grabbed one of my clean game jerseys to put Lily in.

When I pushed the door open, the rain was coming down harder, but Lily was alone, and she came running toward me, jumping into my arms soaking wet. "Good game!"

Fuck, it wasn't that good of a game. We won, St Louis was scoreless, but there was no challenge like there would be on Friday when we faced Los Angeles. Still, it felt good to receive her joy and praise, and even better having her in my arms.

When I set her back on her feet, I grabbed her hand, and we laughed while we ran, trying to avoid the puddles forming across the parking lot. The rain shielded us, and made the parking lot fairly empty, but I still looked around while I opened the door for her. Not wanting anyone to see us the way we were.

With one hand, I held the steering wheel, but with the other one, I held onto Lily's leg. I mindlessly traced patterns on her thigh and listened to her sing along to the music playing on the radio. Things were changing quickly, and it was getting hard to remember that she wasn't really my girl. That she was only staying for a few more days and would be going back to our parents' house.

Yeah, she had at least one job offer so far, and two more interviews, but it wasn't like she would be moving to Miami for me. She had friends, she had a path that excited her, and not at any point was I a part of that.

Like a sore reminder, my phone started ringing, interrupting the song playing, and I hit answer when I saw my dad's number pop up.

"*Holà.*"

"*Tremendo juego, mijo.*"

"*Lo viste en la télévision?*"

"*Si, con Gloria. Los comentaristas hablaron mucho de lo feliz que te veías esta noche.*"

Lil and I looked at one another, both suppressing a laugh.

"*Sólo nos quedan par de juegos y si ganamos contra LA, jugaremos en las finales. Por eso estoy feliz.*"

"*Pues tu te veías como si hubieras anotado con una chica.*" Dad lowered his voice, speaking to me like a man, but aware his wife could hear him if she was close by. Though he was speaking Spanish, and Gloria only knew one through ten, and the seven colors of the rainbow. Meanwhile, Lil seemed to be following along better than I thought she would.

"No." I groaned. "*Sólo me sentía estable mientras jugaba.*"

"*Hablando de sentirse estable, has hablado con Lillian últimamente?*"

Lil heard her name, but I could tell she wasn't completely sure what my dad was asking.

"She's staying with me, Dad. Of course I've talked to her." I replied in English. "She texted Gloria and said she was at your game tonight."

"I got her a ticket, is that okay?"

"Of course," he laughed. "I'm glad you two are getting along. But I wanted to call you before you got home tonight. Gloria is worried she isn't drinking enough water. Can you—?"

"*Ay, dios!* She's a grown woman," I yelled. "I'm not going to tell her to drink her fucking water."

"Look," Dad replied sternly as Lil started to shift uncomfortably in her seat. Tapping her thigh gently, I then took her hand, giving it a silent kiss so she knew not to worry. "If she didn't forget things like that, Gloria wouldn't worry so much. Honestly, it's all I can do to keep her from packing our house up and moving to Miami tomorrow."

"Well Lil will be home soon enough. She's fine. I promise I'm keeping an eye on her."

Suddenly, I was less angry, and more compliant. The last thing I needed was Gloria thinking moving to Miami was a good idea. I wouldn't put it past her either. Dad was retiring, and there was nothing left in Brookville once Lil left. And I loved my dad and wanted him near, but not while I was mentally planning all the ways I was going to make his step daughter come later.

"Good deal," my dad sighed. "Gloria will be happy I spoke to you. Lil hasn't been very chatty lately. I guess she has some new friends, and we are happy for her, but it's just hard."

I rolled my eyes, suppressing the need to gag. It all made perfect sense why Lil was who she was. If they had stifled me the way they did her, I would have rebelled and told them to get lost. Lil was too good for that response, and had spent a lifetime just being a good girl for them.

Telling my dad I was pulling into my parking garage made him hang up quickly, and I whipped into my spot before looking at Lil. *What the hell did I just talk to my dad about? Had it always been that bad?*

"I know how it looks," she cringed. "I haven't been able to tell them I'm a big girl now. Ivan isn't so bad, but he would lasso the moon and give it to my mom if she wanted it. His calls to you are for her, and I'm so sorry you are in the middle."

"I'm worried about you." I turned in my seat the best I could to face her and took her hands again. "How are they even going to let you move for a job at this rate?"

"I don't know," she laughed and rolled her eyes like it was no big deal. "I keep thinking that the more I spread my wings, the more courage I will have to tell them I need some space."

"Let me keep helping you with that," I winked, before getting out of the car.

When we got upstairs, my first stop was the refrigerator to get the leftovers we had from the night before. Lil walked toward the balcony, texting on her phone.

When I had two bowls ready, I carried them outside where the rain was still coming down, and handed her one. She took it with a small smile. "Thanks."

"Your mom on the phone again?" I nodded toward her phone that kept lighting up on the table between us.

"No, this time it's Angel and Jackie. They asked me what I did this evening, and of course, I lied again. Everyone is turning me into a liar," she mumbled as she took a bite of her food.

"Even me?" I teased her. "I feel like you've been super honest with me."

She turned a slight shade of pink, but didn't look up from her bowl. She stabbed at the food a few times and then finally looked up at me. "Even you."

I swallowed hard, not expecting that to be her answer. I wanted to press her for more, but deep down, I knew what she meant, and I didn't want to admit it any more than she did. There were feelings between us. More than what my dad and Gloria hoped would be between us.

There always had been.

Impossible shit that we would lie about to them, and each other, until the end of time.

But not yet.

"Come on." I took the bowl from her hand when it was almost empty then led her to my bathroom.

I started running the bathwater instead of my normal shower, and she watched me move around the room anxiously. "What are you doing?"

"I'm dirty." I tilted my head at her like she should have known that, but also added a suggestive undertone. Getting closer to her, I reached up and pulled the Maddux jersey over her head. "I'm not going to rip this up because your friends got it for you. But I don't want to see it touching your skin ever again."

Maybe I was being irrational, but I meant every word. Tripp's name didn't belong anywhere near her.

When she was completely undressed, I held her hand and guided her to step into the warm water. She sunk beneath the bubbles and then smiled at me as I started taking my own clothes off.

Since the secret was out, I made sure to turn around and give her another glimpse of the tattoo I had of her lily on my body. My hidden secret for so long. Even the guys in the locker room didn't know about that tattoo. If they had, they would have already put two and two together.

"I still can't believe you did that," she laughed, referring to the ink.

I turned back around, completely naked and stepped into the tub behind her. "I can't believe you can't believe it."

She settled between my legs, so easily it was like she was made to be there. As if it was her spot and no one else's. I started rubbing my hands down her chest, kneading her body every-where, and skimming her nipples along the way. My mouth went to her neck and she moaned, tilting to give me better access.

Every part of me wanted to turn her around and make her ride my cock, but I held back and reached for the soap instead.

Together we both bathed our bodies, and for a minute, I wondered how I would be able to bathe, or shower, at all once she was not there with me.

How did I become so dependent on her so quickly? Someone I had never even slept with?

I squeezed my eyes shut and tried to tell myself that half the magic that was going on between us was novelty. She was my step sister, off limits, and untouchable, yet I spent my entire life wanting to touch her. Now that I was, it was like taking a hit of a drug. Once I finally had her in every way, the magic would probably fade a little, and the novelty of being with her would be erased.

It was exactly what we needed.

When I was sure that the game was completely washed away, I turned her around and settled her feet on either side of my hips, making her spread open for me.

"I'm glad you saved this for me," I teased her, running my pointer finger through the folds of her pussy.

"It wasn't intentional," she tried to tease back, but her face contorted as I pinched her clit.

"Maybe so, but I think you always wanted it this way."

"I never knew what I wanted when it came to you."

"Remember when we went camping and I had to help you get some things from the car?"

Her eyes locked onto mine and she nodded without saying a word. Of course she remembered. The way we eyed each other over the fire, shooting daggers at one another for no fucking reason. Our parents sang songs and acted like we were the Brady Bunch.

"That was the first time I ever got hard for you," I confessed. "I followed you to the car because my dad threatened to kick my ass if I didn't help you, and when I got closer, you had taken your hoodie off. It was innocent, but I was a teenage boy with hormones that I didn't know how to control. I knew I would be a dead man if I ever told anyone about that though."

"You called me 'gross.'"

Fuck, I hated that she remembered that. It was probably the only mean thing I said directly to her, and I hated myself so much. "I know this doesn't excuse it, but I was only trying to make sure you didn't see how turned on I was."

"I kept that hoodie on so you never saw my body. Teenage girls are so insecure and the moment I had it off, you said—"

"Fuck," I bit out, hating myself even more. "I'm so... damnit."

"Don't," she smiled. "I'm just glad I know what was really happening that night."

"My dick was wanting you to be *my* first. That's what."

"So this isn't just about me, huh?" She smirked. "You want me too."

"You have no idea," I sighed.

Chapter Thirty One

Lily

If I had been with any other man, those overprotective moments my mother and Ivan exerted into my life would have scared him away. But Cruz knew how eccentric they were and he was still sitting naked in front of me, caressing me and kissing my lips.

We stayed locked on to one another until the water in the bath was nearly cold, then Cruz picked me up in his arms as if I weighed nothing, and carried me to his bed. Before laying me down, he took a towel to my body, but we were far from being dry when he started climbing over the top of me.

He was so hard, and he ground himself between my slick folds, watching the way our skin looked when it was touching that way. My body was flooded and ready, and he was just as eager as I was.

"I don't want anyone else touching this pussy, Lily."

"It's yours," I moaned, leaving out the words *right now.*

"You on anything?" he questioned vaguely, but I knew what he meant. I nodded, and saw his eyes light on fire with my go ahead not to use a condom.

"Have you ever..." I trailed off, trying to be responsible and ask if he had anything I needed to know about, but I didn't want to ruin the mood.

"I've never not used protection, Lil. I'm good."

My hands held onto his face as he held his body above mine. His cock was starting to nudge at my entrance, and we were both losing control by the second.

Leaning up, I kissed him, then widened my legs, creating space for him to nestle between them and ease his way into my body.

"I don't want to hurt you," he whispered.

"Then don't let it be someone else."

My words made him finally push into me, little by little. He was easy, but it was making his arms shake and face start to sweat. I wiped his brow with my hand and then pulled him back down to kiss me again, hoping to take his mind off the control he was using. I could take the pain, I just wanted to feel him.

"I'm so fucking sorry," he mumbled before pushing into me harder, enough to make me burn with pain and scream into his mouth. He pulled away and buried his head into my neck while he pushed a little more, and I bit down on his shoulder.

Within minutes, he started to move again, and the pain that had flashed was quickly becoming pleasure. My body was molding to him, and I was so wet that the ease of the way he glided in and out of me, got easier and easier.

"Cruz?" I whined.

"I'm here, baby." He lifted his head, kissing my face all over as his hips found a steady rhythm.

Tears sprang into my eyes, the moment being so much more than losing my virginity, or starting a new page in my life. It was Cruz and me, together, so gentle and so loving. My heart was going to beat out of my chest, not just from pleasure, but from how much I was falling for Cruz.

Or how much I was finally admitting to myself what he

meant to me. Because he was always something more than I ever admitted.

"It feels so good," I moaned, the tears falling down my cheeks.

Cruz ran his bottom lip along my tear stains and kept them from falling. "So good."

"I don't know what I'm supposed to be doing," I admitted.

"You're perfect. Just let me do the work. Let me move inside your body and build you up."

My arms were wrapped around his shoulders and I held on tighter, taking his words to heart. His lips were skimming me all over, occasionally stopping at mine before running back down my neck. His hips kept the same pace and I could feel the tension building in my core.

When I started to squeeze him, he could feel it, and moaned into my mouth before speeding up his thrusts. The harder he went, the more I felt my body starting to pulse, and I couldn't believe I was about to come from a moment that I thought would be nothing but painful.

"Cruz?" I cried again, not knowing what else to say.

"That's it," he gritted between his clenched teeth. "That's my girl."

I started to lose control and came, clenching around him and making him follow me as we peaked together. The room was full of our loud moans and heavy breathing. I held on tightly to his shoulders, not wanting there to be any space between us.

When he finally slowed, I expected him to pull from my body and get up, but he let his weight down on top of me and slid his arms under my back. His chest was heaving hard, and I took a hand to my heart to make sure it was still inside my own chest. If his athletic body was struggling, I was sure mine had ripped apart all together.

"Lil?" he spoke into my neck. "You can't let anyone else near this pussy. Ever."

I laughed, because it felt like he was joking, or speaking in jest, but he lifted his head and locked his eyes with mine. I swallowed my laughter, but didn't respond. He may have felt at that moment that it was possible, but nothing about us had changed.

Cruz and I slept in each other's arms. I was sore between my legs, and saw the evidence of my virginity on the tip of his dick when he pulled out of me. But he was attentive and unbothered by those small reminders. He had made sure I had a cool rag, water, and slipped *his* jersey over my head before pulling me against him.

When the alarm started blaring, he reached around trying to find my phone and then handed it to me without letting me go.

"I have to get up," I pouted, looking at his closed eyes.

He peeked them open and smiled before closing them tightly again. "No."

I pushed his shoulders and laughed, wiggling my way out of his hold. "I have another interview today."

The reminder made him sit up and he watched me move around the room in his big jersey that hit the top of my knees. "Should I wish you luck?"

I stopped and put my hands on my hips, a half-smile playing on my lips. "It'd be nice."

"Hey," he raised his hands like he had no idea what to do. "The last one made you cry. I've spent almost a week suppressing the urge to find out who made you cry and kick their ass."

"You did that Friday," I reminded him of Mr. Archer. "You're good for a while."

But he was right and I had almost forgotten that he had caught me in tears over being offered the job of my dreams. He kept his word and didn't push to find out more, but it had clearly not been something he let go of.

"No one makes you cry, Lil. You hear me?"

"Yeah," I whispered, loving his version of overprotecting me way more than my mother's.

Walking to the edge of the bed, I sat down, running a hand over his bare chest. "How about I get through these next two interviews and then we have a little chat?"

"Don't leave Tuesday. Or Wednesday. Or whenever you were going to head back home. Stay here until the weekend. Come to my game Friday."

"It's only going to get harder," I shrugged, not saying no, but not saying yes, either.

"It's a big one. I want you to be there."

I knew I was going to stay because I had no reason not to. Other than falling more in love with him, and risking my heart more than I should have been. It would be easy to tell my mom I was staying for a follow up interview on Friday, and then coming home.

"You know my plan is to move here, right?"

"But that will be your new life, and I doubt I'm a part of that version of you. Miami is big, and we could go years without ever crossing paths."

"Or we could make a point to secretly do *this* every once in a while."

"You're too good to be someone I see on the side, Lil. That will never happen."

I shrugged like I wasn't bothered by his words, but somehow, they hurt. I wanted to be his secret, I wanted to be the girl he saw on the side of everything else in his life. Even if that wasn't what he meant, I wanted whatever he would give me.

"How you feeling?"

The change of subject threw me off guard for a minute but I looked down at where his thumb was caressing my thigh and smiled. "Better than I thought I would."

"Good," he squeezed me. "I have practice, you have an interview. Let's meet back here and spend more *quality* time together."

His words made me shiver, reminding me of the times our parents told us we needed to spend quality time together. Cruz had said it on purpose and I couldn't help my giggle. "Mom and Dad would be so proud."

He barked a loud laugh that made my chest flutter before pulling me down into his arms and kissing me. It didn't feel like anything could ruin the day for me, and I walked into my interview that afternoon feeling like a new woman.

Chapter Thirty Two

Cruz

"Remember that guy from Mango's the other night?"

I stopped taking off the wrap that I wore on my ankles during practice, and looked over at Tripp. He sounded lost in thought, and I wasn't sure he even knew he was speaking to me.

"Coach Crazy?" I asked, using Erin's description of him the way I promised her I always would.

"Hunter Ward." Tripp corrected me, but still didn't look at me. He was staring into a blank space in his locker so I got concerned and turned to face him.

"You okay?"

"Hunter is an old teammate of mine. He asked for my help."

"Just because I don't like him doesn't mean you can't help him."

Tripp smirked and finally looked my way. "This has nothing to do with how you feel about him."

"Well that is offensive because the only reason I don't like him is because Rhys doesn't like him. You should be a better friend to me."

"What are you? Twelve?"

I smiled at him and winked, then turned back to my task. I hadn't had any calls or texts from Lily and I was anxious to get home and see how her interview went. But I also knew I needed to let Tripp tell me whatever he needed to get off his chest.

"What does he want help with?"

"I don't know if I should say."

"Is it illegal? Does he want you to shove drugs up your ass?"

"No," Tripp laughed again. "I mean, it's a little twisted, but nothing like that."

"What are you going to do, then?"

"Guess I'm gonna steal his girl, just like he asked me to do."

My head whipped back to him, and my eyes almost fell out of my head. "What?"

"It's complicated," Tripp sighed, then stood and walked away.

I looked over to Rhys to see if he heard anything that Tripp had said, but he was on the phone, a dumb smile on his face telling me he was talking to Ash. His eyes found mind for a second and he nodded at me, wondering what I needed. But I waved him off, not thinking Tripp's gossip was worth interrupting his call.

Plus, it was time to get back to my own girl.

Not my girl.

But mine.

Fuck.

Walking in, I found Lily on the floor, stretching. Fuck she was gorgeous. And the way her eyes lit up and she smiled as I walked closer, made my heart flip around in my chest.

"How are you feeling?" I winked, wondering about the status of her pussy before anything else.

"Good. Better than good."

She was in a straddle position and I dropped down to my knees and crawled in between her spread legs. Kissing her came so damn naturally that I should have been scared, but I just brushed it off knowing that as long as she let me, I was going to keep kissing her.

Her hands came up and grabbed my face, and her tongue slipped into mine. I had a dozen more questions for her, but I figured I could ask those while I took her clothes off.

"How did the interview go?"

"Good!" She said excitedly then went back to kissing me.

"So you got an offer?"

"Nope. They passed."

I pulled back and furrowed my brow, confused as to why she was upset with the other offer, and happy about not getting one today.

"Do you actually want one of these jobs you're interviewing for?" I pulled my shirt over my head, not letting our conversation deter me from fucking her again as soon as I could.

"Of course I do," she moaned, as I pulled her shirt over her head. "But these interviews were set up by an old professor of mine, and it's complicated."

"How so?" I moved to her leggings and started pulling them down, leaving her completely naked on the tile floor of my living room. Taking my own shorts off and throwing my shoes toward the front door, I then pulled her into my lap. She straddled me and I rubbed my nose on hers, waiting for an answer.

"I don't want to be hired because of Professor Grissom."

"And last week, you were?"

"It's the only reason I was offered that job, Cruz. Professor Grissom liked me, helped me, and wanted to do anything he could to see me land the job of my dreams. But I want to be hired because they see something in me. I am well aware I only got these interviews because of Professor Grissom, but I thought showing up and speaking to them would earn me the rest of the way in."

"So what happens tomorrow?"

"I go to my interview, I have dinner with my friends, and then I..."

"Come home and fuck me," I finished for her.

"Yeah," she sighed, like that was the only part of the plan that mattered.

"But I also want you to talk to me."

"I will, I am!" Her arms spread wide, as if to say that was exactly what we were doing. But she was holding back and I wasn't going to force anything out of her. When I asked her what happened tomorrow, I meant the interview, but she glossed over that, and gave me her itinerary. She still had some things to work through, but I wanted to know everything that was going on in her head.

Leaning back on the cold tile, I positioned her over the top of me. Stroking my cock a few times I lined myself up between her folds. Then I guided her down on top of me, letting her go at her own pace. She hissed a few times as she seated herself on top of me, then she sat still with her hands on my chest.

"Move your hips," I groaned. "Ride me."

"Oh my god," she whispered, embarrassed, and turned on. Her hips started to rock and with every new motion, her tits bounced. I was torn between watching them, and leaning up and sucking them. But while I waffled with that decision, she made it for me when she leaned forward and hung them directly over my mouth.

I bit each of her nipples, making her moan more, then licked and sucked them as her movement got faster.

"*Te ves tan bien encima de mí.*" I spoke so low I wasn't even sure she could hear me. But my words weren't for her, they were for me. "*Quiero que te quedes en mi pene para siempre.*"

She paused and looked down at me, tilting her head. Lily had picked up on a little Spanish over the years, and something I said had caught her attention. It caught my attention too, because it was the exact opposite of anything I ever felt.

"Move!" I moaned, hoping to distract Lily from translating in her head. She started grinding her hips again and I pushed up, trying to rub her clit on my pelvis.

"Cruz!" She cried. "This feels so good."

"Grind your clit. Don't be shy.. You take whatever you want from me."

She shook her head, still holding back, worried I would judge her for however she wanted to get herself off. But Lil could have grinded her pussy on my goal post and I would have wanted to write a song about how fucking amazing she was.

"Don't ever doubt yourself Lil. Whatever makes you feel good is exactly what you get."

"I just want everything," she cried.

"Then I'll give you everything."

That felt like a promise. We didn't really know how much time we had left together or where it would all lead, but I knew I would do anything for her.

"Put your hand on your clit. Touch yourself for me."

Her eyes were screwed tight and she shook her head. But at the same time, she ran her hand down her stomach and started making a circle motion with her fingers over her clit.

"That's my girl. Good girl, baby. I love seeing you so fucking lost to pleasure. Have you ever rubbed that pussy and thought about me?

"God yes," she admitted.

"Look me in the eyes and say that," I snapped at her.

She opened her eyes and looked down at me then increased her speed, going harder, pushing herself to the edge.

"Have you touched yourself while thinking of me?" I asked her again.

This time with her eyes locked on mine, she nodded. "All the time."

"And next week when you're alone in your bedroom, and our parents are downstairs having a happy little time, are you gonna touch yourself thinking about riding my cock? Are you dirty enough to do that, knowing how much trouble we would be in?"

"I don't think it'll matter where I'm at. I'm always going to think about being with you like this."

She was so bold and sexy that I could no longer hold off. Spilling into her, I moaned and grunted, my chest was pounding and my legs shaking. Squeezing her hips, I warned her, "You better come, baby. Because I'm done for when it comes to you."

"Not yet," she moaned, before lifting off of my cock and letting my cum slide down her leg and onto my stomach. She took her fingers inside of herself, pulling more cum from her pussy and rubbing it on her clit.

She came with her own hand, having a hard time keeping her knees locked and rubbing her wet pussy all over my stomach. I was already getting hard again, which never happened before, but there was just something about Lily.

I never wanted to stop.

All I could comprehend was need and desire for her.

She thought we were through, and I may have been a mess, but I leaned up and got on my feet. Carrying her in my arms toward the balcony doors, I set her on her feet and turned her around. Putting her hands high on the glass, I pulled her ass out toward me and I sunk back into her core. Her pussy clamped down around me and I moved quickly, too afraid that taking my time would make the intense feelings fade.

"I can't believe what you do to me," I grunted with each push, tears were streaming on her face but she didn't want me to stop, everything was just so intense.

"You knew what touching yourself did to me, didn't you?" I pressed her tits tight against the glass and pushed up into her again and again.

"You've taught me well," she cried.

"Wouldn't it be something if everyone could see us up here? If we weren't facing the ocean, but instead facing the balcony on the other building. They would see us like this. Miss Glenda, in the other building, knows my dad. Could you imagine the look on her face when she saw his two kids fucking each other?"

"It's not like that," she cried out.

"Maybe we need to show everyone what you and I have always known."

I was speechless as I started coming again, and I felt her squeezing me as her legs shook with her own orgasm. The sensation was more than I could fathom. Nothing had ever felt that good, nor had anything meant as much to me. Nothing was certain anymore, I didn't even know who I was.

Once her pussy was full, I pulled out of her and cum started running down her legs again. She kept her face pressed against the cold glass, her chest heaving, and her ass still pushed out.

"You've never looked so beautiful. If you could see yourself like this, it would be your next drawing. Something you'd never want to forget."

"What about a tattoo?"

"I'd put your wet pussy on my skin without question. But ink could never replace the real thing."

Chapter Thirty Three

Lily

After a quiet bath, we climbed into his bed together and made love. It was so quiet and subdued, barely speaking to each other, and without the intensity of before. But still so much more than anything I ever imagined.

We gravitated into each other's arms, needing more of each other without having to ask. Our chaste kiss had immediately intensified, and Cruz gently slid inside of me. When we both came, there was barely any noise, just soft moans and grunts as we climaxed together.

The next morning, Cruz was gone before I woke up. I had either been sleeping really hard, or he was extra quiet. My late interview meant I got to sleep later, and I was thankful he recognized that.

My phone started to ring with Angel's ringtone and I smiled as I leaned over and grabbed it. It was a FaceTime, and without even thinking of where I was, I answered.

"Oh," Angel laughed. "Did you sleep in your birthday suit?"

My eyes widened, and my brain quickly jumped out of my Cruz-induced haze. Luckily the sheet was covering my breasts, so I shrugged and acted like it wasn't a big deal.

"You FaceTimed me before noon," I laughed. "If you get flashed, that's your fault."

She threw her head back laughing, and it made me miss her. It'd been practically a whole week since we'd hung out, and even though I was glad I got to spend a lot of time with Cruz, I still needed my friend.

"My interview is at three today, are we still on for dinner?"

"That's why I'm calling. Jackie wants to meet at a place called Tico's."

Thankfully, I dropped my phone when I heard the name of the restaurant, so Angel couldn't see the way I nearly started hyperventilating when she mentioned where she wanted to go. Or where Jackie wanted to go.

"If she wants Cuban food, I love that place we went to before."

"Yeah but Cruz Martin's cousin is working tonight at Tico's and she wants to sweet talk him into getting more tickets for Friday's game."

"I have to go home Friday morning," I lied knowing I had already told my mom I was staying until Saturday. Of course, those days were supposed to be for Cruz and me, and I knew for a fact that I already had his tickets for Friday's game.

"Oh yeah, I know, girl. No worries, she's just gonna ask for the tickets, and I'll go along with her." *But she won't get them*, I thought to myself.

"It feels weird that she uses this guy, Deon, to get to someone famous."

"Deon knows exactly what Jackie's game plan is. He has no problem getting his dick sucked every once in a while and giving Jackie tickets."

Sucked? I thought she just touched him?

I did a really good job at not flinching when she spoke about what Jackie did to get tickets. Not that it shocked me.

"You must've slept well," she changed the subject before I had a plan and distracted me from thinking of it again. "If I didn't know any better, I would say that it looks like someone had sex."

"Ha," I rolled my eyes. "I wish. This bed is just so comfortable."

"What sucks is you're leaving Friday morning and we never got to party. When are you thinking about making the big move?"

"It depends on if I get an offer today, and when they would want me to start, I'm not sure yet if I'm going to take my first offer, but they wanted me to start in a month."

"I've been looking at apartments with three bedrooms," Angel clapped. "I'll send you some listings."

"Sounds good." I tried to act excited, because that was the original plan for us three. But after the week I had with Cruz, and how far our relationship had gone, I wasn't sure if I was gonna be able to live with Jackie. I could probably keep Cruz a secret for the rest of my life, but I would always secretly resent her for crushing on him and using Deon. Eventually, I would probably yell that she couldn't have him because he was mine.

"Well, Miss Harris, we'd like to offer you the job. We're hoping that you can fill the position in the next couple of weeks."

I smiled and stood up, reaching my hand across the desk to shake Mr. Henderson's hand. "I'd love it, sir. I have to get a few things ready for my move down here, but you tell me when to be here, and I'll make it happen."

"Let's say two weeks?"

"Absolutely."

Everything was falling into place, and before long I would be living full-time in the warm Miami sun with a new job, and a new lease on life. The thought made me bounce out to my car with an extra pep in my step.

Before I even got to my car, my phone rang and I looked down, seeing Cruz's name. "Do you have drones keeping an eye on me?"

"Wow, our parents really have you messed up if that was your first thought."

"I just left the museum so your timing is perfect," I laughed.

"Well then that's just a coincidence." I could hear how playful his voice sounded. It made me feel like he'd had a good day as well. "So how did it go?"

"I start in two weeks."

His excitement made me laugh, and I could hear him telling someone in the background that I got the job.

"Who are you talking to?" I mean, no one else knew how close we were.

"My mom. I decided to come see her after practice today. Waiting on her to bring me dinner."

My heart started racing because that's exactly where I was headed, and I had hoped that his mom wouldn't end up being there when I arrived. Much less him being there himself.

"Oh my God, I got so consumed with this interview that I forgot to call you. You have to leave." I started to panic. "Jackie and Angel will be there soon. That's where we're supposed to have dinner. I think Jackie wants to squeeze more tickets out of Deon."

"Damn Lil, what the fuck?" He sighed in frustration and I felt awful. "All right I'm gonna ask her for a to-go box, and I'll tell my mom to act like she doesn't know you."

"You're the best, you know that?"

"Just for you."

Before I could say anything else he started cursing under his breath, "Your friends are already here."

Oh no.

"Shit, Deon met them at the door. They're headed my way."

I didn't hang up, but neither did he. I could hear him talking to them at his table and them asking him if they could sit down. He was too nice to tell them to go away, but I could tell in his tone that he wanted to.

"I thought I was going to hear from you last week," Jackie whined. "I was looking forward to it."

"Yeah sorry about that. Change of plans."

"That's okay, I'm always available for you."

"Oh, I thought you and Deon were a thing."

I started laughing because he didn't think that at all, but I could imagine the look on Jackie's face when he said it.

"Excuse me," Cruz said and I heard shuffling before his voice was back in my ear. "Señorita?"

"Yes?" I laughed, loving when he called me that.

"You might want to fake a stomach flu and go home. I'll meet you there."

"This is the last time I'll see them for a couple of weeks."

"What if I said I would... oh fuck."

His voice got away from the phone again, and I heard Jackie's in the background. "Can I talk to you alone?"

"What's up?"

"I thought we could have some fun tonight."

"Um..."

"Come on," she moaned, so close I could hear her breath. *"Déjame chuparte."*

What did she just say?

Instead of answering her in Spanish, Cruz took a page from

his dad's playbook and stuck to English, knowing I was listening. "I'm seeing someone."

"No you're not," Jackie laughed. "You have a reputation, and I know all about it. Let me be one of your girls."

Embarrassment for Jackie made me want to throw up. Good for her for trying, I guess, going after what she wanted, but all her self-respect was flying out the door. Was Cruz really into a girl like that? Did he really have a reputation for not caring how, or who, got him off?

"I'm seeing someone," Cruz repeated. "I'm on the phone with her now."

He sounded irritated, but I couldn't help where my mind had gone. Deep down to a place that told me I wasn't special to him, I was just convenient. With me staying at his place, I was an easy target if he wanted to get laid.

"Well that'll end soon," Jackie laughed. "You have my number when you think you can handle me."

Cruz groaned. The same groan he made when I was touching him, or when he was turned on, and I could picture Jackie touching him. Was he starting to regret that she was my friend? Because I knew that was the only thing stopping him. Jackie was gorgeous. Before he saw me sitting next to her at the game, he was letting her know he was interested.

My heart sank, but I knew that was a dumb emotion to feel. Cruz and I were never going to be more, and Jackie was right without even realizing it, because once I left, Cruz would be back to his normal, playboy ways.

Instead of chatting with him, I decided to hang up. I was close to the restaurant and had to get my fake smile ready. When I pulled in, I saw Cruz's car up front, not far from Angel's.

Opening the door, the hostess asked me how many, and I pointed to the corner where Angel and Jackie were talking with a guy I assumed was Deon. Angel was looking for me and started to wave, so I made my way to their table and sat down across from Jackie, next to Angel.

"So how'd it go?" Angel asked. "Are we celebrating?"

"We are," I nodded, then looked at Deon. "I'm Lillian."

"Deon," he waved, "a friend of Jackie's. Move," he nudged her playfully to get up from the booth. "I have to get back to work."

Deon was nothing like I expected. He was handsome, like Cruz, but I expected him to either be annoyed about Jackie's intentions with his cousin, or more into her than just a nudge. But he seemed content, as if nothing was wrong.

While Jackie got resituated, I glanced around for Cruz, wondering if he made it out the back door yet. But Angel tapped my arm and got my attention.

"Drinks on me!"

"I'm not drinking," I laughed, holding up my keys to show her why.

"You can crash at our place, we aren't far."

That was tempting, since I didn't want to see Cruz. It's not that I was mad at him, I just felt a little shame. Everything he said to me, everything we said to each other. It felt like I was just convenient to him, and it sucked to remember that we were what we were, and we always would be.

"One drink," I decided, knowing it would help me loosen up a little. Surely one drink wouldn't make it to where I couldn't drive home.

Angel called for the waitress, who thankfully wasn't the girl from the other night, and ordered a round of margaritas. Then I went into the details of my job offer, and how they wanted me to start in two weeks.

"So you're turning the first offer down? Wasn't that the place you wanted most?"

"Yeah but I just got a better vibe at this one. Meshed well with the guy who interviewed me. I think it will be a better fit." That wasn't a complete lie, and I relaxed knowing the night wouldn't be the shitshow I thought it would be.

Cruz was gone.

His mom would cover for me, I knew she would.

And my first sip of my margarita made me feel warm and relaxed.

My phone started ringing, and before I could grab it, Angel looked at the caller ID.

"Sebastian?"

"Oh my god," I panicked, grabbing the phone from her.

"Who's Sebastian, and why haven't we heard of him?" Jackie urged, always wanting the juicy details.

"He's my...brother." I cringed when I said the word, but I covered it up with a fake sneeze and sent the call to voicemail.

"You never told me you had a brother," Angel practically yelled.

"Step brother!" I tried to fix it quickly. "I barely know him."

"Something must be important if you barely know him, but he's calling out of the blue."

"Yeah, probably," I mumbled, not answering the second call that was coming in from Cruz. I also took a moment to pat myself on the back for using Cruz's real name in my contacts.

On the third call, Jackie grabbed my phone and pulled it away from me so I couldn't reach it. "I'll answer it."

"No!"

"Hola!" My heart was beating out of my chest, and not the way Cruz made it do. This was more of a heart attack feeling and I considered rushing myself to the hospital just in case. "This is her friend Jackie, who's this?"

There was a moment of silence then Jackie's eyes flew open and she looked at me. "Her boyfriend?"

"Oh no," I whispered, while Angel's eyes went between the two of us.

"You have a boyfriend?" She squealed.

"NO!"

"She said you were her brother," Jackie practically purred. "I think she was just keeping you a secret."

"He is my brother," I snapped, trying to grab the phone from her. Jackie laughed like she was innocently having fun, but she had no idea she was talking to the guy to whom she just offered a blow job. Thankfully she didn't appear to recognize his voice.

"I have to get out of here." I took another drink of my margarita because it was all I had to help my dry throat, but I immediately regretted that when I felt the tequila in my veins.

Jackie hung up the phone and tossed it back across the table, making me realize I missed the last of whatever they spoke about. I scooped my phone up and tucked it into my purse so that wouldn't happen again, and then took another sip of my margarita.

"He sounded sexy," Jackie winked. "Now I just need to know if he's your brother or your boyfriend."

"Both," my tequila-fuzzed brain bit at her.

"Right," Jackie rolled her eyes. "That'd be disgusting."

"Why haven't you said anything?" Angel asked, a little more hurt that there was something she didn't know about me.

"He's a complication," I said truthfully. "Someone my mother always wanted me to be close to, but we just never were."

"I still feel like I should have known you had a stepbrother," Angel laughed, but it was half-hearted and weak.

"There's a lot we don't know about each other," I tried to reason. "There is a lot you don't know about me yet."

"I guess," Angel mumbled.

Jackie just looked at the menu, as if nothing had happened, making me steam in anger. For just a second, I thought about calling Cruz and telling him to come kiss me, right in front of her, just so I could see the look on her face. But that would make my life harder. Angel would never forgive me. And like Jackie had said, everyone would think it was disgusting.

"I need to go," I slurred a little. "I need to check in at home and…" What else could I say to excuse myself? They were both looking up at me as I stood, waiting for me to say more, but I couldn't think of anything. So I turned and walked quickly from the restaurant and started fishing for my keys.

Right when I found them at the bottom of my bag, I was no longer on my feet, being carried off into a dark alley behind the restaurant. Kicking and screaming, I was scared to death. Being kidnapped would serve me right, though. Lying, and asking everyone else to lie for me as well. Drinking, and then thinking I would drive home.

When we were no longer where the sun was slowly setting, and hidden in a dark part of the alley, I was finally let down on my feet and looked up, ready to scream. But before I did, my mouth was covered from someone behind me, and I was being dragged toward a car.

Chapter Thirty Four

Cruz

The things I did to stay on Lily's good side. Like hanging out in the kitchen until I saw her leave, and then practically kidnapping her so her friends didn't see her leave with me. There was no way I was letting her drive after having any amount of my mom's margarita.

"Calm down," I whispered, hoping she would stop screaming. Of course, I hadn't realized how bad it looked until I started forcing her into my car. "Hey. It's me."

I turned her around and knelt in front of her as she sat on the passenger seat of my car. Her legs weren't in yet because she was kicking and fighting, but when she saw me, she stopped immediately.

"What the hell are you thinking?" she screamed but somehow also whispered.

"I tried to call you and warn you not to drink the margarita. They're strong here."

"Are you on my mom's payroll?" She yelled. "And how does that explain your kidnapping attempt?"

"I saw you leave and ran out the back. I had already moved

my car back this way and had to get you back here somehow before your friend chased after you."

"No one was—"

Her words were cut off by an incoming call and she reached in her purse to pull her phone out. The caller ID said Angel and I nodded at her that she should take it.

"Hello?"

"Where the hell are you? Your car is still here but you vanished." Angel was screaming so loud, clearly worried, and I decided I liked her a little bit. Anybody that worried about my girl the same way I was, got extra points. Meanwhile, Jackie was at the top of my shit list.

"I took an Uber." I could see her shoulders sag with the lie, and was sure they were starting to weigh on her. She needed to clear the air, to be honest, but we had done some things that would always be a secret, and I guess she was going to deal with that however she thought she could.

"That fast?"

"There was one dropping someone off. I just jumped in." Hell, I was impressed at how well the lies were rolling for her. She barely had to think about it. It made me wonder if the conversations we had were real.

Lil hung up the phone and sighed before quietly putting her feet into the car. "Just take me home."

I closed the door and got in, driving off without my dinner that I'd thrown onto the counter when I chased Lil. My mother was back there and saw the whole thing. She knew something was going on between us, and I figured before long, I would have to explain a few things to her.

Luckily, she let me go and never called me.

I held Lil's hand all the way back to South Beach, assuring her everything was fine, but she kept taking her pulse like she was debating an ER visit. I rubbed her wrist and smiled, and she managed to laugh at herself for the first time.

When we got home, though, she was almost asleep, and I picked her up in my arms and carried her in. She pointed to her own room, keeping her head on my shoulder, but I disregarded her request and took her to my room. I had been sleeping next to her for almost a week and I was used to it. I craved it.

No way was I letting her out of my sight.

She undressed herself as she sat on the edge of my bed and I slid my jersey–now her jersey–over her head before pushing her back to lay down. It was still fairly early, but she seemed exhausted, so I climbed in next to her and pulled her into my arms.

We silently laid together, my hand stroking her hair while her cheek laid on my chest. I knew she was awake, but I didn't expect to feel a tear slide onto my skin.

"Lily?"

"I don't like Jackie."

"That makes two of us," I told her.

She repositioned herself so that her chin was on me and her eyes were looking up at mine. "But I've been a shitty friend, too."

"You've been under someone's thumb your entire life. I never realized how much until you were here with me. It makes you guarded and untrusting. And I get why you don't want them knowing about me. You're right in the fact that Jackie would use you to get what she wanted."

"But maybe I should have realized I didn't want a friend like that before it got this far."

"The lie was told way before you came to Miami."

"True. But I don't want to lose Angel."

"You won't," I tried to assure her. She laid her head back on my chest, and was quiet for a few more minutes before she looked back up at me.

"Would you have taken Jackie up on her offer if she wasn't my friend?"

Fuck. I didn't want to answer that, but I wasn't going to lie to her. There had been enough of that shit. "Maybe." She tensed in my arms, but I tried to keep going and explain. "I'm a lonely guy, Lil. I come across as this fun-loving, hometown soccer player, just living the dream. But most nights are lonely. At least they were before you got here."

"Am I just convenient?" She didn't sound angry or put off, she sounded like she really wanted to know.

"You're the opposite of convenient," I huffed a laugh. "You're complicated. Way more complicated than I planned on ever letting into my life. But you're also worth it. You always have been. You scare the shit out of me."

"How?" She sat up and looked down at me, confusion all over her face.

"Have you lied to me?" I asked her back. "Because I haven't lied to you. I've wanted you before I even knew what that meant. Always thinking it was just some perversion, or sick feeling I got when you were around. I avoided you to keep from doing something stupid. My dad means the world to me, and I loved going to see him. But when you showed up, I no longer knew who I was anymore. My point is, if you were just a convenience, I would have kissed you a long time ago."

"Things are different. We're adults, alone."

"True," I sighed and shook my head. "But running out of the back of my mom's restaurant so your friends didn't get mad at you wasn't convenient. Neither was playing two entire games looking up in the stands and seeing you in Tripp's jersey. Knowing my dad would disown me if he knew about this isn't conven—"

"I get it," she laughed, cutting me off. "I'm complicated."

"But worth it," I reminded her.

She leaned down and kissed me, so naturally. How was I supposed to ever go on with the way life used to be, now that I finally had her where I wanted her? Jackie's offer made my dick hide as far away as possible. So did every other girl I passed, or saw, throughout the days. It was like I needed a shirt that said, "Property of Lily" and an arrow pointing at my crotch. I made a mental note to call my t shirt girl and see about having one made. Lily may be the only one that saw it, but I would wear it around the house every night.

"Hey," I pushed her back a little as an idea popped into my head. "You're coming back in two weeks?"

"Yeah, they want me to start pretty soon."

"Come stay with me. Live here."

"What? I have plans to find a place with–"

"That Jackie bitch. I won't let you move in with her, Lil."

"First of all, I'm convinced you're working for my mother. Second of all, you're right. I don't want to be around her. But I owe it to Angel to see if she still wants to get something together."

"You don't owe her anything. Come live here."

"As...What? Your sister?"

"No!" I shouted. "You know what. We can stay like this."

"A dirty secret that gives me heartburn?"

"Lil?" I growled at her. "Give us more time. No one has to know. Our parents live twelve hours away. We can tell them you're staying here until you find a place."

She bit her lip, thinking it over, but I didn't want her to answer me right away. If she did, she would say no, because that was the kind of mood she was in after everything that had happened.

Pulling her down on top of me, I kissed her and ended the

conversation. Her legs fell on either side of my waist and she pushed herself up a little and looked down at me. Her lips were puffy from our kiss and her hair was down around us.

"If I say yes, then we need to have a talk about some things."

Shaking my head, I was shutting her down. "We can talk when our heads are clear. Right now, I want you to slide those panties over and ride my cock."

Her giggle made my heart skip a beat, and I lifted her up a little so she could slide her thong over. Reaching down, she also pulled my cock from my shorts and stroked it a few times before hovering over the top of me. Seeing her so comfortable with me made my chest puff out a little.

Had she been with anyone else, they may not have empowered her the way I did, and it made me even more thankful we did what we did. Then I grimaced at the thought of her taking that initiative with someone else, and I pushed down on her hips, impaling her harder than she was ready for.

"Fuck," she moaned. It was one of the first times I'd heard her use that word, and I thought maybe I had created a monster.

My monster.

"Mine," I said out loud, pressing my thumb to her clit as she started to shift her hips up and down on me.

Maybe it was the sex, or maybe it was something else, but I decided then and there that not only would Lil move in with me, but we would always be together the way we were in that moment. I wanted to fuck her forever.

Even if we could never tell anyone else.

Chapter Thirty Five

Lily

Sipping my coffee on the balcony, I smiled as I spoke to my mom. "I'm going to stay until Saturday. I'll spend today and tomorrow looking for a few apartments, and then going to Cruz's game Friday."

"I'm so glad you two are getting along and finally being real siblings. It makes my heart feel so full."

I cringed as she spoke, but didn't deny, or say anything. Maybe we weren't what she thought, but we had definitely grown closer, and if it made her happy, then that was all I cared about.

"I'll see you—" I took a deep breath as Cruz wrapped his arms around my waist and buried his nose into my neck. "Saturday."

"Okay sweetheart. Let us know if you need help. We'll be happy to come down and look at places with you."

"That's okay, Mom." Cruz took his teeth to my skin and nipped his way down to my shoulder. "It'll be fine."

She sounded hesitant, like she wanted to hold my hand through finding an apartment, but she sighed and let that pass.

"Well Ivan wants me to meet him for lunch. So I'll call and check in later."

Rushing my goodbyes, I hung up and set my phone down while turning around in Cruz's arms. My back was pushed against the railing of the balcony and his lips found mine without any words.

"Good morning to you too," I laughed when he pulled back a little.

"Never in my life have I dreaded having to go to practice the way I do right now."

"How long will you be?" I pouted, pushing my lip out.

He leaned in and bit it, before kissing me with a quick peck. "A few hours."

"If I promise to be here when you get home, will you teach me some more new things?"

"Like what?" he smirked.

"Like how to take you deeper, into the back of my throat."

His growl vibrated my chest as he pressed against me, holding me close. "Fuck you're perfect."

"I want you to teach me," I moaned, knowing it turned him on. "I want you to teach me everything."

"Right now, the only thing I can teach you is how to get to practice on time."

"Will you teach me about soccer, too?"

"What do you want to know about soccer?"

"How to score," I teased.

"Fuck, baby," he pushed away and backed up like he was scared of me all of a sudden. "You already know too much."

I batted my eyelashes at him as I raised my hand to my chest and pretended I had no idea what he was talking about. But I knew what I was doing to him, and I felt like a goddess. Cruz had the upper hand our entire lives, but now that I knew how much he wanted me, I felt empowered.

When he came back to me, I wrapped my arms around his waist. His phone buzzed in his back pocket and he rolled his eyes without reaching for it. "That is either my lawyer, filling me in on what happened after I punched Archer, or my agent, reminding me I punched Archer."

If he was trying to be funny, it fell flat, because even though I wasn't traumatized by Mr. Archer, I felt bad he'd lost his contract because of me. "Maybe you should get it then."

"Only if you stop worrying," he mumbled. "It's written all over your face, but I promise everything is fine. He got what he deserved, and I avoided getting in a contract with a guy like that."

I nodded as his phone stopped ringing and a text buzzed.

"Grab it and check for me," he leaned down and kissed my neck while I pulled his phone from his pocket. When I lifted the phone, I nearly dropped it as I read the lock screen with the message on it.

> I feel bad about not going with you on Friday, so I decided to make it up to you with a girl I just met. She'll be up for us sharing her.

"Oh my god," I pushed at him to back up, and handed him his phone like it had cooties.

"What?" He grabbed it and read, his face whitening. "Oh no. No, baby, no..."

I held my hands up to stop him, but he grabbed them and shot a text back to whoever that was.

"Remember Erin? She is bullshitting. I asked her to go with me on Friday because she isn't into dick, but she never got back to me. She is saying she will share to be funny, but she won't I swear. Hell, I even have the shirt, I'll wear it today to practice. Fuck... I promise she is just being—"

"Stop," I laughed, trying to stop his ranting. He was friends with Erin, and I could picture her trying to drive him crazy by sending him that text. In fact, it made me want to officially meet her and be her best friend. "I didn't expect to read that, but it's not a big deal."

"It is if you think I'd go for that when I have you here at home."

"I don't. Just go to practice so you aren't late, and come back and teach me soccer."

"Don't. Fucking. Leave." He demanded. "I'll be home in a few hours."

Then he was gone, and I heard the door slam right as my phone started ringing again.

Angel.

I started not to take the call, but I knew I owed her more than I gave her the night before. She deserved to know why I ran out so fast.

"Hello?"

"Oh my God," she sighed. "Are you okay?"

"Of course. Jackie just upset me last night, and I had to go."

"She upset me too. She was way out of line."

"You don't know the half of it," I groaned.

"Well tell me! You're my best friend and I want to know everything!"

I was quiet for a minute, hating the desperation in her voice. "Can you come out to South Beach?"

"I can before work."

"I'll meet you down by the pier."

"Okay," she sounded frantic. "I'm grabbing my keys now."

I walked down to the pier and grabbed a table at the cafe while I waited on Angel. Over and over in my head, I practiced what I wanted to say to her. I was still unsure how much I was going to tell her, but I felt she needed to at least know about Cruz. It was up in the air whether I was going to tell her about Cruz my step brother, or Cruz my lover. That was a decision I was going to make on the fly. Whatever felt right in that moment.

"Hey!" I heard her say, making me look up from my coffee.

My face lit up and I stood to hug her, immediately knowing I was going to spill my guts.

After she ordered a coffee, we sat awkwardly while I found the right words.

"Okay so. This isn't something I want Jackie knowing, and I think you will understand why."

Angel looked hesitant but nodded.

"I'm actually staying with Cruz Martin."

Angel's mouth dropped open and she shook her head in disbelief. "What?"

"His dad is married to my mom. When I decided to come to Miami, they arranged for me to stay with him."

"What?" She yelled even louder, making people on the boardwalk look around at us. "You're joking, right?"

"That was why I was shocked we went to the game, why he was eyeing me funny, why I didn't want to go up and ask him for a picture when we saw him outside Mangos."

"Oh. My. God."

"But," I held up a hand to keep her from freaking out. "I didn't want to tell anyone because he's Cruz, and when I first got here, I wasn't even sure we would get along. It's not like we grew up together."

"Is that who called last night?"

"Yeah. After he left our table he went to the kitchen and

called me. And he knew I didn't want Jackie knowing I knew him. So he lied for me, just like he did when he walked away from me at the game that night. I'm so sorry, Angel. I wanted to tell y'all, but then Jackie started bragging about how she was using Deon and I wanted her to like me and—"

"Stop!" She held a hand up, shaking her head in disbelief. "I'm not actually sure I believe you."

"What?" For some reason, I was laughing, because I thought she was joking.

"This just seems..."

My phone started ringing right as she sighed, unable to finish her thought.

"It's Cruz. Let me get this." Angel rolled her eyes but waved at hand at me.

"Hello?"

"I'm almost home, are you naked?"

My face immediately turned red and Angel noticed, eyeing me as I answered.

"Can you do me a favor?"

"Anything."

"Can I bring Angel to meet you? I mean, I know you met her last night, but I mean, officially meet you. I'm down at the boardwalk with her now."

He laughed, and dang he sounded sexy. "She finally called you about last night?"

"Yeah, I needed to tell her the truth."

"Is the other one with her? Not sure I want her to know where I live."

"No, Jackie isn't with us."

"Then of course. Bring her over. But am I allowed to kiss you?"

"Um..." Now my eyes were wide and my mouth was gaping

open. Angel tilted her head wondering what had me so flustered, but I could also see the doubt in her eyes.

"I'm joking," Cruz laughed. "Get your ass home. The sooner we do this, the sooner I can teach you about soccer."

Chapter Thirty Six

Cruz

Lily threw me off when she asked me to meet Angel. All I could surmise was that she had to prove to her why she ran off the night before. I didn't mind, nor would I have minded if she told me I could kiss her. But since she wanted Angel to be a permanent part of her life, it was probably best we kept that secret. We didn't know Angel, what if she took pictures and posted them all over the internet?

It was a relief that I was meeting one of her friends though. Not that I wanted to be like her mom, but I was curious what Lily's friends were like when we got a chance to talk. Angel didn't do much talking at Tico's, Jackie was the one in charge of that conversation.

When I got home, the balcony door was open and I knew Lily and Angel had gone out there to wait for me. I could hear laughing, so that was a good sign, and I shook my hands out and bounced around as if I was about to defend the goal.

"Hey," I said, popping my head out.

Angel's eyes widened and she stood up, her mouth opening and closing while she looked for something to say.

"I'm Cruz," I reached my hand out. "We didn't get to chat last night."

"I'm Angel," she sighed. "Holy shit."

Behind Angel, I saw Lily roll her eyes and stand up to join us.

"See?" Lily waved between us.

Angel stayed quiet for a few minutes before she finally whipped around to face Lily. "All this time. We took you to a game. We even got you a jersey. You've listened to Jackie go on and on about Cruz, and you didn't think we could handle the fact that he's your step brother?"

"You heard Jackie," Lily countered.

"You knew Cruz way before you knew Jackie was a bitch. You could have said something."

Lily looked taken aback, like she hadn't expected Angel to turn on her the second she met me. Their laughter, before I showed up, told me they were actually getting along and were fine. So what changed?

Instinct told me to jump in front of Angel and tell her to get lost. No one talked to my girl like that, especially in our home. But that was still a secret Lily was keeping, and I had to rein myself in. She also needed me to stop overprotecting her. Lily could handle her friends and herself.

"You know what?" Lily fought tears, her voice strained. "Just leave."

It was Angel's turn to look dumbfounded, not understanding why Lily was the one upset.

"I know I haven't been honest," Lily explained. "But I don't have it in me to defend my choices. So I didn't tell you I knew Cruz Martin? Oh well. As my best friend, you should just get over it. It's not like I blatantly lied, and it's not like you don't understand why. You're upset because you feel like you have some reason to be embarrassed, but you don't. Or maybe you feel betrayed, but you're not. And being upset doesn't mean you can yell at me now that the truth is sinking in."

Fuck, my girl was amazing. Angel was fighting her own tears and backing up into the living room. She grabbed a bag off the coffee table and stomped toward the door. Lily was following her, but I stayed back, not putting myself in between their fight.

"I love you, Angel," Lily said, making Angel stop and listen. Her hand was on the door handle, ready to open it and leave, with her back facing both Lily and I.

"I just wish you had told me."

"Well I have bigger secrets than this," Lily admitted. "You don't know all there is to know about me. But you just showed me that you can't handle it when I *do* talk to you. So I love you, but I'm glad this is as far as my secrets go with you."

Angel pulled the door open and ran. I strode across the room to make sure the door shut tight, and then turned the lock. When I faced Lily again, she was in the exact spot she was in when she spoke to Angel, with her shoulders pushed back and her jaw shaking.

"Fuck," I whispered as I approached her, taking her into my arms. "I know this hurts, baby. I'm so sorry."

"Whatever," Lily sighed. "I tried to be honest with her, but I guess I was too late. I don't regret it. It's my right to have a few secrets. I don't owe anyone anything."

"You don't," I agreed with her, kissing her lips. "We all deserve to have our secrets."

She nodded while wrapping her arms around my shoulders. Scooping her up, I settled her on the counter then backed up so I could look into her eyes. There was sadness, and anger at Angel, but there was that lingering want she always had when she looked at me.

"What do you need me to do? I want to make you feel better."

"You know what I want, Cruz. Don't play dumb."

"I mean when it comes to your friends."

"You've done everything I've asked you to do. I'm thankful for you," she leaned in and kissed me gently. "I stand by what you just said; that we all deserve to have our secrets."

Shoving her legs open, I bit my bottom lip and moaned as I got closer to her. "We deserve to have *this* secret."

She nodded again as I pushed my body between her open legs and kissed her. I had one hand on her neck and the other on her thigh as our kiss consumed us once again. Never had I kissed someone so much.

We kept kissing until she finally started clawing at my shirt. "Take it off."

Backing away, I reached behind my head and pulled my shirt off, loving the way her eyes scanned my body. Her finger reached out and slid down the patch of hair that led down below the waist of my jeans.

"You said you'd teach me how to play soccer."

"Right now?"

"I don't want to dwell on Angel. I want to see better and play your game."

I knew exactly what she meant, so I nodded. I'd give her anything she wanted.

"Lesson one," I grabbed her hand and moved it to the counter. "Only the keeper can use his hands."

Her smile told me I was on the right track, and I laughed as I picked her up in my arms again and carried her into her room where there was a light green comforter. "Lesson two," I kissed her cheek. "The playing surface must be green."

She hadn't slept in there since we started sleeping together, so the bed was made and ready for us to mess it up. When I laid her down, her hands ran up my biceps and I had to pull them off of me, stretching them over her head.

"I'm the keeper," I reminded her. "Don't use your hands, or I'll have to dig out my handcuffs again."

"I thought you threw those away," she laughed.

"I'll improvise." We smiled at each other, our faces close together while I hovered over the top of her.

"What's lesson three?" She breathed.

"There are two forty-five minute halves, separated by a fifteen minute halftime."

Her lips quirked a little. "Sounds like a lofty goal."

"I'm up for the challenge."

"Anything else I need to know?"

"No flops. No faking it." Her laughter was loud and made me laugh along with her. Leaning down, I kissed her neck with a smile and asked, "Ready to play?"

"I think I get it now," she sighed. "I love this game."

She kept her arms above her head and I reached down to start peeling her clothes off. When she was completely naked, my lips found every part of her body, caressing her skin. Her small moans and whimpers made me want to keep going, but the way my cock was pressing against my jeans was also making me want to stop.

Using one hand, I reach down and undid the button and zipper, lowering my waistband just enough to pull my cock out and stroke it. Lily started to bring her hands down but stopped herself, knowing that was against the rules.

"You want my dick?" I teased her.

"You know I do," she practically squealed. "You've made me an addict."

"There isn't anything better in this entire world than you being addicted to my dick."

Lifting up, I shed my pants the rest of the way off, and then climbed up until I straddled her mouth. I held my cock against her lips and teased her, making sure to leave my precum where she could lick it up and taste it.

"Open up, baby" I commanded, angling myself so I could push deep into her throat. "Not just your lips, open your throat and let me in."

As I pushed into her mouth, her eyes started to water so I pulled back out. When I did it again, I pulled her hair a little to get a different angle, then pushed harder.

"This is what you wanted," I reminded her, wiping her tears. "You wanted to see how deep you could take me. All of me. If you want me to stop, just use your hands and I'll stop. But remember you'll get penalized."

She shook her head, unable to speak because her mouth was full, but it was clear she was telling me not to stop.

"Relax your throat. Don't panic, just let me in."

Her eyes closed and she leaned up, taking me further, before she leaned her head back onto the bed. Quietly, I started mumbling in Spanish, unable to communicate in English how good I felt. When she leaned up to do it again, she moaned, and the vibration made me start moving my hips again, fucking her mouth, and losing control.

"You're taking me so deep," I praised. "I'm so close to coming down your throat, *fuck*."

The first half of our game was almost over before I was ready, so I pulled out and jumped off of her, pacing next to the bed while I got my shit together. Looking down at her, with her hands above her head, tears on her cheeks, saliva running down her chin, and her legs open, I knew I was done for. Not just for the night, but for always.

No one would ever be as perfect as Lily. When she left, all of my nights for the rest of my life would be scoreless, because I would never be able to get past how much I'd wish it was her.

"Did I do okay?" she whispered, with a hitch in her tone, worried.

"Too good." I made my way back over the top of her and laid my cheek on her chest. Squeezing my eyes shut, I tried to think of anything else but how much I was feeling for her. "I can hear your heart."

She froze for a minute, but then took a deep breath. Her hands broke the rules, and she ran her fingers through my hair. "How does it sound?"

"Like it's mine," I whispered, almost hoping she didn't hear me.

When I leaned up, I found her mouth with mine again and decided we couldn't play anymore. I needed to be inside of her, I wanted to always be inside of her. So I pushed my cock into her body and started moving.

"Come with me baby," I begged as I started to peak again, making sure I ground down on her clit.

She nearly screamed, her hands pulling my hair, and her head tilted back. Her pussy squeezed me and every nerve in my body was on high alert. My own pulse was pounding in my ear, so strong that I almost couldn't hear her heavy breathing as her orgasm subsided.

Knowing she was satisfied, I let go, coming with my own hiss from the way her pussy continued to hold onto me tightly. My arms were shaking as I tried to keep my weight off of her but once I was spent, I fell onto her body and wrapped her up in my arms.

We laid there, with my cock inside of her, long after we came. My brain was working overtime while she stroked my back.

"You used your hands," I grumbled, still out of it.

"My bad," she snorted. "But oh well."

"Yeah, fuck the rules."

Eventually, I heard her stomach growl, and I looked up into her eyes. "It's probably close to dinner time by now."

"And I skipped lunch," she laughed.

"I should have fed you first, but I was so anxious to make you feel better."

"It worked," she laughed again. "Because until you said that, I forgot that I was upset in the first place."

Chapter Thirty Seven

Lily

I ran as fast as I could, my breathing labored, and barely able to stay on my feet. My scream was loud as I tried to get away but it was useless in the end.

"Got ya," Cruz laughed, picking me up and spinning me around.

My laugh was uncontrollable, and when he set me down, I fell into the sand to catch my breath. Cruz laid down beside me and took my hand, catching his breath as well.

"How can you run that fast after practicing all day?"

"I'll always be able to catch you," he laughed, turning his head to face me.

We locked eyes and smiled, listening to the waves crashing, the water barely touching our toes where we laid.

After having dinner together, we went down to the beach, and walked hand in hand on the edge of the water. Eventually, we started playing around, and I wasn't sure I had ever laughed so hard, or been happier in my entire life.

Cruz took my sandy hand and brought it to his lips, kissing my knuckles.

We didn't have our phones with us, and neither of us had a

watch, but I knew it was getting late. I just couldn't bring myself to leave that spot on the beach, where everything seemed so simple and easy.

The whole world made sense.

When we finally did get home, we showered together and then fell into bed, making love in a way that felt like so much more than sex. He whispered some words in Spanish and even though I didn't understand them all, I loved it more than if I had known every word. It was like he was letting himself be a little more honest knowing I wouldn't know what he was saying.

But I felt it.

Our bodies spoke the same language, and he could never deny what his was telling me while he moved his hips between my legs.

We fell asleep in each other's arms like we always did, completely naked and sated. Neither of us had to be up early since he had a late game, so when my eyes peeled open and I saw it was barely nine in the morning, I turned over and went back to sleep.

When I woke up again, I felt Cruz grinding his hard cock between the cheeks of my ass. His lips were against my neck, and he was biting and licking me as his hands found my breasts and he squeezed.

"Cruz," I moaned his name, knowing he loved to hear me.

"Tilt up baby," he whispered. "Let me inside of you before I come between your ass cheeks."

I angled myself so he could slide into my pussy, but I kind of wanted him to come the way he was. Knowing he could just touch me, and still get off, was making me shake, I wanted to see it and feel it.

As if he knew what I was thinking, he held onto me before I could move and used his hand to press my clit. "Don't you dare."

"I want to see you come on me, just like you said."

"And I decided I really want to see you press your clit against my goal post and come just like that, but it isn't going to happen."

"I will grind myself on whatever you want me to," I said honestly, hoping I didn't sound like an idiot.

"Right now, I want you to press it against my hand and let me fuck you just like this."

He rolled me over until I was on my stomach, his hand between me and the mattress, and worked my clit while he rubbed his body against mine. His cock was still inside of me, but his body covered mine completely, except for my legs which I had spread wide to give him room.

"Ride my hand," he demanded. "I have a big game tonight, baby. Make them sticky."

"You wear gloves," I reasoned, even though that was not the sexiest thing to say.

He laughed nonetheless, and then bit my ear. "I won't tonight. I won't need to. I'll have our cum on my fingers, and poor Los Angeles won't be able to get anything past me."

"I'll be in the stands with your jersey on," I said, trying to sound as sexy as he was. "I'll be up there watching you taste your fingers every so often. Just a reminder of what we did, and what we will do again after the game."

"Oh fuck, Lily. Fuck, that's it. Fuck..." his voice faded as his hips got jerky, unloading inside of me the way he loved to do.

I nearly screamed as I came with him, unable to resist the way it felt when he lost control. He was grinding a few slow movements, just as his lips found my neck again. I giggled because it tickled, and he laughed, trying to do it again.

"Fuck Lil, you are—"

Screams cut him off, and before I could register what was

happening, Cruz was off of me and covering my body with the sheet.

"What the fuck?" He yelled as I flipped over and saw my worst nightmare.

"Mom?"

Ivan and my mom were standing just inside Cruz's bedroom door with matching horrified expressions. Cruz was trying to cover me and keep his dick covered while I started hyperventilating.

"Out!" Cruz yelled, snapping both Ivan and my mom out of their shock.

"Have you lost your mind?" my mom screamed.

"Let's go out here," Ivan guided her, trying to give us a minute.

Mom let him take her to the living room, but not before he gave Cruz a glare that told him he was dead. It was that look that finally broke me, and tears ran down my face. Cruz turned me to face him and started trying to calm me down, but I could barely hear him.

"It's okay, Lil. They'll be okay."

"Your dad looked so angry."

"He'll get over it. It'll be okay."

"No," I cried again. "How will it be okay?"

"Because we're adults. We're not, and never have been, who they wanted us to be. Once they realize that, it'll be okay."

I hurried out of the bed and threw Cruz's jersey on along with some leggings I had tossed on his floor a few nights ago. Cruz watched me start pacing, but stayed in the bed, a sheet covering him from the waist down, and his hands running through his hair every few seconds.

"Don't let them do this to you." His voice was demanding and grave, so low I stopped in my tracks and looked at him. "They have hovered over you for your entire life. They are never going to stop until you stand up to them, and tell them what you want."

"What I want?" I yelled, knowing they could probably hear me through the door. Lowering my voice, I got closer to him and leaned down into his face. "You have no idea what I want. You have no idea how it has been for me with my mom since the day my dad died. I barely remember him, but I remember her. It nearly broke her, and I vowed I would never do to her what he did. I would never hurt her."

Cruz stood up and got close to me, grabbing my shoulders to keep me still. "This won't break her, but even if it did, you have the right to live your life."

I was shaking my head, too scared to tell him what he needed to hear. My heart was racing, I felt sick to my stomach, and I knew if I didn't get out of there, he was going to witness my breaking moment. The one that had been coming since the moment he kissed me.

"I have to get out of here."

"Come to my game," I pleaded. "I'll leave yours, Dad's, and Gloria's name on some tickets along with my mom. It's a big one, and I want you all there. We can all talk when we come home."

I turned around without answering him and left his room. My mom jumped up from the couch, undoubtedly getting ready to scold me, but I couldn't let her. Not yet.

Heading straight to my room, I slammed the door and locked it, then threw myself onto my bed. A little while later, I heard yelling between Cruz and Ivan, but Cruz was mostly telling them that he would talk after his game. I envied how strong he was, and his willpower to not cave even though he knew his dad probably hated him. I wished I could be like that.

After I heard Cruz leave, I decided I would talk to my mom the way Cruz did his dad. I would be strong, tell them I was going to his game, and that we could talk afterward. But I didn't make it as far as I wanted.

There were moments in the past week when I thought I wouldn't be able to handle Cruz. His sexy words, the dominant way he spoke to me while we had sex, the way he took my innocence and tore me completely out of my shell. But somehow, I always came out okay, maybe even stronger.

Not anymore.

I was weak, had been getting weaker, and by the time I walked out of my room with my head held high and my spine stiff, it was too late. One look from my mom and I crumbled.

Chapter Thirty Eight

Cruz

I texted Lil but had not heard back from her.

Not my dad or Gloria either.

"You ready?" Rhys clapped my back as I stared at my phone. "Gonna be a scoreless night for Los Angeles?"

He took the words I said before every game and tried to pump me up, but there was no use. My heart was in a million different pieces and the only hope I had was that maybe they were in the stands, smiling and happy, ready to cheer me on.

Rhys left me alone when I didn't respond, but Sandy, our team's head coach came barreling in looking like he wished he was playing the game himself.

"Martin?" he grumbled, making me stand up.

"Yes Coach?"

"Your agent has been trying to call you, and then tried to barge in here."

I sent him to voicemail every time because I didn't want to talk to anyone but Lily. Whatever he had to tell me could wait until I was sure she was going to be okay. But instead of telling Coach that, I just nodded.

"Told him I would tell you myself, but he wasn't coming in

here before a game. Nike heard about what happened with Archer and wants to offer you the same kind of deal. Of course, I think it all depends on how this game goes, but that should be motivation for you to have your head on straight."

I nodded again, completely in awe. So much riding on the game, and all I could do was think about Lil. It was a huge deal for Nike to want to offer me a contract, and I immediately wanted to call her and tell her. She would be so damn happy, especially since she thought it was her fault I didn't sign with Archer.

There was only one way to know if she was at the game, and that was to go out there and see if she was in the stands. Even if our parents flanked her, I would go up to the wall and tell her face to face about Nike. That would put a smile on her face no matter what, and I wanted to always put smiles on her face.

Jogging out there, I immediately saw my mom but the three seats next to her were empty. My eyes scanned everywhere as the music hyped the crowd up and the lights flashed around the stadium. When I looked back to my mom, she shrugged and pointed to the empty chairs, letting me know they weren't there, and she didn't know why.

My text to her, telling her about Dad and Gloria coming to the game, didn't include the part where they found me fucking Lil. It didn't feel like a good time, and I knew Dad wouldn't come right out and say it while they were in the stands.

"Heads up!" Tripp yelled, making me look up just in time to block one of his warm up strikes. He grabbed the rebound from my hands and went back toward the center of the field while I looked back up for Lil.

The seats next to my mom were now taken, but it wasn't Lil and our parents, it was her friends Angel and Jackie, along with Deon.

"Hey!" I yelled, getting their attention. Jackie immediately started batting her eye lashing and pushing her tits together, making my mom roll her eyes. Instead of giving Jackie the attention, I locked eyes with Angel and she stood like she knew I was about to ask her something. "Where's Lily?"

"I haven't spoken to her," she said quietly.

"What are you two even doing here?"

"The old fashioned way," Deon tried to explain. "No one is in these seats though, man."

"Mom?" I yelled, ignoring Deon. "Text Dad. Ask him if he's coming."

She nodded and started tapping on her phone right as I was told to take my position. I walked backward, keeping my eyes on my mom until I was in the goal and the whistle blew. There was no point in me being in the goal, I barely kept my eyes on the ball or even on the field.

We were twelve minutes into the game when someone on Los Angeles' team seemingly flopped. The referee gave Tripp a yellow card, but when the other guy didn't get back up, they called someone onto the field to tend to him. That gave me a few minutes to jog to the sideline, pretending I needed a refill on my water.

"Cruz!" I heard my mom yelling and waving her arms. As I got closer, way closer than I should have during a game, I watched as she tried to get her composure.

Deon, Angel, and Jackie were still sitting in the wrong seats, watching me and wondering what was going on. I could tell Deon was stressed out, Angel was looking a little sad, and Jackie looked like I had gone over there just to talk to her. She even shoved Deon a little and leaned down as I focused on my mom.

"Ma," I yelled, urging her to talk even though she looked sick. Sandy was yelling at me to get back on the field but I couldn't move a muscle.

Finally, my mom sensed the urgency and blurted out, "She's at Mount Sinai Medical Center."

I heard her wrong, because it sounded like she said she was at the Medical Center and there was no reason Lil should have been there unless...

"Was there an accident?" I asked, taking my gloves off as Sandy threatened to fine me. The game was starting again and our goal was empty, but I didn't care. Nothing else mattered.

"They should have told you," my mom cried, shaking her head.

Backing away, not understanding what my mom meant, I rushed to the bench and down the hall. Without even changing out of my uniform, I grabbed my phone and keys from my locker and raced toward the exit.

My phone started ringing, my agent's name popping up. I knew he was probably having a heart attack, knowing the Nike deal wouldn't go through once I left, but again, none of it mattered.

I dialed my dad's phone number a million times until he finally answered. "You left!"

"Where is she?" I demanded, ignoring the fact that he must have been watching the game on TV and saw me leave.

Dad sighed but was quiet for so long I thought maybe he had hung up. "Where is she?" I yelled again.

"Room 441," he finally said. "She's fine."

I hung up on him, not interested in him placating me. I was almost to the hospital anyway. When I ran into the emergency room doors, all eyes turned to me. The game was on the TV in the waiting room and several people did a double take as they looked between the TV and me.

"I need room 441," I explained.

"Are you family?" the lady at the desk asked.

"My girlfriend is there," I said, as if that would solve her issues.

"I'm sorry sir. That floor is for immediate family only."

"What?"

"You can call—"

"I'm her brother," I yelled, not caring who I had to be as long as I got to her.

"You just said you were her—"

"He's right," my dad's voice told the woman. "He's her brother."

"Oh, Mr. Martin," the lady said kindly. "He said he was her boyfriend."

"He's not," my dad said sternly, looking at me with a mean glare before repeating. "He is her brother."

She looked confused as my dad and I had a stare down. The entire waiting room was looking at us, probably just as confused, but eventually, another woman came up and took control.

"Mr. Martin?" My dad and I both looked at her, but she was referring to me. "You cannot be here," she waved to my uniform, "like that. Go on upstairs. Your, whoever she is, is in room 441. It's better to be there than here."

She looked behind me as a crowd of fans had started to swarm in closer. I nodded and ran past the doors she unlocked, my dad on my heels.

"Son?" My dad called, trying to grab my shoulder. "You need to slow down."

"I need to see Lily."

"You need to know a few things first."

The elevator slowed me down and Dad came in behind me, huffing like he was out of breath. "I need to know if she's okay. I need to know what's going on."

"I need to know more about what I saw this morning?" Dad snapped back. "I need to know what the hell is happening."

I ticked my jaw, unable to explain to him until I saw Lily. There was no time to get into the details of what was happening between Lily and I. And to be honest, he didn't have a right to know anything we didn't want him to know.

Instead of answering him, the elevator door opened and I ran straight toward room 441. It was a good thing I was still wearing cleats because I came to a fast halt that would have put me on my ass had I not been.

Gloria stood up from her chair, anger in her eyes that I ignored, and made my way to Lil's bedside. She was in a gown, hooked up to monitors and wires, but she looked fine. There wasn't even a scratch on her.

Taking her hand, I knelt down and whispered her name.

Her eyes were closed, but she smiled. "Cruz."

"Baby, what happened?" I asked, not caring that her mom and my dad were watching me.

Her eyes fluttered open and she gave me a sad smile before she shrugged. "I've been lying to you too."

Chapter Thirty-Nine

Lily

When I was three years old, my dad died of a sudden heart attack brought on by complications of cardiomyopathy. By the time I was seven years old, doctors had discovered that I inherited that disease. My mom didn't take that news well at all, having already lost my dad.

I promised her I would always take care of myself and that I would be okay, but throughout the years, I was in and out of hospitals—sometimes fighting for my life. My mom carried the fear of losing me every day, and oftentimes, I felt guilty for putting her through it.

She was overbearing and overprotective, but I understood why, and let her help me lead a cautious life. When I headed to college, it nearly killed her with fear. On more than one occasion, I was forced to withdraw from classes for stays in the hospital so that I could regroup and reset. It was why it took me so long to graduate.

Telling her I had job interviews in Miami was hard on her as well, but she knew I needed to live my life. Even the doctors told her I needed to spread my wings. It would be good for me.

From the time I was diagnosed, the only thing I ever asked for was that no one knew about what I was going through. Not even my new step brother. Ivan, of course, had to know, but he was good to me, and agreed from day one that Cruz never had to know.

When Ivan insisted I stay with Cruz, I knew it was because he thought there would be someone nearby that he could trust if it came down to it. It made my mom more at ease and she trusted that even without him knowing, I would be in good hands when it came to Cruz. But she couldn't help but call all the time, ask if I was drinking my water, or worry when I was out of breath.

Just like I had with Cruz and my friends, I started lying to her for the first time in my life. The freedom I found with Cruz was addicting. He still had no idea how delicate I was and he didn't treat me like I was breakable.

He never had.

Now I was looking into his worried eyes and scared I would lose him once he knew the truth.

"You're supposed to be playing a big game," I whispered.

"I'm only worried about you."

"I'll be fine," I smiled. "I do this all the time. It's like getting a little vacation."

"Stop." His voice was stern but not loud. He wasn't interested in my jokes, or how I was trying to make light of the situation.

I glanced up and saw my mom and Ivan watching us, confusion on their faces. To their credit, they were not interfering or angry, just concerned about whatever was going on.

"I need to talk to him alone," I nodded toward Cruz while keeping my eyes on my mom.

She shook her head at first, not willing to leave, but then

instantly changed her mind and nodded. She and Ivan left the room, closing the door behind them, and I took a deep breath.

"Cruz," I whispered, taking my hand to his face. "I'm so sorry."

"Stop," he said again, only with less conviction, and more sorrow.

"I never wanted you to know," I confessed. "I didn't want you treating me like a...I don't know."

"So you'd rather me think you're just an overprotected princess on a pedestal that turned my dad into Danny Tanner the second he married your mom?"

"Well, yeah... kinda."

His eyes lifted, looking into mine, and I could see unshed tears cover the anger. It was finally time to tell him the truth, and explain to him all the things that would probably make more sense now that he knew.

My mom was overprotective, but she had her reasons. My one and only boyfriend bailed when I told him the truth, too afraid he would be the reason I died if we dared to have sex. The college professor that got me the job interviews was the only person in college that knew, and that was only because he let me do a makeup exam after explaining why I missed. He ended up taking me under his wing, and helped me finish college.

But he told ICA about my heart and they offered me the job out of pity. It hurt, made me angry, and made me cry. The director told me straight up that I wasn't qualified, but he wasn't sure turning down a sick girl would be a good look.

No thanks. I couldn't take that position.

As I explained everything to Cruz, he laid his head down on my hand and listened. Every few minutes he would grunt at something I said, but he remained quiet and let me talk.

"A lifetime of knowing me, but never knowing me," I cried

as I finished my story. "A week of not knowing me, but knowing me better than anyone else ever has. I needed what we had, Cruz. I know you're angry, but if you had treated me differently, then I don't regret lying."

"I would have been more careful." His voice was strained, and I could tell he was holding back emotions.

"You would have treated me like a little sister, and I never wanted that from you."

He turned his head to where he was facing me again, and lifted it from my hands. "I wouldn't have wasted years trying to avoid you."

"Yes you would," I laughed humorlessly. "Everyone avoids me when they find out I live with this disease."

"What happens now?" He asked. "Are you going to be okay?"

"I haven't been drinking my water," I smirked. "I forgot my meds the last few nights, and the alcohol I drank didn't help. But once I get back on track, everything will be fine. It always is."

Cruz stood up and started backing away from the bed. He looked so good in his uniform, his cleats clicking on the floor and his hair a mess. Shaking his head, he started looking anywhere but at me, and I knew at that moment that I lost him for good.

"It's okay," I whispered. "We were never supposed to happen anyway. It was always going to end. Don't feel bad. Don't feel like you have to stay because I'm sick. I never wanted that from anyone."

The door opened before he could respond, and our parents walked back in. My mom still had a straight face, but Ivan was trying to lighten the mood. "Everything okay?"

"Yes," I said softly at the same time Cruz said, "No."

Without another word, he made for the door and left, almost running to get away from the situation. My mom ran to me, worried his emotional outburst would affect me again, but it wouldn't. I was used to dealing with everyone else's emotions. It was my own that I had to keep in check and I was at peace knowing Cruz gave me the best few weeks of my life before we had to say goodbye again.

Mom didn't want me talking about what they walked in on yet. She was too scared it would trigger my arrhythmia, but I was fine with that. They knew what they saw, and there was nothing more to say.

Chapter Forty

Cruz

We lost the game against Los Angeles, missing the playoffs. I was sure that was my fault but it didn't feel like it mattered. The next two games were meaningless so I took leave from the team for the rest of the season while I worked on everything I was feeling.

It had been two weeks since I'd run from Lily's hospital room, and the season was over so I had nothing to do but wallow in my own misery. My dad texted constantly, my mom called, and stopped by my apartment with food, and my friends tried every means they could to get through to me, but I wanted to be alone. No, I wanted to be with Lily.

One of my dad's texts said that Lily was doing well. She had been released from the hospital after three days, and they'd taken her home to Brooksville to regroup. I wondered if she was still taking the job at DCG, or if she would ever come get her things from my apartment. I hoped not.

Then I started to hope I could get over her already. That the time we spent together would fade, and I would be able to be myself again. Nights out, friends and women, soccer, living the life I had made for myself, and loved.

It was the Friday night before Lily was supposed to be back in town to start her job, and I was alone on the balcony. I heard a knock on my door, but didn't have the strength to get up and open it. Most likely it was my mom, and she was there to scold me again for everything that was going on.

She used words I had never even heard of when she found out Lily and I got caught in bed together. Not because we were sleeping together, but her mom seeing my ass was apparently something that would scar her for life. But I was just as upset with my mom as I was everyone else because she knew about Lily all along. Not only did she know, she had helped my dad keep it from me. They even planned my trips up there around Lily's hospital stays.

"What the fuck?" I heard from the doorway of my balcony, startling me a little. I looked up to see Rhys looking mad as fuck.

"How did you get in here?" I snapped.

"The door was unlocked."

"Doesn't give you the right to walk in here uninvited."

"Don't be mad at me for being worried about you."

I rolled my eyes and looked back out to the moon that was shining bright over the ocean. Rhys took a seat next to me on what felt like Lily's chair, and kicked his feet up.

"How deep does this run?" He asked me gently.

"Deep."

"Then why are you here?"

"Because every emotion I have is deep. Anger, fear, need, lo..." I trailed off, not wanting to test that word on my lips. It was in my head, but once I said it out loud, it would be more real.

"I don't understand why this isn't easier."

Rhys had been updated on the fucked up situation I was in with Lily. He wasn't even shocked, nor was anyone else on my team. They all knew the moment she showed up in my life that I was a different person.

"We don't all fall in love as easily as you do," I snapped.

"Ouch," he laughed, giving me a pass on that dick move. "But you admit you are in love with her."

Fuck.

I stayed quiet, getting more and more agitated that he was there. He had the nerve to go to the kitchen and make himself a drink before sitting back down next to me. His leg started bouncing, and he was sighing heavily like I was bothering him somehow.

"What?" I finally snapped, sitting up to face him.

"I didn't say anything," he shrugged.

"I'm sorry we missed the playoffs because of me, but I don't regret leaving to find her." Maybe that was his problem. Maybe he was pissed I'd screwed up our season.

"I haven't exactly had an award winning season. Between me, you, and whatever the fuck Tripp has himself wrapped up in, we were doomed."

True. It wouldn't have come down to a crucial game against Los Angeles if it wasn't for his own off the field drama. We tag-teamed the demise of our season—a group effort.

Another few minutes of silence passed before Rhys stood up to leave. "I guess I'm done here."

"That's it?" I laughed. "You came over here to stare at me and drink my shit?"

"It was my turn to check on you, but we all agreed to just make sure you were alive. I've overstayed, really."

"We all? Who?"

"Coach, Erin, Tripp, your mom. We started a group text."

"Are you fucking kidding me?" I stood up and followed him inside, almost laughing at what he had just said.

"We all care about you, but we had to take shifts because you're a handful. We're gonna have to recruit Ash as our fifth if things don't change soon."

"Tell them I'm fine. I don't need a babysitter."

"If we were babysitting you, we would bring you food." I raised one eyebrow at him, ready to argue, but he held a finger up. "Your mom doesn't count, she can bring you food because she's your mom."

I rolled my eyes then waited for him to leave, but he turned back toward me and got in my face. "Things don't have to be this hard," he reiterated. "Figure out what you want and *then* tell us all to fuck off."

I stayed in that exact spot long after he left. Somehow he made no sense at all, but made it sound so easy. Like I could just have, and do, whatever the hell I wanted. But my actions had consequences, my decisions weren't the ones that mattered.

Not to mention, I was pissed.

Then there was the fact that Lily didn't want me to be in her life forever. Not like I wanted her. She smiled at me and said it was okay right before I left, but it wasn't okay. Nothing had felt okay since that moment.

All of her things were still in my extra bedroom, and even though I had only peeked in a few times, I decided to sleep in her bed that night. In the morning, I was going to pack everything up and ship it to her, then cleanse the place of her smell, toss out anything she bought or had added that would remind me of her. It wasn't being childish or petty, it was being an adult and taking care of my own well-being.

When my head hit her pillow, I closed my eyes and immediately thought about the morning I woke her up. The temptation I had to open her legs and slide myself between them was overpowering. At the time, though, I just thought it was lust, something I always knew I had for her.

Flipping over to face the window, I made a mental note to have my housekeeper get new pillows because not only were they uncomfortable, but they would forever smell like Lily. I tried tucking my arm up to give myself some support and when I did, I felt something hard. Lifting up the pillow, I noticed something tucked away inside the pillowcase. Pulling it out, my eyes widened when I saw the sketchbook that Lily had stashed away, not wanting me to see it. She had told me her drawings were like her diary, private, and from her heart.

Everything in me told me not to invade that privacy–again–but what did it matter?

Opening the book, I realized every picture was dated, and started while she was in college. There were sketches of class-rooms, trees, roads, and lakes. A few were of people smiling, and I imagined her sketching them across the park without them even knowing.

Then I saw myself. A picture of me in my uniform when I played in the World Cup. It was two years ago, but she must have drawn it from an image on TV. A few pages further, there was another one of me, a sketched version of a picture that had been online.

"She saw me," I mumbled, realizing that even though we didn't see each other for years, she still saw me. She cared enough to draw me, and they were perfect. Every detail was there.

I flipped to a few more recent pictures, and saw us on the pier eating *La Primada Baracoa* Bars. Her image was staring at me while I looked out into the water. But that picture was all wrong, because I remember keeping my eyes on her every second I could.

Another picture was of my mom's restaurant. Even one of my mom, with her face lit up smiling. My heart loved seeing my mom from Lily's eyes.

The last picture in the book was a heart. Not like one you would draw in a love letter. It was an actual heart, with arteries and veins. Coming out of the arteries were lilies, similar to the one I had tattooed. But when I looked closer, I could tell there were small patches on the heart with the number one barely noticeable. I may have been misinterpreting, but it felt like something she drew when she felt I was fixing her heart.

"Did I fix your heart?" I laughed at myself and set the book down, rubbing my eyes with the palms of my hands.

I needed to do something. Take a chance. Even if my dad never spoke to me again, even if Lily laughed in my face, I needed to tell her just how deep this all went for me. Explain why it all hurt so much, and then beg her to come home with me.

Before overthinking it, I called Rhys and asked him for a favor. He laughed at me because he hadn't even made it home from my house yet, but it felt like it had been hours since he left. Regardless, he agreed to help me, and I started packing a bag before I talked myself out of what I was going to do.

Six hours later, I was on the charter flight that Rhys always had on standby. He made sure the pilot knew where to pick me up, and where I needed to go, so that all I had to do was board and thank him for the ride. Then I called a ride share and gave him the address of the house I hadn't been back to in years. The home I hated going to as a kid, and avoided as an adult, because she was always there.

Only now I was hoping she was there, and that I was strong enough to actually speak to her under that roof. But as soon as the door opened, everything I thought would happen, everything I thought I would say, didn't happen. I was frozen, all those emotions that I had spent that last few weeks trying to tame came bubbling back up, and I lost what little control I had.

Chapter Forty One

Lily

I had spent years practicing how to hide my tears from my mom. Only when completely necessary and unavoidable did I let her see them fall so freely.

Since returning home, tears weren't necessary. I was too numb to cry, so she had no idea how much I was missing Cruz. I didn't blame him for leaving, we said all along that it wasn't forever, but that didn't make me miss him any less.

After hearing from Deon what happened, Angel reached out to me, but other than answering a few texts telling her I was fine, I didn't want to talk to her yet. Jackie didn't even bother. She had clearly learned the truth, that I knew Cruz, and she was probably angry.

The first few days since I got home, I just rested and got back on my medical routines. My mom and I fought about me moving to Miami, but ultimately, I knew I was going to go whether she thought I should, or not. She may not have liked what happened between Cruz and me, but he showed me how to live, even if it was just for a short time.

It was early Saturday morning when I started pulling things downstairs with me. I had enough money saved to get a hotel for a few weeks until I could find a place to live, but I needed to go ahead and ship some things.

"What are you doing?" My mom asked, coming out of the kitchen with a rag in her hand.

"Going to ship these before noon," I explained, situating the boxes near the front door.

"I thought your new boss gave you extra time?" She was panicking, her voice raised up a notch, and Ivan came running in from the den.

"He did," I said calmly. "He also said I could ship some boxes directly to the museum and pick them up once I got my car back."

"You can't really be thinking of leaving again, can you?"

"Mom," I pulled her into a hug. "I know you will worry about me for the rest of your life, but I'm alive. I'm okay. I need to start living."

Ivan took my mom from my arms and wrapped his around her, giving me a small wink. "What about Cruz?" She cried against his chest.

"What about him?" We had managed to avoid Cruz's name for a while, but I guess reminding me of what I left in Miami was her last ditch effort to keep me from leaving. "Miami is a big city. I doubt I'll even see him."

"His face is all over the billboards. You can't possibl—"

"Mom," I cut her off. "Cruz and I are okay. We knew what we were doing. Stop avoiding the subject and let's talk about it."

Ivan's eyes widened, and I could tell he didn't want to hear a word about the fact that his son was on top of me in the bed. He even gave his head a small shake and pleaded with his eyes.

"You didn't answer your phone," my mom started. "We were headed down to celebrate and surprise you. Cruz had a big game, and we thought we could spend that night together, and then drive back up with you. But when we called, you didn't answer. So we drove all night and when you didn't answer the door either, Ivan used his spare key. God I wish I could undo that entire day."

"I'm sorry you had to see that, but Mom, I'm an adult. Cruz isn't a kid. We are not related. There's nothing wrong with two people, living in close proximity, caving and doing what we did."

Ivan looked uncomfortable, but he nodded, trying to agree with me before my mom shot him a look that made him freeze. I would have laughed if I wasn't panicking inside at the fact that we were talking about my sex life with my step brother, and it wasn't even seven in the morning. It was too much to process without anxiety.

Mom huffed a little and walked into the living room, where I followed her and sat down next to her. I didn't know what else to say to her. I didn't feel like I needed to say much at all.

And before I could even think of something comforting to say to her, the doorbell rang. Ivan was still near the front door, and I heard him open it before gasping.

"What are you doing here?"

"I live here," I heard Cruz's voice. "That is what you always said, right? This house was my house."

Ivan must have let him in before I heard footsteps coming toward the living room. My mom was sitting up with her back straight, looking like she was ready for war, and stood up once she saw Cruz.

"You are not welcome here," she screamed, completely irrational. Ivan and I both yelled at her, but Cruz held up a hand to stop us.

"I live here," he repeated, like that was the main point of him being there. All it did was make my mom more upset, and I shot daggers from my eyes to his hoping he shut up.

"Cruz," Ivan said calmly. "Son, you are always welcome here, but you caught us at a very rough moment."

"Good," he nodded. "Because I've had a few of those moments myself, and I think we need to work them out... as a family."

Those were the exact words we heard every time Cruz was in town while we were young. Ivan wanted to go camping as a family. Mom wanted to have dinner as a family. We all had to decorate the Christmas tree as a family.

The words weren't lost on any of us. Ivan looked like he was getting ready to throw Cruz out, but when I looked at him, in his eyes, all I saw was pain and I fought the urge to run to him and wrap my arms around him.

"I had a right to know," Cruz said angrily. "You should have told me."

"Don't blame them," I yelled. "I told you in the hospital that it was my decision. I begged them. Not to mention, didn't you tell me we all deserve to have secrets?"

"Even my mom knew," he yelled back at me. "I was the only one that didn't." I had no idea that Mariana knew about my heart issues. Mom and Ivan never told me that she knew, so I looked at both of them in shock. Cruz turned toward Ivan and ran his hands down his face before pointing at his dad. "You spent every one of my trips here trying to convince me we were one big happy family. You reminded us every day, and almost every time we were on the phone, that I had a sister, that I had a family. You wanted us to be one big happy family so much, but not enough to tell me the truth about Lil."

"You didn't live here," Ivan explained. "Lily was always sick when she was younger. When we got to spend time together without hospitals, or distances between us, Gloria and I tried to create a family for you both. It was a small piece of normalcy in what was a very chaotic childhood for you both."

"It made me angry," Cruz admitted calmly, then glanced back at me. "I was scared every trip here that if I looked at her the way I wanted, or in a way you thought wasn't appropriate, you would disown me. She was never my sister, Dad. She was my crush, my first dance, and the girl I used to think about every single day. Too young for me to be feeling the things I was, and when I turned eighteen, I never came back for that exact reason."

I heard my mom gasp next to me, but Cruz didn't seem fazed. He came on a mission, to say his peace, and that was exactly what he was doing.

"You should have told me," Ivan tried to reason. "I was a teenage boy before. I would have understood."

"You don't understand," Cruz laughed. "I basically fucked my way through Miami trying to get her out of my head. I wasn't always a kid, I've been an adult for a while now, and nothing has ever changed. When you called and insisted she stay with me, I knew it would be trouble. I knew I wouldn't be strong enough to resist her anymore."

Mom was crying, like it was the end of the world, but my heart was beating wildly and I started walking toward Cruz. He tucked his hands into his jeans, he had a plain white t-shirt on and a leather jacket that he only got to wear because it was colder in Brooksville than in Miami.

"This is unbelievable," my mom mumbled, making me turn back around to face her before I got to Cruz.

"It wasn't just him," I confessed. "I hated our 'family' trips because I didn't want Cruz to be my family."

"You never said—" my mom started to say but cut herself off.

"I promised you a long time ago that I would never break your heart the way my dad did. That meant I went along with almost everything you needed from me. I have lived my entire life to make you happy, Mom. But being with Cruz meant I got to live for myself for a while, and for the first time in our lives, we got to be together without someone constantly trying to tell us how nice it was that we were siblings."

"That doesn't make it right," my mom started to cry again, before walking out of the room, back to the kitchen.

"And it doesn't mean you had a right to know about Lily's heart," Ivan added.

"*My* heart," Cruz said. "Her heart has always belonged to *me*, and while I do respect that you kept it from me because she asked you to, I always had a right to know."

Chapter Forty Two

Cruz

Gloria ran from the room in tears and Dad followed her into the kitchen. Leaving us alone meant I finally got to concentrate on Lily, who was looking at me with her eyes wide.

"Come on," I grabbed her hand and led her upstairs to my old bedroom, "We need to talk."

There were a few boxes for storage in there, but the bed was still made up with the same quilt I used all those years ago. I had never had many personal affects there, but there were things I had left behind that I knew would still remain.

Once the door was closed, Lily pulled her hand from mine and wrapped her arms around herself while walking slowly to the window. I took my jacket off and tossed in on the bedpost before following her.

"I'm scared to talk." Her voice cracked and I turned her around so that she could see into my eyes how serious I was.

"Then I'll talk," I snapped. "I left because I was scared. I had to get out of that room and away from the fear I had when I looked at you in that bed, knowing what you had been going through for so long."

"You never came back."

"You told them everything was okay. It wasn't okay for me, but if you were telling the truth, then I wanted to make sure it was okay for you."

"I was lying again," she sniffed, making me laugh a little.

"You have to stop that. No more lying. No more sparing anyone's feelings but your own. Tell me you're okay, and I will leave. I promise. But please don't lie again."

"I'm not okay."

I wrapped my arms around her and she buried her face into my neck. My hand made soothing circles on her back as I rocked her back and forth trying to calm her down.

"I'm not either. My friends have had me on a watch list for two weeks."

"Why didn't you call me, or text me?" She pulled away to look into my eyes.

"Because," I said slowly, making sure she understood. "I thought you were okay."

She nodded a little, like it was finally sinking in, and then fell back into my chest. "I thought it was what everyone needed to hear."

"What else, Lil? I want you to tell me everything you are feeling, not what you think anyone else wants to hear."

She backed away and sat on the edge of the bed, glancing past me out the window. "I used to come in here and sleep after you left. It smelled like you, and seemed like an innocent enough guilty pleasure. I'd sneak back into my room before Mom and Ivan woke up, and they never even knew."

I swallowed, thinking of how I had intended to sleep on her bed at my place before I found the sketch pad. "Did you ever find my secrets in here?"

She smiled up at me and shook her head. "Did you have secrets?"

I got on my knees in front of her and reached down under the bed, feeling around for a few seconds before finding the envelope I knew was still there. Pulling it from between the boards, I handed it to her, wanting her to be the one that opened it and looked inside.

"Oh my god," she sighed, pulling out a few pictures I had taken but knew I had to delete from my phone.

"I know," I laughed. "I was creepy, but I knew if my mom or dad saw them on my phone I would be grounded for life. So I had them printed and kept them hidden here."

There were five pictures, and all of them were of her when she had no idea I was around. One of her on the couch with her feet up, one of her laughing at the park, one of her across the fire from me on our camping trip.

"I forgot I had that shirt," she pointed to the one of her sitting in the grass in the front yard. Her t shirt read, "I'm a keeper."

"I loved that shirt," I laughed. "I used to pretend you wore it just for me."

"Maybe I did," she mused, not remembering. But the next picture she remembered, and her eyes started to leak again. "I was at my dad's grave."

"Dad had asked me to tail you just to keep an eye on you. Obviously I just thought he was being overprotective for no reason, but I didn't mind following you. It was one of my last long trips here before I graduated."

"I was sixteen," she nodded. "And I was so pissed. I barely even remember my dad, but he invaded every aspect of my life. I had to live with his disease while he got to live in heaven. For a while, it didn't seem fair."

"I never got close enough to hear you, but I knew you were talking to him."

"Yelling," she corrected me. "I was yelling at him because he was the reason I didn't get to go on the school trip. Mom wouldn't let me go because she couldn't chaperone, and I hated them both for it."

I was still on my knees in front of her, so I spread her legs and wrapped my arms around her waist. "I wish I had known."

"We would be different people if you had known," she ran a hand through my hair. "And I quite like who we turned into, Cruz."

Looking up, I crooked a smile at her and then kissed her lips gently. "Come home with me."

"Not sure my heart can take it," she joked.

"*My* heart," I reminded her. "It's always been mine. And I promise it's safe with me."

"Our parents are going to freak out," she laughed.

"Is that a yes?"

"It's always been a yes when it comes to you."

"Your first love?" I asked, like the kid I felt I was inside my old room.

"Yeah," she whispered. "Was I yours?"

"Yeah," I said back to her. "And my last."

Her breath hitched, and I kissed her again. We stood up, but I really wanted to throw her on my bed. I had a lot of dirty dreams about her in that bed, but we were on thin ice with our parents, and fucking her in their home seemed like a step too far.

"Now that we are good," she shrugged. "Let's go face those two lunatics together."

"Sounds better than doing it alone."

I grabbed my jacket and she tucked the pictures back under my bed. "These can stay here and be our little secret."

"Oh," I stopped and set my jacket back down. "One more thing."

I reached behind me and pulled my shirt over my head.

While I worked my arms out of the sleeves, I smiled at her face as she tried to discern if I'd suddenly had a change of heart, and was going to fuck her right there.

But then my shirt fell to the floor and she saw exactly what I wanted her to see.

My new tattoo.

Her heart with the lilies, this time over my heart.

"I wanted one where everyone could see. Don't be mad."

Her jaw was open and her hand was up close to my chest, but not touching the fresh ink.

"We have a lot in common because I went to sleep in your bed, and accidently found your hiding spot."

"Oh my God," she whispered, not letting me know how much trouble I was in for peeking again.

"I didn't have time to get to San Francisco, but I know a guy in South Beach now. I had a few hours while I waited for my flight, and wanted it done."

"What if..." she trailed off, not asking what I knew she was thinking.

"Didn't matter," I laughed. "Just like the first one didn't matter. Whether you wanted mine in return or not, your heart always belonged to me. And I wanted it on my body forever."

Chapter Forty Three

Lily

Cruz and I walked hand in hand down to the kitchen. There was a huge breakfast prepared, and my mom pointed to our seats at the dining table. "Sit."

We took our usual spots across from each other but instead of scowling, Cruz sent me a wink. Ivan was helping my mom bring everything to the table and then sat at one end.

Once my mom was finished, she sat at the other end, and just like when we were kids, we were having breakfast like one big happy family. Only Cruz and I were frozen, not sure what kind of trap we had just walked into. He and I were good, but did my mom have enough time to realize I wasn't a kid anymore? Was she magically okay with Cruz and me?

"I'm not okay," she sighed, being magical enough to read my mind. "But I have lived my entire life scared out of my mind for you, Lillian." She grabbed a bowl of scrambled eggs and dished some on to her plate, then passed the bowl to Cruz while she spoke. "You know I loved your father, but I hated him so much, too. We didn't know anything about what he was dealing with when we had you, but I hated him for making you sick."

"Mom," I reached for her, but she shook her head and kept making her plate.

"Let me finish."

I nodded and made my own plate, taking a look at Cruz.

"I committed my life to saving yours," my mom continued. "Meeting Ivan felt like meeting an angel because I wasn't alone. When we decided to get married, I slept better at night knowing you would have a brother. Someone to be your family after I'm gone, one day." She looked up to Cruz, and then to Ivan, before finally settling her eyes on me. "I'm not okay with...whatever this is...but I'm not going to lose you over your choices, either."

The rest of the meal was silent, no one having anything else to add to an already tumultuous situation. But when we were back in the living room and sitting all together, I decided to rip the band aid off of one more thing.

"I'm going to stay with Cruz until I figure out what Miami has in store for me." I grabbed his hand and held it in my lap, hoping they understood that it wasn't a sibling roommate thing.

Ivan's eyes shot up and he looked between Cruz and Mom, waiting to see if either of them were going to say anything. If it hadn't been such an uneasy subject, I would have laughed.

It felt like forever, but eventually my mom sighed. "And you will drink your water?"

Cruz snorted and shook his head in irony. "If y'all had told me the importance of her hydration, I would have drilled her a well."

"I'll drink my water, Mom," I assured her as she tried to smile at Cruz.

"And log your heart rates?" Mom asked again, to cover all the bases.

"Mom," I laughed, "I'll do better, I promise."

She started crying again, but I knew it was just a lot for her to accept. Deep down, I think she thought I would come home after a few weeks in Miami and decide the big city wasn't for me. But even without Cruz coming for me, I was going back.

In fact, I couldn't wait to get back to the warm Miami nights.

We stayed one night with my mom and Ivan, in separate beds, in our old rooms, then left for the airport. Cruz had a private jet waiting to take us straight to Miami, and that included taking anything I felt I needed right away.

My mom was still struggling with the fact that Cruz and I were together, but Ivan seemed to be coming around to the idea quickly. When he gave me a hug goodbye, I made him promise to take care of my mom, and he laughed like that was never even a question.

"*I always have, and I always will,*" he said to me.

For some reason, I felt shy with Cruz once we were alone again. We had decided to be together, but everything felt different. There was a difference between being the girl in his bed, and being the girl in his heart.

"*You've always been here,*" he said to me, tapping his chest where his heart was. "*The only difference is, I am admitting it to us both.*"

After a few days of adjusting and getting settled, Cruz started his offseason workouts and minicamps, and I started my job at David Castillo Gallery. It went as well as could be expected considering it was my second choice in careers, but I knew I would be good at what they wanted me to do.

I came home each night of my first week, and told Cruz all

about my day. Then he told me about his workouts while I cooked dinner.

Cruz had been used to eating out, but my diet played a huge role in my health. So he made sure the cabinets and fridge were stocked with everything I could possibly need. It made finding something to cook super easy, and since I loved cooking, I immediately fell into the role.

The only thing we hadn't done since we got back was make love. Cruz had been worried my heart couldn't take it, which caused our first fight. It was exactly why I didn't tell him about my heart in the first place. If he started acting like I was made of glass, I wouldn't be able to take it.

Thankfully, he calmed down, and we agreed to take things slow. He showed me some papers my mom slid him before we left, that were instructions from my doctors. No physical activity for four weeks was the requirement. I was sure my mom handed those to him thinking he would just focus on the food guide, but not Cruz. He zeroed in on the activity suggestion, and was taking it as far as he could.

Four weeks after my hospital stay, I walked in the door from work to find Cruz in the living room kicking a ball from his knees to his feet, and back to his knees with impressive precision. I set my bag on the counter in the kitchen and kept walking toward him, completely turned on from watching him do what he did best.

"Didn't you get enough of that at workouts today?" I laughed. "Not that I'm complaining."

"Oh," he laughed, and then grabbed the ball with his hands. He tossed it to me and I caught it as he added, "I brought that home for you."

"Me?" I turned it over in my hands, trying to catch on to whatever game he was playing.

When I looked up, I realized his t-shirt said "Property of

Lily" with an arrow pointing toward his groin. I laughed, about to ask him where the hell he got that shirt, but he stopped me before I could say anything. "Yes you. We are having more soccer lessons."

He pulled me closer to him and started unbuttoning the suit jacket I wore to work, quickly discarding it onto the couch behind him. Then he unbuckled my pants and let them fall to the floor, making me step out of the wide leg. I was left in nothing but a silver silk camisole, a pink thong, and silver pumps.

"I need to tell you something." He took the ball from my hands and kicked it a few times before kissing my lips. "I love you."

I sucked in a sharp breath, loving hearing those words from him.

"I have loved you for so long," he continued. "I should tell you every day, and starting now, I will. I promise."

"I love you too," I smiled. "I always have."

There had been moments when we hinted at the L word, but it was the first time we used it in a complete phrase that left no room for misinterpretation. It made my heart race, but also made me feel whole.

Cruz pulled his shirt off, then slid his shorts to the ground, leaving himself in nothing but tight boxers. I could tell through the thin fabric that he was hard, and I felt my knees wanting to give out in anticipation of being with him again.

"What about the soccer ball?" I asked, distracting myself from his cock. "What are you teaching me today?"

"Nutmegging," he smirked. "This is the ball I used all day today. Its fucking dirty. Stained and has been kicked by more cleats than I care to think about." He tossed it from one hand to the other. "Then Tripp kicked it, and it hit my goal post." He shook his head like the ball had done his goal post wrong.

"Cruz?" I moaned, falling for the deep timbre of his voice, and wanting him to get to the point so I could launch myself at him.

He got closer to me and slid his finger up my thigh and under the fabric of my thong. "Already wet?"

"I knew what today was. I practically ran home."

"Me too," he groaned. "I've missed you."

"We didn't have to wait, Cruz. I told you my heart is fine."

"And I promised to take care of it."

"Well you have it beating nice and strong."

He smirked then reached over to the side table next to the couch. Flipping a water bottle in his hand, then uncapping it, he handed it to me. "Drink."

I rolled my eyes, but did as he requested, not wanting to risk him changing his mind about where the night was going.

"Good girl," he whispered when I handed the bottle back, half empty. "Now get on your knees and spread your legs."

I lowered down to my knees, then spread them open like he told me to. He kissed me again before backing away and setting the soccer ball on the ground. "Ever heard of nutmegging?"

"Cruz," I moaned, "Don't play with me. You know I haven't."

"We don't use that term too much in the US, but," he shrugged before kicking the ball between my legs. Since I was on my knees, the ball stopped and I started to grab it but Cruz stopped me. "It means to kick the ball between your legs."

I looked up at him, and he had his cock out, stroking it while getting closer to me. He was biting his lip with a smirk, and found himself to be quite funny.

"Settle your pussy on the ball. Get comfortable." I shook my head but did it anyway, taking some of the pressure off my knees. He held my jaw and forced my mouth open, then shoved the tip of his dick onto my tongue. "Remember everything I taught you?"

I moaned because the memory alone was erotic.

Licking the bottom side of his cock, I made sure there was enough saliva coating him. He liked it to be messy and noisy. Then I took his tip and wrapped my lips tight around his glans, pulling as hard as I could without using my teeth.

It was crazy how brave and bold he made me. I just knew that everything I did was a turn on to him, and it made me want to try and test him the way he did me.

He held my cheek and stopped my movements long enough to get my eyes to glance up at him. When I did, he ran his thumb along my bottom lip. "*Te amo.*"

Using what little Spanish I knew for sure, I answered him back. "*Yo también te amo.*"

Chapter Forty Four

The last couple of weeks were more of an adjustment than I realized they would be. Living with someone, no matter how much I loved her, was hard. There was a lot of compromise, and even though Lily had put all her things in my other room to make it easier, I didn't like her thinking our living situation was temporary.

There was no way I could ever let her go now that I had her. It felt like twelve years of waiting for her was finally my reality, and I wasn't fucking it up. So while she was at work one day, I had Tripp come over and we rearranged my closet, making space for her things. Then I made sure that there were always groceries, and added to my housekeeper's responsibilities to keep everything from Lily's list of recommended nutritional details in stock and fresh.

But the hardest adjustment was balancing my fear of hurting her with my need to fuck her. It was the longest, and hardest, nights of my life because every night I held her in my arms and had to resist my instinct to spread her legs open.

It was worth it, though, because no amount of need for her was worth risking her health. She may not have liked that I was treating her differently, but I wanted a lifetime with her, and not taking care of her wouldn't work for me. I tried to make her understand that even without her having a heart issue, it was always going to be my goal to take care of her. She was just going to have to get used to it.

"I'm going to come so fast," I snickered, not even denying that I was a hairpin trigger after so many nights without her.

"Me too," she moaned, inadvertently grinding on the ball that was between her legs.

I reached down and tore the fabric of her thong, tossing it to the side. "I want you to come on that ball, baby. I want your cum all over it, so when I take it back to workouts tomorrow, I'll be able to think of how special that ball is when it dares to touch my goal post."

She froze, realizing what I was asking her to do, but I wasn't giving her time to get shy. I grabbed her shoulders and started moving her around, making her pussy grind on the ball. Within minutes, she was moaning, and I pushed my cock back into her open mouth.

"Fuck you look good sitting on that ball and sucking me off."

She started grinding back and forth, chasing her own pleasure. Her right hand was wrapped around the base of my cock and her left was holding my thigh, using it to keep her upright on the soccer ball.

I loved pushing her out of her comfort zone, and that was all I intended when I brought the ball home. But now I was thinking of having it dipped in gold and put on the shelf as a trophy. It wasn't like I could actually take it back to the field. Once someone else touched it I would have to kick their ass and it felt like that would lead to too much tension among the team.

"Oh," she moaned, taking her mouth off of me long enough to steady herself again.

"I have never been more jealous of a soccer ball," I hissed. "This was such a bad idea."

I went to move her off the ball but she stopped me and shook her head while licking the tip of my cock. "You asked for this. Now you have to wait your turn."

A few more bounces and her head fell back, her mouth open. She was still holding onto my cock like a handle, but was too consumed with her own pleasure to keep her mouth on me.

Didn't matter. Her small touch, and the way she looked grinding the Nike logo that was stamped onto the synthetic leather, made me start spurting all over her chest. I grabbed myself above her hand and finished myself off as she screamed my name.

Once we were both able to refocus on each other, I stood her up and kicked that dumb ass ball across the room, nearly hitting the chandelier in the dining area. She gasped, but I threw her over my shoulder, not giving a shit that my own cum was spreading all over my body.

"That ball was a bad idea," I mumbled, throwing her into the bed.

She giggled, seeing how unhinged I had gotten. Probably loving the fact that I was no longer taking it easy on her, or going slow. My cock was already hard again, something only she ever did to me, and I pushed inside of her hard and fast.

I pulled each of her legs up over my shoulders and held on tight to her thighs so I could have all the control I wanted. Her smile faded quickly and she placed a hand over her heart. It was something she always did, but now I knew it was a reflex when she felt like it was going to beat out of her chest. I also knew if I stopped, or slowed down, she would kill me, and neither one of us wanted it to be our time yet. We had way too much to look forward to in our lives together.

Once her pussy started squeezing me, I held myself inside

of her and let those pulses finish me off. I came without even moving, being squeezed so tight that I had to put my hand over my own heart to make sure I was still alive.

"Fuck," I repeated, over and over again until I finally pulled out of her and fell beside her.

Without me having to even pull on her, she wrapped her legs around my body and kissed the side of my face. "Mom and Dad would be so proud of us," she laughed, making me flinch and look down at her like she had lost her mind.

"I fucked you so hard you thought about our parents?"

"Kinda," she laughed. "I was just thinking of the last time we were in this bed like this. Poor Mom."

"Okay," I held a finger up to stop her. "Real quick. Remind me to get a new bed. No more thinking of our parents after sex. Also, I don't remember ever thinking they would be proud of us for this."

She leaned up and looked down at me, a soft smile on her face. "They would be proud that we gave them exactly what they wanted. Us, together. A family. Maybe it's not how they envisioned it, but it's exactly what they wanted."

"Even better," I agreed with her, kissing the top of her nose.

"Oh, by the way," she pulled back, her face full of serious concern. "Did you change the locks?"

"They're coming in the morning," I laughed. "Definitely not taking any chances."

Epilogue

Cruz

After knocking on the old wood, I stepped back and nervously ran a hand over my mouth. A million different scenarios were racing through my mind, none of them good, but it didn't change what I was there to do.

"Cruz?" My dad answered, with confusion in his tone and on his face.

"Can I come in?"

Dad laughed and opened the door wider, making room for me to enter, then closed the door behind me.

"It's your house, son. Should I be worried?" He asked nervously.

"Maybe. Is Gloria here?"

"Is Lillian okay?" His voice had changed from humored confusion, to stern and demanding.

"Of course," I whipped around. "She stayed home."

Gloria came walking down the stairs and saw me, looking around to see if her daughter was with me. "Cruz? Where's Lillian?"

"She had to work," I explained, motioning for them to join me in the living room. "I made a quick trip without her."

In the past year, Gloria and Dad had done a better job of letting me be the one to worry about Lil. Except when I wasn't with her, because they occasionally forgot she was a grown woman.

They accepted the decisions Lil and I had made with our relationship, but I felt like they were always waiting for the moment I fucked everything up. No doubt, that's why they thought I was there.

"I only have a couple of hours. We are double-dating with Rhys and Ash tonight once the girls get off work so I need to get home."

Dad sat down and furrowed his brow, before Gloria felt around for the chair behind her and sat as well. Taking their cues, I chose the couch and leaned my elbows on my knees, trying to think of how I wanted to go about talking to them.

"The suspense is killing me," my dad huffed sarcastically.

"I wanted to thank you both for supporting Lil and me this past year." I turned to Gloria and focused my words on her. "I know I'm not the one you pictured her being with, but it means a lot to me that you gave us a chance."

Gloria laughed a little, feeling uncomfortable. "It's been... interesting...but she's happy, and that is all I want."

That was going to make the next part of my speech easier.

"I love her," I told Gloria. "I think I've loved her since I met her. This past year has been more than I ever expected to have in my life. Sometimes it doesn't feel like I deserve her, but I'm not going to let her go. Ever. Can I have your blessing to marry her?"

Gloria let out a cry, tears coming down her face, while Dad smiled knowingly. "Once we sat down, I figured that was why you were here."

"Oh Cruz."

"I promise, Gloria, no one will ever love her as much as I do."

"I know," she whispered, then stood up. Her arms reached out so I stood as well, and accepted her embrace. "When are you wanting to ask her?"

"Soon. Maybe after my last game. I want it to be a time when you are all in town and can be there. I want her to see she has the love and support from everyone."

"We wouldn't miss it," Dad clapped my back. Letting go of Gloria, I turned to him and gave him a hug as well.

"Does this mean I have your blessing, too?"

Dad leaned back and tilted his head. "You don't need mine."

"You've been the only dad she's known. She will want to know you're okay with giving her away."

Gloria's tears were still coming down and she hugged my dad, burying her wet cheeks into his chest as he answered me. "You have both of our blessings."

Once Gloria stopped crying, she offered me a cup of coffee, and we sat together for a bit. I told them about my upcoming games, and that I would use my new charter flight connections to get them to the game in style. Gloria was more excited than I had ever seen her, and told me she couldn't wait to see the look on Lily's face.

When I was just about to leave, I decided I had one more thing I needed to clear the air about. Standing there in the exact spot I got angry at my dad for hiding Lily's heart disease from me, I looked him in the eye.

"Thank you," I swallowed hard. "You took care of her heart for me when I wasn't ready to do it myself. You made sure she had everything she needed, tried to give her more than she thought she wanted, and honored her wishes, empowering her more than you probably realize. I've got it from here, Dad."

Instead of a hug, Dad reached his hand out to shake mine, trying to fight back the emotions on his face. "I know you do."

Lillian

"Gonna be another scoreless night for Atlanta," Cruz yelled toward the suite where Mariana and I watched the Inferno with a few of his teammate's friends and family. It was their redemption game after coming up short the year before.

Cruz swore he never regretted walking off the field that night against LA, but beating Atlanta to solidify their spot in the playoffs was going to feel extra sweet to him.

The entire game, I was either holding Mariana's hand, jerking side to side as if that would help Cruz from where I was sitting, or pacing the back of the suite with Erin. She had spent most of the game next to Ash, but like me, she had to get up and move every once in a while.

Right before halftime, Atlanta started driving down the field, and was wide open. When their midfielder took the shot, Cruz blocked it and then wrapped his hands around the ball to prevent a rebound. But as he did, the midfielder kicked anyway, and took his cleats right to Cruz's hands.

"Fuck!" I heard Cruz yell from across the field.

The other player was penalized, but Cruz was shaking his hands and pulling his gloves off in obvious pain. Trainers ran out to him, and Mariana had to hold me back and remind me I wasn't Cruz's doctor.

"He'll be fine," she whispered. "He needs to shake it off."

I got up to stand behind the seats during that last minute of the half, and when the whistle blew, I mumbled about needing something, and went out the side door then down the tunnel where the players would walk. Rhys saw me against the wall and laughed, but gave me a wink before he passed by. Tripp stuck a hand out for me to high five and also laughed. They knew I was worried about Cruz. It was what we did with each other—overly panicked and overprotected one another.

Just because Cruz didn't have a heart condition didn't mean he didn't need me.

"Chica loca, ¿qué estás haciendo?" Cruz asked when he saw me.

I ignored trying to translate after I heard the word "crazy" and reached for his hands. "Let me see."

Blood was everywhere and his fingers were already swelling. "It's not as bad as it looks."

"Looks like your hand is broken."

"Nah," he shrugged. "It's just a little ugly. Won't stop me from blocking the ball for another half. Nor will it stop me from doing anything else."

His low timbre made me look up and into his eyes. Then I looked around to see who else may have heard him, but it was just us. The team had already gone through, and everyone else was doing their jobs.

"Come here," he whispered, then pulled me into a door that was slightly ajar.

The door slammed shut, my back was pushed against the wall, and Cruz's lips were on mine before I could even see where we were. Just like all of our kisses, it instantly escalated, and I forgot to even care where we were.

"I love your shirt," he moaned, holding my neck so my lips couldn't get too far from his.

"Uh huh," I hummed back, thinking of my "Cruz doesn't Lose" shirt that I had made.

"I need you to bend over, Señorita," he turned me around and took his mouth to my neck as his hands skated down my stomach and into the waistband of my jeans. He popped the button open and started pushing them down before I could even register what was going on.

"Wait!" I put my hand against the wall to steady myself but Cruz didn't stop moving. "That isn't why I—."

"No time to wait," he kissed my neck again. "If I'm not inside you before the end of the half, they'll have to play without me because I'm not going back out there until I fuck you."

"But—"

"You know damn well I can't kiss you without wanting to fuck you. And I can't play with a hard dick."

He had lowered my jeans around my thighs and was grinding against my bare ass. His fingers were against my clit and when he wasn't speaking, his tongue was tasting every inch of my skin he could reach.

I folded over for him, giving him a better angle to push inside of me. When he lined himself up, he pushed hard and I nearly screamed from how good it felt. His free hand found my mouth and covered it as he pumped his hips.

"This is all I needed," he whispered. "It's impossible to feel pain when being with you feels so fucking good."

With his hand still over my mouth, I moaned again and started moving my own hips. Cruz took his fingers off my clit and moved them to my ass, spitting on my tight hole before pushing a finger inside of me. He loved playing with me like that, and thought he was pushing a boundary with me, but there wasn't any part of my body that I didn't want him claiming.

"Fuck baby." His breath was ragged and I could tell he was

gritting his teeth. "If I didn't have to be back on that field, I'd fuck you all night long."

"You're playing the game wrong," I moaned, trying to tease him. "This is halftime."

"You and I have always made our own rules."

With his finger finding a rhythm with his cock, I was completely done for and started pulsing. My knees nearly gave out but when he had taken his hand off my mouth, he had already wrapped it around my waist, knowing I wouldn't be able to stand on my own.

He started coming with me, forceful and hard, almost pushing his own finger farther inside of me than he intended. I could already feel the mix of our cum sliding down my legs before he even pulled out and knew I was going to be a mess for the rest of the night.

"You're going to smell like sex," he whispered as he pulled out and kissed my cheek. I pulled my jeans back up quickly to contain the mess and then turned around to look at him.

Nothing looked better than a freshly satisfied Cruz Martin. Except for maybe a satisfied Cruz that had just played half a soccer game. It felt like I should have pulled my phone out and taken pictures of him to add to the stash under his old bed. Something I wanted to remember and maybe look at every once in a while.

"Oh my God," I gasped, finally realizing where we were. "We have to get out of here."

"Pretty sure the ball boys have been trying to come in for the last five minutes," he laughed.

I looked around at the chairs and a few tables. It was basically a resting area for the ball boys and luckily for the most part, they were on the field during halftime. But I was panicking and started to open the door to leave.

"Not yet," Cruz laughed. "I'm gonna head back to the field, you are going to get the blood off your neck."

"What?"

He held his hurt hand up and shrugged, reminding me that it had been bleeding before he pulled me into that room.

"Oh my God, you needed to get that looked at," I cried.

"Trust me," he smiled and leaned down to push his lips against mine. "Nothing is getting past these hands now. Pretty sure they've never felt better."

After a short kiss, he opened the door and made his way to the field, leaving me to figure out how the hell I was going to convince everyone that we *didn't* have sex at the most inappropriate time and place. There were no mirrors in that room, so I did the best I could, and when I opened the door, I realized the ball boys were standing there waiting.

"Oh um," I laughed.

"Cruz said you didn't feel well," one of them shrugged. "So we are waiting."

"Thank you." Who knows if they believed me or Cruz, but they were kind enough not to embarrass me if they didn't. I was just glad the ball boys weren't actual boys and had enough sense to get back to work once I walked away.

The game was just restarting when I entered the side door from the tunnel and back into the suite. Erin was pacing in the back and when I walked in, she was the first one to see me.

"Oh no!" Her eyes widened and she came rushing to me. Taking my hand, she pulled me toward the back of the suite and into the single bathroom that was thankfully empty.

"Girl you look like you just got fucked," she whispered. "We need to fix you."

I looked in the mirror and realized I was worse than I thought. Cruz's blood was still on my neck in a few places, and on my cheek. My shirt was twisted and my eyes looked about as happy as I had ever seen them.

"I look happy," I whispered to Erin, who was getting a paper towel wet in the sink.

"It's a good look on you," she laughed. "Just figured it may not be the best time to sport this particular style."

"Simone would know," I laughed.

"Mmm," Erin moaned as she started wiping my neck with the towel. "That girl knows all about style, and the freshly fucked look is definitely in her portfolio."

The day Cruz met with Nike to sign his contract, I went with him, but not before I made a trip back to Sean LaLa for the perfect outfit. Nike wasn't requiring my presence, but we had decided not to hide and Cruz wanted me with him.

Erin went shopping with me that time, and she and Simone hit it off. Now they were an official couple, who we often doubled with when all our schedules worked out. Cruz, Simone, and I even went to Erin's games for her new team in Fort Lauderdale. It was a group of friends a million times better than the one I thought I needed.

As for Angel, she and Jackie were no longer friends, and she was dating Deon, which meant we saw her on occasion. Angel and I were never going to be as close as I hoped we would be, but we didn't have any ill feelings toward each other either. Seeing one another every once in a while was enough for me.

When Erin had me cleaned up and presentable, she and I made our way back to the suite. Atlanta had yet to score and when I sat down with Mariana, she filled me in on how well Cruz looked despite his earlier injury and that he must have had it looked at during halftime. I just smiled and nodded, sparing her of any awkward stories of how he spent his halftime.

When the final whistle blew, and Miami was up 3-0, the

guys celebrated in the middle of the field while Mariana and I hugged one another, and everyone else that was in the suite.

"Your boyfriend was on fire that second half," Erin squealed as she ran up to me. We jumped around in an excited hug. When we stopped turning, my back was to the field and Erin backed away, pulling her phone from her pocket. "Okay, say cheese."

Giving her a confused look, I shrugged, but then I felt Cruz's arms wrap around me from behind. Erin held the phone up and I smiled, letting her take the shot before turning around and letting Cruz pull me over the short wall that divided our seats with the field.

He took a minute to hug his mom and Erin, and a few others that were in the box with us, then pulled me onto the field. We walked with his good hand holding mine towards the goal as fans were still screaming and cheering.

"I'm not humping that goal post," I joked as Cruz pulled me along.

His head fell back in a laugh before he shook it and eyed me. "No one is going to watch you hump my goal. No one but me. But I want to show you something."

He knelt down and pointed to something written in marker on the white post. I had to squat to see it but in his handwriting were the words:

Ask her to marry you.

"Who wrote that?" I laughed, not understanding what was happening.

"You know how I write my goals on the posts because I love the irony?"

"Yeah," I gasped, finally realizing what he meant.

"Put this on there a few games ago and I wanted to show you before they changed the goals out for the playoffs."

He was still on one knee, running a finger over the marker, before making me stand up from my squat.

"I want everyone here to see the moment I ask you to marry me."

"Oh my God."

He positioned himself to where it was more obvious what his intentions were and the crowd still lingering on that side of the field started screaming. My right hand went to my mouth and I started crying as he pulled my left hand toward him.

"Lily," he smiled. "Will you please let me take care of your heart forever? Let me love you and make you happy everyday for the rest of our lives? Will you marry me, *Señorita?*"

I was nodding yes before he even finished his words. He reached up behind him and I saw Ivan standing with my mom, along with Mariana. Ivan winked at me and handed Cruz a ring.

With his bloody hand holding mine gently, he used his good hand to slide the ring onto my finger. He popped up and pulled me into his arms, spinning around as those around us clapped.

When he let me down, I turned to my mom and Ivan, who weren't at the game and shook my head in disbelief. "Where did you two come from?"

"We got here around halftime," my mom hugged me. "We went to the suite, but you weren't there. Mariana had said you went to the restroom but when you didn't come back, we decided we still had time to sneak back out and surprise you."

"I helped with that," Erin laughed as she stepped forward and hugged me, then turned to Cruz and whispered. "You and that bloody hand almost got her in trouble."

He shrugged and smiled, then moved on to hugging his mom and dad.

"You knew about this?" I asked Ivan, when he pulled me into a huge, fatherly hug.

"Cruz asked for our blessing and had us flown down here. Unfortunately, even that fancy plane couldn't come straight through the weather near Jacksonville, so we had to divert and got scared we wouldn't make it."

"Thank you," I cried into his chest. "Thank you for being in my life and bringing Cruz with you. Thank you for loving my mom and coming around to who Cruz and I are as a couple."

"Gloria and I have had a lot of talks in the past year, and we both know that you two are exactly what you should be to each other."

Still in Ivan's embrace, I looked around at Mariana laughing with Erin. Simone was giving Cruz shit for something and making him roll his eyes. My mom was standing to the side with her hands together, as if in prayer, only her eyes were open and she was looking at everyone.

"She's happy," I whispered.

"And probably thanking your dad for looking out for all of us."

2 years later
Cruz

"Calm down," Lily whispered to me as I held her hand.

The sound of the hospital was all around and it felt like sensory overload when all I wanted was peace and quiet to think about my wife. She had been admitted the night before after she passed out in the living room. I rushed her in since she had been weak, tired, and barely able to hold her head up.

"Cruz?" She whispered again. "I'm okay, I'll be…" she never finished her sentence before her hand weakened on mine and her head fell to the side.

"Lily?" I jumped up, scared. "Lily?"

A nurse came running in and checked her, before gently tapping my arm. "She's okay, Mr. Martin. We gave her something to help her rest, and she just couldn't hold her eyes open anymore. I promise she is in good hands."

It had been two years since the last time Lily was in the hospital for her heart. That was the night I walked out thinking that was what she wanted me to do. I didn't stick around and figure out how it all worked and what happened while she was there. It was a decision I had regretted before, but now I almost hated myself for it.

Luckily, Dad and Gloria had moved to Miami over the summer and were only a phone call away. Since the sun was coming up, I expected them to be joining us as soon as visiting hours started.

Since I had been up all night, I laid my head down on Lily's hand and closed my eyes. I fell asleep to the sound of her heart beating steadily on the machine.

"Cruz?" I heard my dad's voice and felt his hand on my shoulder. "Wake up."

Lifting my head, I saw Gloria in a chair on the other side of Lily's bed, looking down at her daughter with a soft smile.

"What time is it?"

"Ten," Dad said behind me. "We got here at seven but didn't want to wake you until we had to."

"Everything okay?"

"Yeah, the nurse just came in and said the doctor would be

here in a few minutes to update us and let us know when we can get her out of this place."

I rested my head back down and squeezed my eyes shut, holding back tears that I never cried. The only time I had ever cried was the moment Lily came through the double doors of the Catholic church we got married in. She looked so damn beautiful that I nearly fell to my knees.

My dad escorted her to me and when the priest asked who gave her away to me, he spoke proudly and said, *"Her mother and I."* Then he gave me a wink and her hand, and it took five full minutes before I stopped my eyes from leaking. I nearly started again when she was saying her vows, but added in how she would be my Sister Lily forever, and I laughed instead.

Fuck I loved her so much. "How did you do this for so long?"

My head was still down, and neither Gloria nor my dad answered right away, but when I glanced at Gloria she simply shrugged and said, "I just lived my life in fear. Smothered her. Protected her the only way I knew how. But no matter how much I did, we still had these moments, Cruz. You will always have these moments, and I wish I could say it got easier but it doesn't."

As she finished speaking, Lily started stirring and her eyes fluttered open. Once she was focused on the room, she gave us all a small smile, and then looked at me. "I'm sorry."

"Don't, *Señorita*." I tried to smile, and reached up to run my hand over her cheek. "We will get home soon. Definitely before your exhibit opens next week."

Her smile got wider as she remembered her exhibit. Lily still worked at David Castillo Gallery, and once they realized how talented she was, they decided to dedicate a wall for her sketches. She took some of her older pieces and did a few new ones for the display, and I had never seen her more content. It was incredible watching her work with such passion.

Scoreless Heart was the name of her exhibit, and told the story of all the ways her Cardiomyopathy would never win. Love, family, and friends were stronger than whatever her heart went through, and she drew about it almost everyday. I had honestly never been more proud of anything in my life—not even my own personal achievements.

"Knock, knock," the doctor came in, feeling more cheerful than any of the rest of us.

I stood up and kept Lily's hand in mine while Gloria stepped aside and stood in the corner with my dad. It had to be hard for her, letting me take the lead, but she did so with grace.

"How's she doing, Doc?" I asked, pushing her hair on her head a little. Dr. Henderson had been Lily's doctor since she moved to Miami, and was used to us being overly protective, but it was his first time seeing us in the hospital.

"Well," Dr. Henderson said as he browsed the notes, then looked up directly at Lily. "This had nothing to do with your heart, and everything to do with the fact that you, Mrs. Martin, are pregnant."

Gloria gasped from the other side of the room, and Lily's eyes were wider than they ever had been. I was frozen, in shock, and in a little bit of disbelief. "How?"

"Well, Cruz," Dr. Henderson smiled, "When two people love each other..."

Lily laughed, stopping the doctor from speaking, and he looked over and winked at her. "Am I okay to have a baby? I'm on the pill, too."

"Being on the pill has always been hit or miss because of the array of medications you take. As for being okay, we will definitely have to make some adjustments, and you will be at high risk, so buckle up for a long ride. But given how well you take care of your health, and your age, you should have no problems carrying a healthy baby safely to term. It will also help that I will be referring you to the best obstetrician in the city who handles these kinds of high risk pregnancies all the time."

Shock and excitement were mixing with each other inside of me, and I had to sit down before I passed out. Lily was holding my hand and I could tell she was still tired, but trying to be present for me.

"I fainted," Lily explained to Dr. Henderson.

"I know," he said gently. "Your body and heart are working overtime to create a new life. Be extra careful, and stay calm. Do your breathing exercises, and keep your feet up. No physical activity for a while. Let's make sure you are under the proper care, and we have a plan before you resume normal activities."

With that, the doc wrapped everything up and made his way out of the room. Dad and Gloria started squealing over the fact that they were going to be grandparents, hugging both of us and feeling relieved that Lily was going to be able to go home later that same day.

"We will head out and let you two soak in this news together."

"Don't tell anyone!" Lily yelled as they exited the door. "We want to do that!"

"So no plane banner rentals," Dad joked. "Got it."

Once they were gone, I looked back to Lily and we stared at one another for a long time.

"I'm going to be a dad," I finally choked out, tears finding a new reason to form in my eyes.

"You are going to be the best dad in the entire world," Lily smiled.

"And you are going to be the best mom. I love you so much Lily."

"Love you," she whispered, before I leaned down and kissed her.

"This is a lot to take in," I sighed when I sat back down in the chair.

"How are you feeling about everything Dr. Henderson said?"

"Confused, but I know he's right. Your meds are always changing, and there was always a chance this could happen. We knew that risk and we talked about being okay with bringing a baby into this world."

"What if he or she inherits my heart?"

"Then he or she will be in good hands because we will know just how to take care of them. Dad and your mom are close now too. It'll be okay."

She sighed and smiled again, leaning her head back and looking at the ceiling. "If I am doing the math correctly, I'm probably fifty days pregnant, but since I'm not regular it's hard to guess. Just assuming I'm right, though, that would mean in two hundred and thirty days, we will be parents."

"Ugh," I sighed playfully. "And since the doctor said you can't have any physical activity, that means we have two-hundred and thirty scoreless nights ahead of us."

Afterword

Cruz has been my favorite male main character since I started writing. This was close to being a friends to lovers with a sprinkle of second chance, but I wasn't sure it hit those tropes enough to claim them. But, those are two of my favorites to write and I think that was why Cruz became my favorite.

Want more Rhys? Check out Reckless Goals.
Nothing is more reckless than falling in love.....
<u>Rhys</u>
Despite being in my mid thirties and one of the world's best soccer players, I had never reached my main goals in life—to be a husband and a father.

But after being left heartbroken and alone on the night I planned to propose to my girlfriend, I realized how reckless that goal was.

Love, in general, was reckless....
In order to keep from self-destructing, I'm forced to train with college soccer star, Ashlynn Keller. She was young and naive, too caught up in her own life goals to focus on her game.

We were on very different paths in life, but we found common ground on the playing field. It may have been wrong, but sparks started flying between us. And when we finally gave in to each other, we realized that being a little reckless was exactly what we needed.

That is, until my ex showed up....

Acknowledgments

Just like with Reckless Goals, this whole process has been far different than any other book so I need to make sure everyone that has worked with me knows how much I appreciate them!

As aways, my family is my number one support system! **TJ and the girls** are the only reason I get to keep doing this. They are understanding, patient, and encouraging. When I wrote, THE END, on this book, we had a dance party and the girls put a crown on my head. They don't read my words, but they know what it means to finish an entire book.

I also want to make sure I thank my friends: **Gail, Ashton, Lori, Sara, Rachel, Autumn, and Tits.** Just like every book I write, these babes talk me off the ledge and help me focus on what is important when those tough times seep in.

Next, I want to send a **HUGE thank you to Amanda.** Your continued support on this series has meant everything to me.

My cover designer KB Barrett. You finally understand how crazy I am and still love me... its wild.

Brenda, my editor. ALL THE LOVE for being a part of this one and grinding for me when times were tough for you.

To my beta readers, Michelle and Meg. Thank you for your honesty and feedback. As always, you two may want to reread this book since y'all made me change so much haha.

A special thank you to **Hiramys, who translated for**

me. Hiramys was raised in Puerto Rico and has always been obsessed with books. She has both a BA and an MA in English literature. She is also a tenured college English professor at the University of Puerto Rico in Aguadilla. **Hiramys,** you've been so helpful making sure I got it right, helping me make Cruz extra sexy, and helping me create the vibe I wanted for this book. Stand by, because I'm sure Cruz will have something to say in Twisted Assist, too! Haha

Kandace and Issa. Kandace, again, I cannot do a series like this without you having my back when it comes to content. You're my personal hero!

To my admins, Jenn, Elizabeth, Caitlin, and Katie. So much more than admins, you all are my friends and I really don't thank yall enough.

My street team and ARC team: Thank you all for your trust in me! Every share and review make me weepy, and my heart is so full. I think I wrote this exact same thing in the last book but damn its so true!

Also a special thank you to **The Author Agency** for taking over the promotions for this one! You ladies are amazing! Are you ladies ready to deal with me through Twisted Assist?

TO MY READERS! I saved y'all for last because this is where I really get weepy. For those of you that let me write and love my words, I can't thank you enough for how much you empower me. Often times, there is rough criticism when storylines don't go a certain way and sometimes I feel pressure to change who I am as an author. Then I read YOUR words—the DMs, the reviews, the reactions—and I remember that MY readers get me, and allow me to write the stories I long for as a reader myself. I LOVE YALL SO MUCH!

About the Author

Katie Rae is a wife and mother, first and foremost. She and her husband, TJ, have been married twenty years and have two girls who she homeschools. They live in South Florida and enjoy boat days, sunshine, and family time.

Visit www.katieraebooks.com for signed paperbacks, merch, events, and extras.

Join Katie Rae Reader Group to chat all things books.

Also by Katie Rae

Miami Inferno FC Series (Interconnected Standalones)

Reckless Goals

Scoreless Nights

Twisted Assist

The GAMES Series (Interconnected Standalones)

The Games We Play

The Lies We Tell

The Love We Make

The Way We Dance

The Way We Fight

Men of the Military (Complete Standalones)

Ranger (Army)

Raptor (Air Force)

RECON (Marines)

Rogue (Navy)

The Boys of Summer Novella

Pretty Boy

Man of the Month Club Novella

Love Bites

Another One Bites the Dust

Silverbell Shores

Now and Then